THE MOORLAND MURDERERS

Also by Michael Jecks

The Jack Blackjack mysteries

REBELLION'S MESSAGE *
A MURDER TOO SOON *
A MISSED MURDER *
THE DEAD DON'T WAIT *
DEATH COMES HOT *

The Templar mysteries

NO LAW IN THE LAND
THE BISHOP MUST DIE
THE OATH
KING'S GOLD
CITY OF FIENDS
TEMPLAR'S ACRE

Vintener trilogy

FIELDS OF GLORY
BLOOD ON THE SAND
BLOOD OF THE INNOCENTS

* *available from Severn House*

Visit www.michaeljecks.co.uk for a full list of titles

THE MOORLAND
MURDERERS

Michael Jecks

SEVERN
HOUSE

First world edition published in Great Britain and the USA in 2021
by Severn House, an imprint of Canongate Books Ltd,
14 High Street, Edinburgh EH1 1TE.

Trade paperback edition first published in Great Britain and the USA in 2022
by Severn House, an imprint of Canongate Books Ltd.

severnhouse.com

British Library Cataloguing-in-Publication Data
A CIP catalogue record for this title is available from the British Library.

ISBN-13: 978-1-78029-122-2 (cased)
ISBN-13: 978-1-78029-824-5 (trade paper)
ISBN-13: 978-1-4483-0562-9 (e-book)

All Severn House titles are printed on acid-free paper.

MIX
Paper from
responsible sources
FSC
www.fsc.org   FSC® C013056

Typeset by Palimpsest Book Production Ltd.,
Falkirk, Stirlingshire, Scotland.
Printed and bound in Great Britain by
TJ Books, Padstow, Cornwall.

This book is in loving memory of my brother
Alan John Jecks
27 September 1950 – 27 November 2020

ONE

Tuesday 28th July 1556
Okehampton, Devon

When, after what felt like an age, his vicelike grip slowly released me, and his hand fell away, I was aware only of the thrill and elation sparking in my chest. It felt like a punch, like a physical blow. He was beaten! I had won!

Oh, I know that many people do not understand the thrill, but I feel sorry for them. Every man should know the sensation of utterly thwarting an enemy, of beating him into the dust, of knowing absolute victory over him. When a man can see he has bested an opponent, the exhilaration is astonishing. There is nothing quite like it. And this time, especially since I had no idea at that moment that my companion was soon to die, I felt invincible, invulnerable. This enemy was vanquished. I had overcome him.

Naturally, I retained my gentlemanly decorum at the sight. I merely indicated a little pleasure.

'*Hahaha!* I win!'

His only reply was a grimace of defeat as he stared at the dice while I scooped up his coins. His round, swarthy features were unpleasant. Now, as realization struck and he knew how far he had plumbed the depths of utter failure, his face took on a more gruesome appearance. He looked like a toad trying to swallow a wasp.

Meanwhile, the women about us crowed and clapped at my great success. They must have marvelled to see an elegant gentleman such as I. I doubt they had ever encountered such a well-dressed fellow in their lives before. One buxom young wench caught my eye and I gave her a broad Lucky Jack smile. It is a smile that rarely fails to win a return from any woman with blood flowing in her veins, but as I did so, she was distracted by some young fellow walking from the door and banging it

behind him. She didn't catch sight of my grin, or else she would
have been all over me like a cheap jerkin.

No matter. I could work on her later, when I had her
undivided attention. With my purse bulging like this, she would
surely be keen to make my acquaintance.

Where was I? I was sitting in the parlour of the Green Cock,
a noisome, smokey chamber, where they burned dried turf in
an attempt to warm the place. Seriously, they didn't have
logs or coals, only blocks of dried earth and grass. The town's
name is seared into my memory with burning letters: Okehampton,
in the county of Devonshire. I can only urge you never to go
there. Personally, I would not return for a hundred pounds in
gold. A team of oxen couldn't drag *me* back. And as for those
moors . . . Well, you can keep them. Give me a cosy fireside
in the Cheshire Cheese or the Sign of the Boar any day.

Of all the miserable dives I have been forced to visit and
endure, there can be few so miserable as this. There were none
of the basic amenities of life such as I was used to in London:
decent wine and sack, good brothels, food for a gourmand.
Instead, just a collection of independent-minded peasant women,
dangerous men, mud and ale – or cider – all under the watchful
eye of a dilapidated castle. Oh, and miners – a group of lazy
brutes under the command of a vicious man who had the look,
common humanity and feeling of a stoat. I had thought to have
escaped – just – capture by the Queen's officers, and to
have found a refuge of sorts when I reached this cesspit of a town.
It hadn't occurred to me that civilization ended at the borders
of Middlesex. Other parts of the country held some essentials of
culture, but here? There was nothing for a man of my style within
the environs of the city of Exeter, and beyond that, where I was
now, it was more or less a territory of cut-throats, outlaws and
thieves. The Queen's writ did not reach this far.

I was not staying here, no. It was merely an opportunity to
find a ship which had brought me so far to the west, to the land
where English was hardly understood, let alone spoken. I was
on my way to the coast so that I might discover a helpful
shipman to take me to France as quickly as possible.

If I were forced to remain in Okehampton for any period,

I would surely go lunatic. Or 'mazed' as they say there. They don't even use English as a gentleman would.

Yes, yes, yes, I know. Certainly, it would have been better for me to have headed east and south to the Kent coast, or perhaps up to Essex, but the fact was, I was simply keen to escape London and capture. I happened to be near to Temple Bar when I heard the rumours of my imminent capture, and did what I am best at: I took to my heels instantly. It was a matter of pride that I had already managed to travel so many miles in only a matter of days.

However, even the most determined traveller must rest occasionally. Not only the traveller, either. After six days of hard riding, my horse had grown recalcitrant and mulish. So here I was, desperate to continue on my chosen path to the coast to find freedom and safety from arrest, but without a beast to carry me. I was stuck. The coast was yet a long march, I had been told. And so I took advice and sought a place to rest while my beast recovered a little. Yet seeking a good hostelry west of Exeter was mortifyingly difficult.

It was more than I could manage. This tavern was the best I could find. It did at least have a room with a mattress on which I might rest. I had taken it, trying to ignore the miserable certainty of fleas and worse.

As an inn, it did have some wenches who were built in a pleasing, if peasant-like fashion. If I failed with the first who had taken my interest, there were always others who looked less like something from a stable, and didn't smell like a sodden sheep. I should be able to entice one or two to my chamber to give them an introduction to the ways of a gentleman of leisure from London.

To return to that evening, however, the man stared at me with a suspicious glower as I casually took up my purse. My forearm was a little bruised where he had grabbed me when I first made to collect my winnings, and I made a note not to deride him too much. If he were to punch me, he would knock my head from my shoulders and make play with it as a football, I had no doubt.

He made some grunting sounds, which I suspect he fondly considered to be English, but I could only shrug my shoulders in bafflement. I held up my hand and beckoned with all four fingers. 'We agreed on the terms,' I reminded him in case he had forgotten. Cautiously, I held up my purse and filled it with his coins. I did not have a warm feeling of security here. As I mentioned before, this was far beyond Exeter, and that city was the extreme limit of civilization and culture. Here, I dare say, the bones of many strangers and travellers might be found littering the moors and commons.

This is the difficulty, you see, of leaving London and enlightenment far behind. On a journey of some hundreds of miles, a gentleman like me could expect to encounter two fresh dialects before lunch. Here in Devonshire, each village appeared to have its own. Most of them didn't appear to speak English of any form; I rather believe that the locals of one village would find the language of their nearest neighbours incomprehensible. How any commerce could exist in such an environment, I could not imagine.

He made another grunting comment. Or request, perhaps. I could not tell.

'Very likely,' I said affably. After all, I may have drunk five or six of the pints of ale served by the barmaid who, if one ignored the squint and leering grin, could have appeared moderately appealing, so I was in an amiable frame of mind, even if I should have been suspicious of this stranger.

He had come to me soon after I had arrived. A broad-shouldered, full-bellied man of some five-and-forty years, with a shock of brown hair that had never seen a brush, and a chin that could have burnished a cuirass, the stubble was so thick. He entered with two other worthies, one of whom stood near the door and leaned against the wall. The other walked past my table to the bar and stood there with his arms crossed, while their master, for he was confident enough to be Sheriff of the county, ambled to my table and sat on a stool opposite me, baring his teeth in a manner which I suppose he felt was friendly. When he indicated a game, holding some bone dice in his grubby palm, I glanced at him with some suspicion. Such fellows were not, in my experience, so keen to thrust their friendship on others. For example, the entire room had gone silent when I first entered. At first, I thought it was only my fashionable jerkin, with the slashed sleeves to show off the silk lining, and my poise. Clearly, such a man as me must excite interest wherever I go. Especially in a place like this, where four-fifths of the population had never travelled as far as Exeter. However, I was quick to agree to his proposal. It seemed expedient: he had hands the size of a bullock's hams, after all, and the man at the bar was glaring at me with a look that indicated I had options in life and had best select the correct one.

Slamming the dice down on the table, my companion looked at me expectantly. I gazed at them without enthusiasm. Now, I may not be a distrustful person generally, but when a stranger comes, offers a game and provides his own dice, I think it's only fair to be dubious. So I shook my head and called to the tavern's host. He had a set of dice, apparently. Soon he passed me a small leather pouch with a set of five. My companion tried to argue that his own were better in some way, but I was forced to insist. One must not allow the lower forms of peasant to feel they can browbeat a man of a higher order.

Especially if the thieving scrote planned to fleece me.

Soon I had all his coins. It was a satisfactory end to the evening, and I was about to rise to find my bedchamber when he shook his head, glowering, and muttered something into his beard.

'What?'

Another incomprehensible mumble.

'He says he'd prefer to bet again.'

This was from one of my audience, a likely-looking wench with a gleam in her eye that told me she was potentially available for a mattress wrestle later. It didn't occur to me at the time, but I could understand her much more clearly. Her language was less befuddled with ale, of course. That might have helped.

'No, I fear not. This is enough for me,' I said.

A snarling rasp and my wrist was grabbed again. His face was as black as midnight in a mine. The man at the wall lumbered upright where he had been leaning, no doubt saving his brain for complicated calculations such as which foot to move first, and glared at me. He looked like the contender for half-wit of the county, but his hands, I noticed, were large, strong and well scarred, like a man who had fought often, and who tended to win.

'But if he wishes to lose even more,' I said hurriedly, 'I'll be happy to take his money.'

At that lordly remark, many of the others in the audience clapped or cheered, from which I guessed my companion was about as popular as an outbreak of the pox. The heavy leaned back against his wall and moved his gaze to the door, staring at it with all the interest and concentration of an intellectual bovine studying a painting.

We were playing a simple game, which is, after all, the only sensible way to play after the better part of a gallon of ale. 'I have all his money – what will he risk this time?'

My translator approached the table, hitched up her skirts and placed her buttocks on my lap. This displaced my codpiece, but just then I saw no reason to complain. She was a dainty weight, and her chemise was well filled at eye-level. I leered at her bounties with anticipation. Perhaps, when this game was over, I could persuade her to help warm my mattress in an energetic fashion.

'He says he's no more money, but he'll bet his horse against the money he owes you already,' she translated.

'What sort of a horse?' I asked, not unreasonably. You could not believe the condition of the poor beasts in this town and all about. I have seen poor nags on the streets of London, of course, but the state of some of the sumpters and rounseys I had seen west of Exeter had to be seen to be believed.

'It's a good riding horse. I know it,' she said, casting an arm about my shoulder and wriggling slightly. Yes, I had correctly guessed at her profession. She remained there for the duration, only removing her shapely backside when others called for drinks, and when she had to fetch turves for the fire, but she was soon back.

'Very well, then,' I said. 'Let's play.'

Thus it was that I was soon the proud owner of a knock-kneed, aged, spavined thing that would have looked better had it been dead for a week. Perhaps it was, and still dared not lie down in case it received another beating, for there was little doubt in my mind that the poor devil had routinely been whipped to within an inch of its life.

After viewing it, my new companion and I returned to the tavern to settle our transaction. He insisted on forcing me to drink a foul brew from apples – 'scrumpy' – which at first made my belly recoil, but which, after two more pints, tasted less like something made by a pox-doctor and more like something that might persuade a wench to consider a little bedroom gallop. Oddly, after the second of these, I began to discern a certain number of words as he spoke, although I did not dispense with my translator, who made a most appealing lap-warmer.

'He says you're not so bad as some of those who pass by here,' she said.

'No, well, I am a gentleman of London,' I said modestly, trying to nuzzle at her.

'You won a lot from him,' she said.

'Aye. It's the way of things. It's why I'm called "Lucky Jack",' I chuckled.

'Are you?'

'Of course,' I said with a mild belch. 'You only have to look at me to see why.'

'I thought you said you were called Peter? Peter the Passer, you said?'

'Yes. Lucky Jack is a nickname,' I said quickly. After all, I did not want everyone to know my name. That could have been dangerous.

She glanced down at me then, and for some reason I felt a slight nervousness. It must have been the cider, I told myself.

Shortly afterwards, I went outside. I wanted to empty some of the cider from my bladder, but I also wanted to see the horse again. I was not sure it was in a fit state to carry me to the next town, let alone the coast.

There was little light outside. As I stood at the door and stared about me, the stable's light spilled out into the yard, and it gave rise to strange shadows and fancies. I could have sworn there was a swirling in the light in front of the doors, and vaguely glimpsed figures moved just out of the light. When I looked to the right, there was the strong appearance of a figure under the eaves of the stables, and what looked like another man near the gate to the field to my left. But that was a twisted blackthorn, the figure at the eaves was a pair of fence posts leaning, and the light's movement was more likely the ale I had drunk.

At the rear of the tavern there was a distinctive odour at the back wall, and I pulled my codpiece aside and enjoyed the relief. Then, I resolved to cross the yard to the stables. For some reason the cool air did not so much invigorate as befuddle. I discovered that my legs had grown wobbly, and the bright moon seemed to sway like a lantern on a cord. I smiled at the thought that the moon was being blown by the breeze, and then felt distinctly queasy. It took a firm resolve to swallow hard and continue on my somewhat wayward path to the stable door. There, I had to grab at the door's jamb to settle my legs. My heart seemed to be thundering, and I had to close one eye to peer inside. Yes, I could make out the stalls. I walked in and had just reached the animal when I caught a glimpse of a shadow up in front of me.

'Christ's pains!' I cried as visions of the Queen's men and the rack leapt into my mind, but then something struck me on the pate and, what with my tiredness from journeying, the ale, the scrumpy, and the sudden crack on my skull, I collapsed with a little sigh, thankfully toppling into a pile of clean straw.

It is not as if I am unused to being hit on the head, after all.

When I came to, it took a while for me to remember where I was.

From experience, the mind needs a few moments to climb into the saddle and trot after a blow like that. Some people can wake from a deep sleep already fit and prepared for the day; others, like me, prefer a more leisurely beginning to their daily round. Usually it takes me a half pint of wine, some bacon or a pie before I feel ready to take a canter through the day's events. But when I've been stirred from an unexpected rest like this, when someone has decided to play skittles with my skull, it takes me a little longer to recuperate. There is the little matter of the damage done.

So my first thoughts ran to the physical. Were all my limbs still with me? Thankfully, yes. I lifted my hands to my face, but it seemed apparent that no items were missing – my nose was whole, and my brow had no new injuries. The same was not to be said of my pate, which thudded painfully. I patted my belly, and there were no apparent wounds there. Then my hands went to my purse – and found only laces.

I cursed long and loudly and with all the imagination at my disposal, which was not terribly extensive. With my brains rattling in my skull, I was forced to resort to simple crudeness. And it was unsatisfying. Rolling slowly, I was able to rise to my knees, and thence to clamber to my feet. It was a painful journey, and the space about me seemed to cant like the deck of a ship in a storm. The worst of the pain was from just over my right ear, and when I put a hand to it, there was blood on my fingers. That was enough to make the stables whirl still faster, and when I closed my eyes, the sour taste of bile came to my mouth. Clearly, I had been more severely beaten than I had realized – or the cider and ale had not agreed with me. I had to put a hand out to a supporting timber and from there tottered to the door. Soon I was crossing the small yard to the rear of the tavern, and when I entered, I hunted for a sight of my gambling companion. It will not surprise you to learn that he was not present.

There was a definite problem for me now. My journey was to have continued, funded in part by my winnings, but mostly by the other contents of my purse. I had to repay the host of the tavern, I had to purchase food for my journey, and I had to pay a shipman for the journey itself. Without money, I was as good as imprisoned here in the tavern. And if I were unable to pay for my billet, I would soon be in a prison for debt, I had no doubt.

I ground my teeth and could have pulled my hair in frustration. All this because some peasant had decided to take advantage of a poor traveller. No doubt he had thought to gull me with dice that had been subtly modified with quicksilver inside, or shaved edges, so that they would always fall the way he wanted them to. Perhaps, when I won the games, he had sought to recover his losses by robbing me both of my winnings and my original coins? Well, if he thought he could get away with that, he was wrong!

It was impossible to run away from the tavern and continue without any money. I needed my money back. So I put my hand to my injured skull and slowly walked into the chamber, groaning loudly and bemoaning my fate.

'Robbed! I have been set upon and robbed!' I cried.

*   *   *

There are few men who can be as uncooperative and suspicious as those who own taverns. I suppose they are used to seeing men try to drink their houses dry before 'remembering' that they have left all their money at home. This fellow, Mal, was no exception, and as I made my slow and painful way to his bar, I was concerned to see that he had picked up a stout cudgel and was allowing it to slap unpleasantly into his other hand while he gazed at me in a thoughtful manner. It was not an encouraging look. As to my gambling companion, there was no sign.

'See? My purse has been cut from me!' I declared, holding up my laces. 'The man who gambled with me, he must have chosen to get his money back! He set upon me and robbed me!'

There was some murmuring at that. The large man at the farther end of the room unhitched himself from his post at the wall and began to walk towards me. I did not like the look on his face. The man at the bar, I saw, was no longer there. He too had left. I moved around so that the wench who had wriggled so enticingly on my lap was between us. His expression was not reassuring to this traveller. It was the sort of look a cat might wear while stalking a rat.

The host was not taking my word. 'Shew 'un th'aid.'

I stared at him. His brows darkened. He had looked rather like an ape beforehand, but now he was an angry ape with the suspicion that the figure before him had stolen his favourite fruits. His stick rose menacingly.

'He said to show him your head,' the maid translated with a sigh. She rolled her eyes as though thinking me the purest form of fool she had encountered. It made me scowl – but briefly. The movement pulled the skin over the lump on my scalp, and that hurt.

I submitted myself to her inspection. She came forward and glanced at my head. She pulled a face when she parted my hair, making me wince and flinch in pain, and her hands came away with my gore on them. The sight of blood can make me feel queasy at the best of times, but the sight of my own has always had a marked effect. I could feel the colour drain from my face, and the world began to whirl about me once more.

'Get him a stool!' the wench burst out, and since her mouth

was close to my ear, I started like a child caught stealing a biscuit, and fainted away.

As regular readers of my chronicles will know, I have had some experience of waking after being struck over the pate. This time I could have hoped to return to the land of the living with my head resting on the wench's soft thighs, or perhaps on a fragrant mattress, with a down pillow under my head, the odour of meadowsweet all about me, but no, I had no such good fortune.

I was still in the bar of the tavern, lying on what smelled like the residue of a tannery's settling tank, and I curled my lip at it, trying to rise. Instantly, my head reminded me that I was not in the very best of conditions, and I closed my eyes and allowed myself to return to a prone posture.

'Why did you leave me on the floor?' I demanded in a pained manner.

The landlord had at least laid his cudgel aside. He shrugged and said something that sounded like, 'Yofell off er 'un.'

'You fell off the stool, and you were a weight to pick up,' the maid said. As she spoke, she was dipping a cloth into a bowl of something.

I was alarmed, and tried to scrabble away from her. After all, there was no telling what sort of unguents such peasants might be tempted to try on a fellow. It was not as if these were experts in the physician's panoply of tools of torture. They would probably have little idea of the modern approach to nursing an injured man like me, and when it came to bleeding me to settle my humours – well, I wasn't keen on their testing my veins with whichever butcher's knife came first to hand.

She approached me again. I sprang up.

That was a mistake. I fell back with a whimper. Trying to leap up was foolish.

'Sit back, you great lummox,' she snapped. 'Do you want to injure yourself more? I'm washing the wound with egg white. It'll help seal the cut.'

'But you're wiping my brow. The injury was above my ear,' I said suspiciously.

'This is where you fell and hit the stool,' she said calmly.

I pursed my lips. My head rang with pain, and I was growing

seriously angry with my treatment in this benighted town. 'Where is the thief who knocked me down?' I demanded of the host.

He looked a little askance at that, almost apologetic. 'Ah, 'e war off'n zoon as 'e yerd yoom gawn.'

I looked at my delicate translator. She rolled her eyes again. It was an irritating mannerism. 'He was off as soon as he heard you leave to go for a piss. He had lost his money and his horse – what, did you expect him to sit in here and demand free drink from Mal here?' This last indicating the host.

'See? This poltroon followed me to the stables and knocked me down to rob me! I'll have the bailiff on him. What's his name? Where does he live? I expect you to go and demand my money back before he can hide it!' I said emphatically. I looked about the room, and noticed that neither of the two brutes who had come in with my playful companion were among those present. They must have left with their master.

'It'll wait till morning,' the wench said.

'I think not! I want my money back. He will conceal it, bury it or pass it on to an accomplice if we don't get after him,' I declared, full of passion. I knew any thief would do that. If it had been me who had stolen a purse that full, I'd have hidden it. I tried to rise, but the mere attempt was almost enough to send me off again. The two injuries – one at the side of my head, one at the fore – were enough to make the room whirl and bob before me, and I was close to vomiting again, while two peasants with blackthorn staffs took it in turns to belabour and pummel my pate. Or so it felt.

'You are going nowhere,' my maid said. 'You need to go to your room and rest.'

'But my *money*,' I said. It might have sounded rather like a wail, but I was desperate. My freedom, my opportunity to escape – possibly my life – depended on that money.

'We'll get it tomorrow,' she said.

TWO

Wednesday 29th July

You may be wondering what I was doing down there, so far from the security and distractions of the city.

I was fortunate enough to have been discovered by my master, John Blount, at the time of the rebellion, when the damned fool Wyatt decided to gather an army of Kentish men and march on London. Not that he might not have succeeded – the city was in a pretty temper of its own, and no one was particularly enthusiastic about the new Queen, Mary Tudor. She was a Catholic, after all, and seemed set on marrying a Spaniard! But, for all that, she was already on the throne, and we English have an aversion to overruling God's choices in such matters. He had seen her crowned and anointed in His name, so the majority felt that the decision had been made.

Wyatt and others disagreed, however, and sought to remove her and place Lady Jane Grey, or perhaps Mary's half-sister, Elizabeth, on the seat of government. But Mary gave a pretty speech in London when the rebels approached the city, and I reckon many men thought it would be unchivalrous to see her evicted so quickly. And I think she promised treasure to the guilds, which probably helped.

I had little interest in such matters. As far as I was concerned, no matter who ruled the kingdom, I was likely to feature only as a casualty. My worst fears seemed ready to come to fruition when I was conscripted and forced to hold London Bridge against the peasants of Kent. Not on my own, of course, but it was not a pleasant experience. Cannon-fire, matchlock-fire, arrows – they threw everything at us, and it seemed to be mostly me they were aiming at. I managed to survive that and was able to evade injury but, in the thick of things, I was noticed by others in the fighting, and they formed the rash assumption that I was a fellow ideally placed by nature and training to remove some of those obstacles that occasionally put themselves in the way of the well-meaning and righteous. By which I mean I was employed to be an assassin.

It must be stated here that although I am naturally of a courageous bent, and am more than content to risk all for a good cause, yet I dislike the actual reality of violence. I do not like blood. I do not like the sight of it, the smell of it or the feel of it. That is particularly true of my own, but I extend the same courtesy to that of others as well. I am not a natural murderer for hire. For that reason, I tend to hire a fellow I know, who is very competent at removing those people who have grown to be an irritation to my betters.

Thus far, it had been a most convenient arrangement. I earned a goodly sum to keep me in a pleasant situation; I was given a new suit of clothes every year; I had a house and a servant; and I received a bonus with every problem dispatched. All was well at the outset of the year.

But events conspired against me. The Queen, ever a suspicious woman, had heard rumours of a fresh rebellion, thought up by Ashton and Dudley. These two blockheads decided to rob the Exchequer to pay for an army. Armed with bullion, they crossed to France, where a warm welcome awaited them, and there they plotted as best they might. But in England, matters were not going their way. Their co-conspirators had been discovered, and soon many were in the Tower. And it was now that Lady Elizabeth, Mary's half-sister, became implicated. Her servants, her friends and even her comptroller were arrested and questioned, and it seemed clear that a case was being made against all.

The first I knew was when my master was captured. He was a servant to Elizabeth's comptroller, Sir Thomas Parry, the fat Welshman who had managed her affairs since her childhood. To be a friend or associate of Sir Thomas or John Blount was now to be suspected in my own right.

Praise be to God, suddenly Elizabeth was released. It was all a misunderstanding, we heard. The Queen even sent her a massive diamond and assured the Lady that she had never truly been suspected; there were allegations from some of her staff, but no matter. Elizabeth was released from the Tower into the care of some of Mary's most trusted officials.

I was utterly confused by this turn of events. Mary was a pleasant enough woman when I met her, but I would never think of her as forgiving. I could not help but remember poor Lady Jane Grey being executed on Tower Hill. She saw her husband going to his execution, and saw the corpse brought back, knowing it was to be her turn next that same day. A woman of only seventeen years. That was enough to persuade many in London that Mary was not a kindly soul.

Still, Lady Elizabeth was released from the Tower, and all should have been well.

Which it was. For a month. One month. Then a cloth-brained fool of a schoolmaster took it into his head to declare himself the Earl of Devonshire, and claimed that he and his beloved 'bedfellow', Elizabeth, were rightful King and Queen of England, or some such nonsense, and tried to raise an army about him.

News of this came to me while I was sitting in an inn outside the city, and it was adequate to make me leap up and hurry from the room in an instant. Why? Because if this contender for village idiot of the century could claim he was King, and that Elizabeth would be his Queen, Mary would in short order have all Elizabeth's household and known acquaintances arrested before the rebellion could take hold. My master worked for Parry, and I worked for both. If there were to be arrests and incarcerations in the Tower, I did not intend to be one of them.

So it is surely no surprise that I fled. I found a mount and paid considerably more than it was worth, leapt into the saddle and was away that same day. And since that day I had not stopped running until I reached that benighted town.

You will understand why the thought of being unable to leave the country was not appealing. I was certain to be invited to the Tower at Her Majesty's pleasure, and if you have heard half the tales I have heard of that dismal place, you will understand my sense of urgency. Besides, if she were to learn that I was assassin-in-chief to her half-sister Elizabeth, I wouldn't give a clipped penny for my chances of escaping with my life.

Yet it could not be denied that my head was not in the best

of fettle. As soon as I was left alone in my chamber, before I felt the first bite of the flea, I fell into a deep slumber.

When I woke, it was past dawn already, and the tavern was a place of bustle and noise. I rose, grimacing at the pain in my head, and clothed myself as best I might. My jack, to my despair, had been well covered in my gore, and the material was stained and messy. When I hunted for my hat, I realized I must have left it in the ordure of the stable the previous evening. Picking it up had been the last thing on my mind at that time. Still, I tied the laces to my hosen, tugged on my boots, buttoned my jack, pulled my sword's baldric over my head, tugged at the strap of my powder flask and shot, grabbed my great wheel lock and shoved that away into my belt. I felt sure that were there a mirror large enough, it would show me as a stern, handsome, warlike creature who would put the fear of God into any who dared thwart my intentions.

I turned and instantly closed my eyes. The pain from the two injuries was enough to have forced a weaker man to his knees – but I am made of stronger stuff. I reopened my eyes without a murmur, strode to the door and pulled it wide.

Or, rather, I tried to. It refused to open. I tried the latch once more, but the door remained stubbornly immovable. Peering through the slats of the door, I could see nothing. That was good. At least there was no guard set outside my door. If they were keeping me here to pass me over to a local bailiff, and have me taken back to London, they must surely have set a man to watch and make sure I didn't escape.

Then a fresh thought settled in my stomach like cold suet. They could not have realized I was running from the Queen's men, surely? That would be ridiculous! I had only arrived here myself yesterday, and did not use my real name of Jack Blackjack, but my *nom de guerre* of Peter the Passer. In any case, the Queen's messengers would take as long as I had, surely. No one had overtaken me on the road, after all. I had heard that her messengers could exert themselves to extraordinary levels on occasion, but for them to get here so soon, they would have to have flown!

No, it couldn't be that. It must be because these locals were seeking to protect me. They wanted to make sure that I was safe from another attempt at robbery, perhaps. Anyone could have broken into my room in the middle watches of the night and taken my sword or gun.

'Hoi! Hey! Let me out of here!' I bellowed. After all, the simple fact was that I had no idea why I was being held, and the easiest way to find out was to ask. 'Hello! Hey!'

It was some moments before my knocking on the door and shouting resulted in a figure approaching. 'What do you want?'

I almost sank to the floor in relief. 'I am glad to hear your voice, maid. Please let me out of here. Why have I been locked in? Who locked this door?'

'I did. As if you need to know why! It's because you killed old Daniell Vowell, and folk here are not happy to have a murderer walking our lanes.'

Standing with my mouth agape, I had no idea what she was talking about. I was as confused as a hound chasing a cat's scent who suddenly meets a lion. 'Eh? Who?' I asked, but there was no answer. All I could hear was her footsteps disappearing down the corridor.

That was a blow, I will admit. What was she talking about? She had not struck me as lunatic last evening, but the wench must have been moonstruck to accuse me of murder, surely? She had helped me to my room, although she declined my various offers, and to be honest, it was better that she did. My head was swimming, and I could not have performed at my best if she had come for a mattress-walloping.

I heard her footsteps disappear, and although my mouth remained open, and I wanted to beg her to open the door, not a sound came. I was so flabbergasted, I could only give a squeak when I tried to call to her.

Weakly, I tottered to the bed. I sat on it with all the posture and elegance of a boned chicken. It truly felt as though the life had been sucked from me. I could hear a rushing noise in my ears, and my head swam. It felt much as though I was going to be sick, as if I had partaken of too much wine and ale, and in order to forget the onset of nausea, I took to enumerating my woes, which just at that moment seemed to be multiplying at an alarming rate.

Life was so unfair.

To be named as a murderer was intolerable. I was being held here against all reason, when I was the injured party, with two wounds at my skull to prove the matter. Here I was, accused of slaying a man, while I was also being hunted from London, in all likelihood, because I had a reputation for being an assassin – although I had never intended to be cast in that role – and someone had robbed me of my money, too. All I wished and desired was to be able to leave this benighted town and continue my journey to the port and freedom, but everything conspired to keep me here.

The window was unbarred, but I was on the second floor, so the drop to the ground was much too far for me to jump. When I looked out, I could see many hand- and foot-holds. The building was of timber frame, with limewashed wattle and daub filling the gaps, but the builder had stinted on the daub. Whereas some houses and taverns had the wooden beams flush with the plaster, here the beams had a half-inch to an inch of wood projecting from the wall.

I peered more closely. A bold man could climb through the window, place a foot on the wooden beam that supported the window frame, cling to the window sill as he manoeuvred himself from one wooden support to the next, and after a few moments of cautious clambering be down on the cobbles outside in the yard and safe.

Or he could allow himself to slip along the wall, feet on one beam where it projected, and with his fingers clinging to the upper beam, which was just reachable, make his way to the next chamber, which was surely not locked like mine, and escape.

Yes. A bold man could. However, my innate respect for danger forbad me from making the attempt.

I returned to the bed in a mournful temper. In all truth, I could have wept for the injustice of it all.

The sun was approaching noon, I reckoned, when I heard steps returning along the passageway outside.

'Hello? Maid?'

There was a grunt, which made me think at first that a bear

had escaped the local pits and had come to dismember me. Then I remembered Mal, the host of the tavern. It was him.

He had a key, and it rattled and squeaked when he pushed it into the keyhole and turned it.

I was prepared. I took up my pistol, made sure it was wound up, and held it out as the door opened.

He looked surprised to see me. Behind him, I saw the maid again, this time holding a board, on which stood a quart of ale, half a loaf of bread and some cheese. She eyed me without expression, but the host took up more of my attention. He was gripping his cudgel again and, at the sight of me, hefted it as though considering a third bout for my skull.

I thrust the pistol at him.

'Mf' 'a'?' he said, cross-eyed as he stared at the muzzle.

'What?' Really, these country clods could at least learn a basic understanding of plain English and how to speak it.

'He said, "What's that?"' the maid said helpfully, peering around his broad shoulder.

I gazed at her uncertainly, and he reached up to grab my gun, but I was trained to fight in the streets of London. I was more than a match for this fellow when it came to defending myself. Drawing the pistol away, I snapped, 'If you try to grab it, I will fire it at you!'

The man's brows drew down in a scowl, but he had enough wits to withdraw his hand.

'Good. Now, stand back. I refuse to remain here in this room a moment longer.'

She shrugged and stepped away, elbowing the host from my path as she went. He complied with a bad grace, keeping between me and her as far as he could. I walked out into the passageway and held my gun pointing at him.

'You wait here. Don't follow me, or I'll loose the gun,' I said grimly. It clearly worked, because although the man scowled, the maid shrugged as if it was a matter of no moment for her, and so, walking backwards, my gun pointing at them, I made my way along the passage. The bedchamber was on a second level, over the tavern's kitchen, and there were steps outside which led down to the yard. I hurried down them and strode out to the stables, thinking to saddle my beast and make my exit. And I would have been at Plymouth by supper time, had I not been interrupted.

'Mass' Pass'r?' A voice called, but I didn't break my stride. Truth be told, I had forgotten that I had given my name as Peter the Passer yester-e'en when I arrived here. Since leaving London, I had used several names, and just now that name didn't register. I continued on my way.

'Pass'r? Oi, *you!*'

The uncouth bellow was enough to set my bruises all a-jangle, and I turned to see the cause of this unnatural row.

Behind me stood a slim man with shabby jerkin and hosen. He wore a tattered cloak that had seen better decades and was all bespattered with mud. His face, fortunately, was open like many a gull I have known. There was no guile or viciousness in his features.

I almost stopped and went to chat to him, but even as I had the thought, two more men appeared. These were from a different mould – large, broad and with the sort of closed, suspicious face that I have seen all too often before on the visages of bailiffs. I would have taken to my heels, or preferably my horse's hooves, but there was no escape today. Even as I had the thought, another man appeared and stood leaning against the doorway to the stables. He, too, was a sturdy fellow, and I recognized the fellow immediately. It was the man who had been in the tavern the night before, leaning against the wall. Today he looked different, as though he could cope with two thoughts in every hour. But a henchman doesn't need brains. Just looking at him reminded me of a bully boy from London. He had the look of a man who was fully experienced at handling himself in a fight. This was not some pretty fellow who would squeal at the sight of blood and run; this was a professional fighter who would think little of removing my head to see how it fitted on my shoulders.

I swallowed and determined to make the best of a poor situation.

'Good day, Master,' I said, fixing a suitably servile smile on my face. 'Can I help you?'

'You'm for'ner yer?' the man said.

He must have been only five and twenty or so. His face was

unmarked with any of those little signs of experience. All in all, he had the look of a fellow who was on his way to a meeting with like-minded individuals in a tavern that sold good rum or brandy in large quantities, and was reluctant to be delayed by the appearance of some stranger.

I allowed my smile to broaden. 'Why, yes,' I said. 'I am passing through on my way to Plymouth, and—'

My explanation was curtailed by the fool of a host, who suddenly appeared in the doorway to the tavern, pointed at me and roared something . . . well, I assume it was something to do with my parentage and general demeanour, because he didn't sound happy. Whatever it was, the three heavies started to make their way towards me, the round-faced fellow looking apologetic.

He opened his mouth to say something, and I acted.

I have spoken before about the need for quick thinking and faster running. When fellows are after you, there are some basic principles to hold in your mind. First and foremost, if you are as fleet of foot as I, it is worth always concentrating on the fact that whoever is behind you is not likely to catch you. Only those fellows in front pose a risk. So don't waste time glancing over your shoulder to see whether they are close enough to grab you – if they were, they would already have done so. No, the main thing is to hurry forwards. Because you need to be somewhere else, farther away, out of their reach. It doesn't really matter where, precisely, as long as you are not in the vicinity of the men chasing you. In this case, I had an easy choice: run to the stables, where gorilla number three was waiting to pull my head off; run towards my round-faced friend, in which case his companions, gorillas numbers one and two, could have a splendid game of human racking, each grabbing an arm and seeing who could rip his from my shoulders first; or possibly run in the opposite direction and escape.

It took me only a moment to weigh up the options. Then I was off.

Now, obviously a fool would decide too late which was the better direction to take. In my case, it was easy. My back was to the two with the apologetic commander, and I was facing the stable. Left of me was the entrance to a pasture of some sort, with what looked like a fence, hedge and fields beyond. That was appealing, but a field means rough ground, and that is harder to run on. Added to that was the fact that I could see a cow or bull staring at me near the gate. That meant an additional risk, plus the fact that the field would be enclosed. I would have to fight my way through thorny hedges, no doubt, or get held up at a gate or two. All unpleasant delays which might well lead to an even more undesirable capture.

Naturally, I chose the alternative. I span on my heel and bolted to the right. And it was clearly not something they had expected, because I heard a muttered oath and a man fall, I think. Meanwhile, my gaze was fixed on the far horizon and the joyful sight of the roadway passing through this horrible town. I knew that if I could make it to that road, I would be able to pass around the castle, on up the hill (where my youth and strength would allow me to power on ahead) and thence on to the long road to Plymouth, which was, so I had been told, in that direction. Best of all, it was all on a flat, if badly potholed, roadway, with a surface that had ruts and stones but which was still preferable to the tussocks of grass on a pasture, with holes where hooves had sunk deep into the soft soil. At least on a road I could see the risks.

That was all in my mind as the road suddenly came into sharp focus, but at entirely the wrong angle. It was most confusing and curious, and I studied it for a little while.

You know how it is when something distracts you from your chosen path? When, to pick an example, you are riding fast on a safe, easy track and approach a hedge, and you bend down and clap spurs to the beast's flanks preparing to jump, and the horse suddenly stops, and you find yourself flying through the air without the brute as company? There is invariably a moment of peace and rational thought, during which the mind performs some extraordinarily swift calculations, such as: If I left the horse when he was at full gallop, that means I am now flying towards that stump at a speed roughly the same as a horse can go, which means that the pain on landing will be roughly the same as . . .

The fact is, a similar occurrence affected me now. I was

flying through the air, and I can clearly recall the thoughts which passed through my mind:

> One: Why am I not still running?
> Two: How can I be flying through the air?
> Three: *Why* am I flying through the air?
> Four: When will I stop flying?

The last was the first question to be answered. I suppose I was only in the air for a second, if that, but it felt at the time as though it was a considerable period. I had time to put both hands in front of me, and as soon as they struck the ground, I knew the answer to the fifth question: Will this hurt?

Yes. It did. My hands failed to stop my forward momentum, and every stone and gravel chipping in the yard caught the palms of my hand and ripped the flesh from them, shortly before my chin joined in the fun. The feeling of my jaw hitting the ground, the sudden wrench at my neck, the crunch of teeth slamming together, the rasp of stones on my chin – all formed a distinctly unpleasant experience which was not assisted by the continued pounding of my head injuries.

But I forgot to mention the answer to the 'Why' question. That was soon provided as I lay there, winded and in agony.

The maid from the tavern was just beside me, leaning on the broom, whose handle she had deployed to send me flying. I was about to scrabble to my feet when she wielded it expertly like a quarterstaff at the back of my head. I subsided with an oath of my own, my head ringing unpleasantly. I swear there were stars whirling before my eyes as I gazed at the ground.

'What did you do that for?' I demanded, blinking to dispose of the stars.

'To remove this,' she said, placing what felt like a none-too-dainty foot on the small of my back and retrieving my gun.

I would have protested more, but for the feeling of flying again. This time it was the impetus given to me by a pair of hands the size of bucklers grabbing me under the arms and lifting me to my feet. I found myself gripped by the two bully-boys of the round-faced man, and suddenly his apologetic smile was before me. He glanced at the two holding me up and shook

his head at the maid. 'You didn't 'ave to 'urt him, Agnes. We'd
have had 'im in a trice as it was.'

The maid shrugged and leaned on her broom. 'Your boys
were too slow. He'd have left them standing.'

I could understand them, I realized. Perhaps the knock on
my pate had dislodged something, so that now all their words
were perfectly clear. I shook my head. It was preferable to
remain uncomprehending, I decided – especially now that my
arms were likely to be pulled from their moorings. I glanced
from left to right. No, these boys were unlikely to let me slip
away.

The man took the gun from 'Agnes' and studied it carefully.
When he looked up at me, he still wore that faintly apologetic
smile. 'My apologies, Mast' Pass'r. We don't usually welcome
volk to our town in this manner, but you'll 'preciate that when
there's been an attack—'

'Yes, I was attacked, and look, you can see where my head
has swollen! But you treat me as if *I* were a villain, instead of
the churl who knocked me down! In faith, I swear, I have never
been to such a nest of vipers as this! And now you hold me
against my will?'

'Yes, well, you understand poor Daniell is dead, and there's
only one man who everyone agrees must have disliked him.
That happens to be a stranger – you. So, if you want, we can
argue the matter out here or you could accept my hospitality
for a while. How does that sound?'

Of course, when he put it like that, it did change the complexion
of the matter. I followed him into the tavern once more, my
feet scarcely having to touch the ground, with the aid of his
men. Passing inside, they incidentally managed to knock my
brow on the lintel, which made me yelp in pain. That was the
fourth injury to my skull, and it served to remind me of my
missing hat. I turned, thinking to go and hunt for it at the first
opportunity, and found my gaze blocked by the stableman guard.
It seemed to me, gazing into his eyes, that the search for my
hat was suddenly uninteresting.

'So what is all this about?' I demanded as I took my seat at
a table. 'All this fuss over a peasant who robbed me?'

with the repellent Daniell and, after being beaten about the head for a period, now was suspected of being a murderer. Which was a step down from my actual job as assassin, which does at least carry a little cachet, I think.

But the simple fact of the matter was that right now I was staring into the face of a man who appeared to have ice flowing through his veins. He had just told me that his father had been murdered and I was his only suspect, but meanwhile he was treating me with the courtesy of an equal. It was like being questioned by an affable priest while all the while behind him the Inquisition stood with braziers and brands waiting.

'You will understand that I would like to know what actually happened to my father,' he said, and lifted a finger. Instantly, Agnes sprang into action and brought him a fresh jug of wine. He even filled a goblet for me, and I took a large gulp. A quantity went down the wrong hole and left me coughing and spluttering for some while. In the end, one of his henchmen struck me on the back so hard I thought he must drive my spine through my mouth. I stopped choking just to ensure I didn't receive another 'helpful' buffet.

When I could speak again, I managed, 'I don't know. I was out cold in the stable.'

'So you have said, yes . . . But let me explain. My father was a tin miner. He has many men working for him, and they all respected him greatly.' He held up a hand when I attempted to offer my condolences. 'Now, the point is, all those men relied on my father to keep the land for them. He must protect them from the rampages of others who would come and steal their wealth. And for that work, he naturally took a small gratuity from each of them. The miners had a lot of respect for my father, you see.'

Ah, so blackmail and extortion, I thought to myself. It was the way of the world. No doubt his 'small gratuity' was enough to keep a man like me very comfortably. Which begged the question, why had his father been dressed like a peasant?

'They will all be very sorry to hear that you killed their master and protector.'

'I didn't kill anyone! I was victim of—'

'So you say. On the moors, you know, the miners run their

'No, over the man who was killed last night, the man people say you killed.'

The little fellow sat at the head of the table, and I gained the impression that he was used to command. It was there in the way he looked at me before seating himself, as though I had no right to take my seat before him. There was enough disdain in his eyes for me to scrabble to try to rise to my feet. I had the distinct feeling that this was rather like a meeting with royalty – or, rather, it was like meeting a man who ran a gang of cutpurses in the city. The sort of man who could cut your legs away and laugh at you for not standing until he was seated. I've met a few like that. And to think I'd thought him a young innocent!

This one was a cool operator. First, he spoke over the tavern-keeper as the man tried to browbeat him and tell him to take me to the town's gaol – I won't repeat the name the host used for me, which was exceedingly disrespectful – and soon had the host running to fetch ales and brandy for our merry little group, and demanded logs for the fire instead of the turves, and called for a pottage to warm him.

By now, I was sure that I had got the man's measure. He was obviously the Coroner, brought here to question me as a witness in the death of 'Daniell'. I swallowed and prepared to make as much of my injuries as was practically possible. 'How can I help you?' I said, using my feeblest voice.

'Peter Passer, you call yourself?' the man asked. He looked as apologetic as a rider paying a woman for knocking down her child.

'Yes, that's me,' I said. I nodded encouragingly and had to wince at the pain.

'The good landlord here tells me that you were assaulted last evening.'

You noticed, too? Yes, he could speak passable English, without the difficult *zur*s and *zider*s of the others. He could almost have arrived here from Middlesex.

'That's right. Someone attacked me and knocked me down. I wanted to go and look for my hat, which must still be on the floor where he hit me. And he stole my purse! Look, it was here,' I said, displaying the cut laces. 'I think it was that cur

Daniell, because he lost to me in gambling. A perfectly fair game, it was, too,' I added huffily. After all, not many games were as fair as that. 'He followed me outside, struck me down and robbed me.'

'He played fair? It would have made a change,' my companion murmured.

'Coroner, I don't know what happened after I was hit, but I heard that this man Daniell was killed, and I had nothing to do with that. I was beaten, robbed and left for dead. That is all I know.'

'So you didn't stab Daniell and murder him?'

'I was unconscious, in the stable,' I reminded him.

'You see, if you had made up being attacked, then, well, that would be an easier story. It would explain why your hat was there, beside the body. If you hadn't been knocked down, but had followed after Daniell, stabbed him in the back and – I don't know, perhaps the laces of your purse got entangled in his belt or something, and when he fell, he pulled your purse with him. That would explain why he was found on his belly, but not where your purse had gone, would it?'

'My hat was with his body? Where is it?' I said. A wonderful hopefulness wafted through my body. All I needed was to retrieve my hat, find my purse, saddle the horse, and I could be away!

'I am sure you can have it back. No doubt you will be allowed to leave before long. Just as soon as we have had the inquest . . . and when we learn why you killed him.'

'Why would I kill him? He was the man who attacked me! Are you sure my purse wasn't near him? Perhaps it fell into the vegetation? His attacker, in the dark, didn't see it, or—'

'Or, perhaps you realized he was following you, or when he knocked you down, you weren't badly injured, and you chased after him and slew him with your dagger. I see you have it there. May I see it?'

His words were, of course, only a matter of form. One of his fellows reached down to my dagger and pulled it from its sheath, passing it over.

'It is interesting always to study the weapons used to kill others,' the fellow observed. 'Look here, for example. Dark

stains of some form of dirt up near the quillons. Who but that these might not be blood? A man could wipe in the dark and not see these, after all.'

'It's nothing of the sort!' I protested.

'How can you be so sure?'

I gabbled my innocence, my honourable upbringing, respected father (I didn't swear an oath to that), and, in s did all I could to deny any taint of guilt in this matter.

'So you say,' the fellow said. He smiled at me, and beca I have always been an excellent judge of character, that sm was soothing. He looked like a disappointed father who, aft breaking off a switch to punish a wayward son, learns tha witnesses saw another boy fleeing the area. Suddenly, I was sure that I would be freed. I could feel the anxiety draining from me and began to plan my escape. First, find out where the body lay so that I could search for my purse, then retrieve my gun and demand my horse to be saddled and bridled, before taking my leave of this noisome little town. The sooner I was on the ship the better.

I glanced over at him, hoping that my sycophantic approach would help, and then looked up to where Agnes was standing, still grasping her broom. To my surprise, I saw that she was agitated, rather as though she was fearful of this round-faced Coroner.

'Oh, by the way, I'm not the Coroner,' he said with a quiet little cough. 'My name is David Vowell. I'm here because Daniell, the man we think you killed . . . well, he was my father.'

I have been unfortunate enough to have suffered many of the knocks life can throw at a man who was only ever doing his best to survive, but this one really did seem unfair. After all, I was being sought by the Queen's men because she thought I might have been involved in some plot with her half-sister. I mean, only someone deranged could have thought that self-possessed, devious and cunning vixen Lady Elizabeth would have confided in a common man like me – but leave that to one side. The fact was, I was fleeing for my life even though I had done nothing wrong, and in fleeing I managed to find my way to this hellhole, met

own affairs. They have their own justice. All perfectly legal, but . . . well, it can be a little rough and ready. But do not let me delay you. If you wish to go, I will not stop you. However, the road will take you past many mining camps. It may be a little hazardous . . . if they learn that the murderer was you.'

'I didn't—'

'So you said. But if you were able to give us some intelligence that indicated who might have been guilty, of course that would make life so much easier. For me . . . and for you.'

I looked up at the henchman at my side. He looked down at me. His face was like moorstone, and I swear, were he to grin, his skin would crack. Glancing at his hands, I reflected that they were as large as shovels and as heavy as mauls. He looked in every way a miner. It was pleasant to think that I might escape from here, only to be met by a gang of similar men, all seeking knowledge – mostly of how all the bits of Jack Blackjack (or Peter the Passer) might be disorganized and investigated.

Swallowing hard, I looked at my companion again, took a long swig of wine and licked my lips. 'What do you want me to do?'

'Well, first, I would like to know how it was that your hat ended up on my father's body.'

It was late. Very late. My 'friend' had gone, and in theory I could have slipped away myself. Yes, I had lost my money, but remaining here was fraught with danger. Escape was appealing. And yet David Vowell's manner, when he spoke of the men on the moors, the army of tin miners and others who revered his father, had been convincing. He had been entirely believable, and if he was to be believed, those men had sympathy for his father. If they captured me, it was plain as the stalk on an apple that I would be forced to suffer a great deal. And then – well, it didn't seem likely that I'd make it to the coast. His conviction was communicated to me perfectly. If only I had someone with me to help. John Blount would not suffer these fools – but he was probably languishing in the Tower with his master. He was not likely to be able to help me ever again.

At that thought, I felt unutterably lonely, a mere orphan in this world of brutish men. I could have wept. Except I wasn't alone exactly. When David Vowell left, one of his henchmen remained. The man who had been here the night of Daniell's death, leaning against the wall, was to remain. I suppose he was here to ensure that no Londoners made a moonlit escape.

Seeing my expression, Agnes came over to me when they left. She brought with her a flagon of wine and a reasonably sympathetic expression. She might even have regretted helping in my capture. 'Drink that. It'll help.'

'It'll help me to escape?' I said bitterly.

'No. But you won't care so much about being stuck here.'

'I should just ride away. I have two horses.'

'They told the stable to keep your horses. Yours and Daniell's. The hostler is guarding them.'

I gave a half sob on hearing that. Trying to sound a little more masculine and brave, I tried to change it to a grunt. Listening to myself, I pulled a face. It sounded as if I was growing Devonian.

She poured a goblet full. To her credit, she looked almost apologetic. I suppose it was guilt at having tripped me and caused me this additional trouble.

Trying to make conversation, I said, 'Who was he? Daniell's son – who is he? *What* is he, if not the Coroner?'

She sighed and leaned against the bar. 'I am sorry. It's not your problem, not your fault, but you have fallen into the middle of a battle.'

At those words, I felt a shiver run down my spine.

'The miners are a powerful group here. Daniell spent his life on the moors and built his own group by his efforts.'

I remembered that face again – the ugly, dirty skin, the thick, pugnacious chin, the little eyes like chips of coal, the compact, wiry frame. Why had I agreed to play dice with him? He was clearly an evil, malevolent spirit. Only a fool would want to spend time with a fellow like him. I had been exhausted from travelling. I should have gone straight to my bed. His was the sort of face that would come back to me at night after eating too much pork and cheese. The mere thought that I could have tried to attack him was . . . well, it was ridiculous!

'Daniell was always a violent man. He had to be, to control his men. The miners are a law to themselves up on the high moor. You wouldn't understand it, but to live out there, in all weathers, you have to be a strong man. And to control them, you have to be stronger and more determined. But he wanted something better for his son. So he had David sent away. He paid for the Bishop of Exeter to allow David into the school. That's where he learned his manners.'

Where he learned to talk English like a baron, I thought, and how to offer fierce bullying and torture with a dollop of honey.

'And now he's back. He got into trouble in Exeter and came home. And he's going to have to take over control of the moors up here if he wants to take over his father's business.'

'Tin mining, you mean?'

She curled a lip at my stupidity. 'Yes, not that he will dig himself. Do you see him getting his hands dirty? No, he'll be visiting the landowners all about and doing what miners do best. It's a business that matters to the Crown, so miners are protected workers. He'll explain to the landowners that their best pasture has tin under it; he'll tell others that the stream that feeds their fields is going to be diverted to drive a water wheel, or send water to wash the ore they dig. And only if the landowners pay their money will their lands be protected. If they pay, the miners will go on to the next one.'

'And it's legal?' I asked. This sounded like a good proposition for a man of business.

'If they say so. Their parliament makes the laws on the moor. And only miners can vote.'

I nodded with some admiration. If only I had been born with such opportunities. To be able to threaten all about at will: that was power, and power was money. If they could extort money just for not digging up a pasture or removing a stream, they were kings here on the moors.

'Why does he want to keep me here?'

She shrugged. 'Who can tell what's in his mind? He wants you to tell your story to the Coroner, of course. If you leave, there are no witnesses, and no one can tell who was responsible. He is his father's son: he wants someone to pay. And you were there; your hat was beside the body, as he said.'

'That's not my fault!'

'It is your business, though. If no one else is found, they will want someone to be held for the next court.'

I chewed at my lip. 'I must escape.'

She gave an unsympathetic sneer. 'Wonderful! Without a horse? No money? And if you were to run, the news would be all over the moors in no time. You may get ten or fifteen miles, but you would be found and caught and brought back here—'

'And then . . .'

'Or worse,' she added.

'What could be worse?' I said.

She said nothing but looked at me thoughtfully while scratching her armpit, as though there was something infinitely worse than being caught and dragged back to this awful place.

'Well?' I said.

'You don't want to think about *that*.'

She was convincing. I decided not to mull it over.

'But I have to get to Plymouth! If he wants me to talk to the Coroner, I will, but I have to get away as soon as I can. How long will the Coroner take to get here?'

'I don't know. It depends on how busy he is. He lives close by, so it shouldn't take him long to get here. And he has his own reasons to see to Daniell's inquest.'

'What do I care of that?'

'No reason why you should,' she said with a shrug. 'He and Daniell had their own disputes, though.'

I was not paying much attention to her. My thoughts were more personally focused. 'Meanwhile, I have to find my purse – and I want my hat back.'

'The hat is being kept here for the Coroner. As to your purse, you'll have to find that yourself, if you want to. At least that way, you'll learn who was responsible for knocking you down.'

'Ha!' It was meant to sting. Of course I would. As I have said, anybody finding my money would slip it all into his own purse. Whoever knocked me down had almost certainly taken my winnings, secreted them somewhere secure where I would never find them, and thrown away my purse or burned it. It was enough to make a man weep. Any one of the peasants here would grab my money with both hands. I had seen the look in the eyes of the men in the tavern when they saw my winnings

– and not only the men. This maid had worn a similar look of Devil-may-care greed. If she could, she would have warmed my bed for me that night in exchange for a handful of coins.

She glanced at me but didn't offer any more sympathy; she merely shrugged and went about her business. I don't think she was a sympathetic soul. Rather than offering apologies for my predicament, or some more appealing compensation, she gave the impression of being disgruntled. I suppose, since she had thought that she might be able to persuade me to share some of my winnings, she was feeling out of sorts as well. Without money, she was less interested in me, the strange chit.

Well, I didn't plan on leaving my money behind. I *would* get away, and I *would* get my money back.

The only problem was *how*.

THREE

Thursday 30th July

I woke next morning with a crick in my neck like a bent iron bar. Trying to move my head was next to impossible. When I rolled over, there was a crack, and I felt a red-hot skewer shoot up into the base of my head. Pushing my cloak from me, I climbed out of the straw and slowly rose to my feet, rubbing the back of my neck.

Yes, straw. On hearing that my purse was gone, the landlord had decided that I was no longer a valued guest. My food and drink could not be paid for, so I was undesirable in his tavern. Ejected from my room, with my gun and sword confiscated in lieu of payment for the first night's victuals, I was pointed in the direction of the hayloft, where I shared my bed with a number of rats. Still, there were fewer fleas here than in the tavern's bed.

It had not been a pleasant night, all told. I spent much of it running through the events of the past two days, from my arrival here in the town to the appearance of the old miner, my injuries, the theft of my money and then the appearance of Daniell's son.

I was not the only man to resent the keeper's decision. David's man, left behind to keep an eye on me and prevent my attempting to escape, was clearly disgruntled, too. My companion was obviously as experienced at watching people as he was at leaning against tavern walls. The fellow had the expression of a man who had been looking forward to an evening of cider and mutton stew but who, since he was forced to remain with me, had discovered such simple pleasures were denied him. Instead, he had a stool in the doorway to the stable. It made my rustling bed feel all the more comfortable. Not that his glower made me happy. He still looked as though opening my gizzard to investigate my interior would be more satisfying for him.

Walking over the courtyard to the tavern, I demanded food and drink, but the surly tavern-keeper refused me. He maintained a grim determination to deprive me of any sustenance. However, my companion had a quick discussion with him, which involved his picking up the tavern-keeper by the jerkin, shoving him against a wall and holding a brief but very intense one-way conversation with him. I think the lack of sleep had made him crotchety, and it was all I could do not to clap approvingly as he explained in words of some curious dialect how the tavern-keeper's face could be easily modified by the use of a miner's hammer, and went on to describe the sort of accidents that happened to those running taverns who chose to make miners sleep on stools in a hayloft, and how a hungry, tired miner could become quite temperamental if forced to forgo his breakfast.

At least, that is the sort of thing I would have been explaining if it had been me who was shaking the man like a terrier snapping the spine of a rat. Sadly, the finer nuances were missed by me, since I couldn't understand many of the words he was using, but the result was a gratifying alacrity on the part of the host, and he bustled about accommodatingly, roaring at Agnes to come and prepare eggs and bring bread.

I made as good a breakfast as I could on weak ale, eggs, bread and a little ham, and when I sat back, my belly comfortably full, and took in the maid's taciturn expression, I was hurt. After all, I had not done her a bad turn; if either of us had cause to be disappointed or bitter with the other, it was me with her, for tripping me and ensuring I was captured by the miner. When I attempted a mild pleasantry, she gave me a look so cold I could feel it chill my spine. That, you see, is what happens when a wench thinks a fellow is wealthy and he is careless enough to lose his purse: she goes from near infatuation to utter contempt. But I knew that when I retrieved my money, she would be keen again. Hah! If she kept up this show of rude disinterest, I would ignore her and pick one of the other women in the area as my bedmate. Let her see how she liked that!

She cleared away our trenchers and pots, and shortly after I walked from the room, my silent guard behind me. I had the impression that he might not be terribly fast, and that I could outrun him – but what would have been the point? I had no idea what the roads were like heading south, and I was painfully aware that if the miners were to disapprove of my escaping, there was a lot of moorland where my body could be disposed of. The first night, someone had been talking about the dangers of the moors, and how a man could fall into a bog and disappear. I hadn't thought much about it at the time, but now it was plain that any path I took to the coast would lead over the moors, and the thought of falling into some filthy mire, the mud entering my mouth and choking me while I sank under . . . well, it made my stomach queasy again.

Outside, I walked about the yard. Musing over the fickle nature of fate, I stood for a moment at the place where I had emptied my bladder against the wall. It had been only a short while afterwards that someone had knocked me down. I glanced back at the stables, and on a whim crossed the yard again. I wandered inside, thinking about the day that Daniell had gambled and lost his horse to me. I had fallen about *here*, I thought, near the second stall. Not that the straw would show my imprint. I was merely glad that I had a soft place to land when I was hit.

What was peculiar was that I was sure I had seen a shadow in front of me. But the man who knocked me down must have been behind me. And I hadn't noticed my own shadow because it was dark. But ahead of me there had been a glow – perhaps a candle? And that shadow, which had surprised me. And then I was knocked down. The shadow had not come from the man behind me, then.

There must have been two people in the stables with me that night.

This was something I had to think about. I saw the hostler busying himself about the place. Walking into the stables, I patted my brute on the rump, and she took a half-hearted kick at me, but she still wasn't feeling up to it and missed. Still, it was good to know the monster remembered me.

Her stall had been cleaned and swept, I saw. There was no muck about, only fresh straw, and I pulled a face, knowing that the tavern-keeper would be charging me for all the work done to help my horse recover. At this rate, I would never regain my pistol and sword.

In the next stall but one was the profit from my gambling. Whereas my own rounsey was a sturdy brute when fit, this looked as though it had been kidnapped on the way to the butcher's yard. Certainly, it hardly looked capable of supporting a man on its back. I went to the animal's head and studied it without enthusiasm. Bones protruded at hip and shoulder, and the thing was as short as a foal. I wondered whether the animal would be able to make it to the stable door and back without toppling over. Surely this beast would be better off sold. Again, probably to the butcher. There was no point trying to load the animal with my belongings as a sumpter. Even one pack would break its back, from the look of the poor creature.

'He's a poor old fellow,' a voice said.

Turning, I found myself confronted by a tall, sallow man leaning on a dung fork. He was the sort of figure I would have expected to find in a stable. A mean-looking, ill-fed lad of some two or three and twenty, with a pale, mousey-coloured shock of hair above a face that wasn't entirely ugly, I suppose. He didn't have the clean, chiselled good looks that I had been graced with, but not everyone can be as fortunate as me, obviously.

'He looks a poor fellow, certainly. Badly fed, poorly treated and no doubt prey to every illness known to equestrians,' I said. 'If I'd known this midget was my winnings, I'd have told the fellow to keep his bet and be damned! As it is, I suppose I can give him to the landlord here as partial payment for my room.'

This was a thought that hadn't occurred to me before. The value of a horse, even one in the condition of Daniell's, was more than the cost of my board. I decided to make the offer as soon as I could. At least tonight I might have a bed again. The thought made me simultaneously smile and scratch at a couple of flea bites.

'He's well enough. A good temperament, and he can travel all day long without complaint,' the hostler said, snapping a carrot in half and feeding one piece to the dwarfish beast.

'Really? He looks as though he has been badly bred – a mixture of pony and hound.'

'He's strong and reliable,' the lad said, and apparently took umbrage at my insulting of his charge. He picked up his fork and made his way to my horse, feeding her the other half of carrot. I saw him peering over her back at me as he got on with whatever it is hostlers get on with, and I left him to it.

Walking out, I almost walked into the guard again.

He really was a horrible sight. His face pallid from lack of sleep, he loomed over me when I left the stable. Bloodshot eyes took in my appearance with apparent disgust.

'Well?' I said.

'What?' he said.

'What are you doing, blocking my path?'

'You'm killed my maister, and I'm yere to see you don't try to escape before Coroner comes. Then us'll see you 'ang.'

I considered him without pleasure. He was a most unappealing companion. 'You do know what justice means, I suppose? I am innocent until a court is held, and then I can rely on the jury to listen to the evidence and decide my innocence.'

He bared his teeth at that. 'You b'ain't vrum yere. You'm be glad you don't be up on thickee moor. Don't have that law there. There t'iz *our* law – Lydford Law.'

'What does that mean?'

He chuckled in what I can only describe as a highly unpleasant manner and walked off to a bench.

I decided to ignore the foul-mannered ogre and wandered out to the roadway.

'Where be you to?' he demanded as soon as my direction became apparent.

I turned to him with exasperation. 'My horses are in the stable, my purse is stolen, my gun and sword are held by the tavern-keeper – even if I wanted to go somewhere, how do you think I could? If you want to make sure, you are welcome to join me, but if you have nothing better to say or do than sit there and complain, well . . .' I was short with him, but I felt I had the right to be. However, I had already run out of potential insults, and the sight of the anger rising on his face made me recall how he had lifted the tavern-keeper in one hand and thrust him against the wall. I was, I realized, lighter than the host of the establishment. It made me reflect that perhaps baiting him when he was already exhausted after sleeping little, if at all, was perhaps not the best idea. I turned on my heel and left him with an imperious gesture of contempt that I rather hoped he did not notice.

Lydford Law, I mused. What on earth that meant, I didn't know. This was Okehampton, after all. There was another place not far away called Lydford, I had heard. I shrugged, content to remain in blissful ignorance. I had no idea then that I might learn all too much about the style of justice that existed on the moors.

No, I thought, it was probably nothing more than a local term that meant some form of insult to men of higher degree like me. I would not allow him to distract me. He couldn't worry me. I wasn't at all perplexed.

The town was a mean, ragged little place that once may have been important. I guessed that because in the distance I could see a castle. It was quite an imposing building, and I imagined a moderately important lord must have had his base there, because it had a good, defensive appearance. A place like that, surely, must be the seat of a man of importance and influence.

On a whim, I walked towards it. There was a river to my left for most of the way. Someone had mentioned that there were two rivers here in Okehampton, both flowing from the hideous wasteland that was the moor, and continuing somewhere to the north, I suppose. This river was full and fast, but only small. It was nothing like the Thames in London, of course. It could not compete with that. Except, perhaps, in terms of its freshness. The water here was clear and wholesome. I happily drank a handful or two, which I would not have attempted in London. The turgid brown mess that passed for water in the rivers there is not appealing.

Left of my path, a series of wooded hills rose, and there was a small plain that was obviously used as pasture. The castle stood proudly on its hillock, with a great wall protecting it. As I drew nearer and reached a ford in the river, I could see it more clearly. It was obviously no longer in use. The great wall that encircled it had been neglected, and the long corridor leading from the barbican to the gatehouse was infested with weeds and mosses. I gained the impression of a great building that was sliding into decline, rather like the sad manor of Woodstock, where I had first met Lady Elizabeth. There, the holes in the roofs and broken windows meant much of the building was unusable. Here, the castle's walls were obviously decaying, and there was no sign of life.

It made me sad. Somehow, it reminded me of my life. Once successful and flourishing, but now a faded and pale reminder of what it had been. Perhaps others would see me like this castle: a decaying reminder of past glories. I was struck with a sudden melancholy, soon joined by a feeling of resentment. Why should I be forced to flee the country? How would I survive in France if I could not even understand the locals here in Devon? I would become a laughing stock over there, no doubt. A shambling figure of derision, mocked by even peasants and their brats.

I turned, thinking to return to the tavern, but when I glanced back along the roadway, I saw the heavy-set frame of my guard standing there, watching me.

He put me off the idea of going back straightaway. I didn't want to pass him in the street. He scared me. In the past, I had been assured of friends and companions who would help me to evade danger and protect me when I needed their assistance. Here, I had nothing. All those about the town seemed to assume my guilt, and if they could have their way, they would condemn me to an early grave with a stretched neck.

I was a sorrowful, lonely man, standing there before the castle. Life, I felt, was so unfair to innocents like me. All I had ever done was my master's bidding. Yes, it was to see other people slain, but that was not my choice.

Yes, life was decidedly unfair.

I continued towards the castle. A ford led to what I later learned was a great deer park which sprawled across the hillside, with thick woodland interspersed with horrible, prickly furze and low-lying heathers. Ahead of me, past the northern wall, the main road to Cornwall curled about the castle's foundation. A way ahead, I could see that there were more woods, and smoke rose, so I guessed that there were more houses along there.

A pair of tiny, thatched cottages stood near the ford, and a woman was weeding the raised beds in her little garden. Various leaves were there that I didn't recognize, but there were also onions and garlic, and she had a form of wicker tray on which she had collected beans and valerian flowers. Other plants looked familiar, not that I was particularly interested. I was still nursing my grievances.

The peasant woman studiously ignored my presence, but when I asked her who lived in the castle now, she straightened from her bending, her hands in the small of her back, stretching her neck. Once, I dare say, she might have been an appealing woman, but now I guessed that children, hard work and the weather had beaten her features and figure into submission. Her belly sagged as much as her breasts, and her face was as mournful as a hungry mastiff's.

I was, by now, growing accustomed to the rasping tones of the locals. Slightly nasal, with ragged, harsh consonants and a lazy speech that rolled everything into one long 'Wehroohaarwehr' noise that was as incomprehensible as the cry of the baker's boy back at my home in London. Every time he passed, he would scream something – I don't know what. It was one of those daily noises that signified nothing. I certainly couldn't make out any words in his strange shrieks, but that he was saying *something* was unarguable, and people would flock to him to buy his fresh bread, not because they knew what he was saying, but because they recognized his specific voice.

However, here in Devon, people did appear to understand whatever their neighbours were saying, and I was a little concerned that I was also beginning to comprehend. Thus, if this woman had said something that sounded like 'You'm unna naw wat 'un were zayin'?', I would instantly have known she had tried to say, 'You want to know what he was saying?' It will save us all a lot of time if I translate from here, I think. Otherwise, you will grow as confused as I was.

So when I asked, 'Who owns the castle?' she replied, 'It's the King's.'

That, of course, made me smile, since we hadn't had a king in some years. 'I think you mean the Queen's,' I said condescendingly.

'No. King's.'

'There is no King.'

'You tell him that.'

'I would, but, you see, he's dead.'

'You say? Not anyone's told him.'

'Who?'

'The King.'

'I see. The King.'

She gave me a quizzical look. 'Yes, the King.'

'The King of England.'

'No,' she said contemptuously, and turned her back.

'I see,' I said. Clearly, the woman was deranged.

At this moment, an even older and tattier peasant walked up, bent under a load. He had a sack of something on his back, held by a strap that passed over his forehead. He glanced at us and, without breaking step, made some comment deep in his throat which I could not understand even a tenth part of.

As he walked away, I asked her what he had meant. She responded as I have indicated above, and continued, 'He said I shouldn't be talking to the likes of you. You're a foreigner.'

I bristled at that. To be called a foreigner in my own land was enough to make my hackles rise. I had just been thinking about my exile to a foreign land where I would understand nothing of the local language, and here was this old fool accusing *me* of being a foreigner.

Making a comment about peasants, I stalked off after the man.

'Hoi! Hoi! You, there!' I called.

He had taken the path leading past the castle, but as I followed him, he suddenly turned left and entered the castle grounds, walking up a narrow path which took him to the barbican's gate. Without glancing round, he entered and disappeared from view.

'Wait!' I shouted, but he paid me no heed. After a moment or two, I decided that I could not let this miserable creature ignore me without remonstrating, and I hurried my steps as I followed him up the hillside.

Not that the hill or anything else could be seen. As I entered the barbican, a long, dark tunnel led upwards to the main court. The gates here and at the farther side of the gatehouse were both open. A portcullis was visible, the oaken points of the stakes dangling in the slot of the ceiling, and I swallowed to think that they might fall on to a man if he were unlucky. Beyond, there was a long corridor between two walls of grey moorstone, with paving slabs underfoot – although grass was attempting to reconquer the path – and at the top of the pass was the gatehouse. I hurried up here and soon found myself inside a narrow space, which widened as it rose further up the hillside.

This was a castle built for strong defence, clearly, but also for comfort. To my right was a great hall, with a large buttery and kitchens, while on my left were a number of buildings that would once have held pleasing apartments, beyond which was a chapel. Ahead of me was a great keep, with squared walls that looked as though they could withstand even the Queen's artillery.

However, of the old peasant there was not a sign. I peered about me, pushing at rotting wooden doors, but saw nothing of him. Then I heard a slight noise from the hall and went to it. Warily glancing inside, I reassured myself that I was not entering a trap and strode in.

It was a good-sized chamber, with a soaring roof that only lacked a few shingles. I could see the sunshine, such as it was, through them. As I walked further inside, there was a sudden scuffle, and I all but leapt from my skin. A flurry of noise from behind me made me whirl and then shoot a look skywards again. I was in time to see a large black bird rise from a perch and disappear through a largish gap in the roof. A crow or raven, no doubt, I thought as I turned back.

And gave a bleat of alarm.

It's hard not to when a fellow materializes out of thin air in front of you, wielding a very rusty but horribly dangerous-looking knife inches from your heart.

All I could think was, where the hell was my guard now that I really wanted him?

*　　*　　*

'Who're you?' the old peasant demanded.

It was the old man I had seen carrying his pack past the ford. I tried to answer, but at first only a gibber made it from my lips. There is something about the sight of a blade near me that always does that. I tried to step away, but I lurched as a heel caught a stone and I went tumbling down. Which took me away from the knife, at first, which was a relief, until I saw the old fool drop to my side, the blade again perilously close to my heart.

You may complain at my saying the knife was sharp, but it was. And yes, it was also rusty. But when a rusty piece of metal is sharpened, there is a clean, greasy-looking patch of shiny silver metal on an otherwise dull background. This was an appallingly sharp-looking knife. And while it was short, at only four or five inches, that was more than enough to kill a man, as I had heard many times from my expert of sudden death, Humfrie. When I was commissioned to arrange for the death of a man my master decided was unnecessary or irritating, it was to Humfrie I turned. When we had been forced to dispose of enemies of my master or his superiors, Humfrie was the man who undertook the task, for a consideration. He was fond of reminding me that two inches of steel was more than adequate in the right place.

Just now, however, I was not thinking of Humfrie but only of that waving blade. The old man was moving it as if to persuade me to give it my closest attention, and if that was his object, he was succeeding. I could not take my eyes from it.

'Who're you?' he snarled.

The blade moved to my left, then to my right. It absorbed all my powers of concentration. If it had been a diamond the size of a penny, I could not have studied its movements more assiduously.

'I . . . I am—'

'I don't care who you are!'

'I am just a traveller, that's all!'

'What are you doing here in my castle?'

'Your castle?'

'Who else's?'

'I . . . I don't know!'

He waved it once more for good measure, and then settled back on his haunches. Down in Dartmoor, so I have heard, they had certain evil creatures which they called piskies, small fairy-like creatures who would all too often perform misdeeds for travellers. They would lead a man astray across the moors and into a bog, or send him witless. If they didn't look like this evil old man, I should be surprised.

Shorter than me by a good six inches, he had a thick, grizzled beard, a fringe of similar hair passing round his pate, and a pair of eyes that were as intense as they were black. His skin was like six-year-old leather, wrinkled and brown as a chestnut. But there was no doubting his strength. When he suddenly stood and gripped my jack, he exerted a pull like a cart horse. I was smoothly drawn upwards, and he waved his knife under my nose.

'You don't look too dangerous,' he said with a tone that implied disappointment.

'I'm not,' I said quickly. 'I'm just a traveller on my way to Plymouth.'

'Why are you in here, then?'

I explained about staying at the tavern and Daniell's death.

'That miserable son of a mongrel? Someone will win his reward in heaven for killing that thieving son of a poxed Plymouth wench. He's lucky it was fast.' He spat on the ground for good measure. Glancing at me measuringly, he pulled a face and reluctantly shoved his knife into a sheath at his belt. 'I suppose you aren't a threat.'

I was effusive in my reassurances on that.

'Shut up. You make my ears burn,' he said.

'You knew Daniell?' I asked.

'He was the worst bastard to work the moors, and they'm all bastards up there,' he said with feeling.

'I heard he was master of most of the miners.'

'Oh, aye, that was what he would say. He was their master, right enough. Any that didn't acknowledge him was soon out of business. They found their claims would move, from a good site to a poor. Or their huts would be broken down, or their walls torn apart, or their tools stolen, or . . . he had many ways to persuade people to do his will. He was the most powerful man on the moors, and now his son will try to take over from him.'

'I didn't like his son.'

'He's cast from the same mould. Nothing would be too cheap for him to steal it.'

'You know them both?'

He looked at me then from beetling brows. 'Mayhap.'

'You had a dispute with them?'

'Aye.' He gazed at me for a long, serious moment, before suddenly sighing. 'They took my own claim and destroyed all my tools. Threw them into a mire while I watched, and then set to beating me. I couldn't work the moors without my tools, so after they left me for dead, I made my way off the moors. I've been off them ever since.'

'All alone?' I said, glancing about us. It did not seem to me to be the height of luxury. But then I was from London. Civilization ended many leagues to the east.

'Aye,' he said with a glower.

'It must be lonely.'

He snorted. 'When you have lived on the moors, there is no hardship you cannot endure. All is so much better than staying up there when the wind blows. It was no place to bring . . . It is easier down here.'

'I suppose so,' I said, for I was keen to escape. Humouring him seemed the best way to ensure that I would walk away from here without being pinked by his knife. 'I should return to the tavern, I suppose.'

'You are staying there?' Suddenly, a different expression came into his eyes. 'You know the folk living there?'

'Some. A wench, the host, the hostler.'

'Which wench?'

'Agnes. She is a tallish woman, but . . .' I had been about to describe her figure in some detail, but something made me refrain. 'Ah, pleasant company. She served me wine and seems very competent at her job. Better than the host, certainly.'

'Oh,' the man said.

'What is your name?' I asked.

'Most people here call me the King of the Castle. But my

name is Ned. Ned,' and paused, glancing at me before he said, 'Ned Gubbings.'

Of course, that meant nothing to me at the time. Why should it? I knew nothing of this area.

Walking down to the barbican once more, I mused on the empty buildings. Why should not a man who had been thrown from the moors take up residence in such a warren of buildings? He must be hardy, though, if he intended to stay there over winter. I had seen little enough of the town and the moors all about, but I had seen enough to persuade me to leave this place as soon as the Coroner had returned my purse to me.

At the bottom near the portcullis, I glanced over my shoulder. Ned Gubbings was there at the first gate in the wall, staring after me with a kind of suspicious hunger, so it seemed to me. As I watched, a huge black raven fluttered down and rested on his shoulder. It sat there and stared at me. That bird sent a shiver up my spine. I assure you, if I were a superstitious man, I'd have run to call for the nearest priest and denounced the man and his bird as sorcerers or worse. I hastened from there as fast as I could, back down the barbican to the ford.

'Where have you been?' my guard demanded. He had a face as black as a charcoal-burner's. 'I was looking for you.'

'I was bored with your company, so I flew to the moon and back,' I snapped. 'If you can't keep up, you shouldn't be guarding me, should you?' I stomped off before he could register my contempt. I didn't want him to hit me.

It was late in the morning when the Coroner arrived.

I have seen many coroners in my time, from the heavily paunched, unimaginative fellows who would barely give a corpse a brief glance before demanding food and drink, to the sallow, anxious types who would start at a mouse's squeak. Most of them, in my experience, are lazy, corrupt and mendacious. They are happy to demand *deodand* and the other fines, and no doubt they take their share without advising their masters. Personally, I have always thought it a sensible job for a man with little feeling for other people, but unpleasant, especially when a body has gone putrid. If a body has gone green, I would prefer to pass on investigations before my face achieves the same hue.

At least Daniell's body was not yet that far decayed. He was out behind the stables, and fortunately there was a broad space there, for half the town had appeared. I even recognized the peasant woman from the road near the castle, although there was no sign of Ned Gubbings.

Daniell Vowell lay on his back out behind the stables. His eyes were open, but a bird or rat had got to him overnight, and I didn't care to study him too carefully. Various bits and pieces of him had been nibbled.

'I hear you were gambling with him the night he died?' the Coroner said, when he got to me. Sir Geoffrey de Courtenay had a quiet tone, and it was a great relief to hear his accent; largely, I could understand him.

He was a slim, stooping man, with wings of grey hair over his ears, and a sharp, intent gaze. Dressed moderately conservatively, he wore a black cloak over a jack of some dark blue material. If I had been him, I would have had some scarlet piping at the edges, perhaps a run of fine yellow thread down the middle to emphasize my slim waist, and a hat to set it all off. But not this fellow. Sir Geoffrey de Courtenay was not a man from my mould. In looks, he had a hawklike face with heavily lidded eyes. It was obvious that he didn't trust his fellow man. He was suspicious of me, of the tavern-keeper, of David, and everyone in between, but he held the deepest misgivings for the foreigner – me.

I kept my eyes away from the body before me. The Coroner had instantly demanded that all the men of the town should be called in order that he might hold an inquest into the death, and there were some thirty men all about, along with women and children. An event like this was not to be missed, after all. Spectators from the town welcomed the opportunity to come and gawp. No doubt some were here to make sure he really was dead, if he was such an irritating man to the local landowners.

'Yes, we were playing dice.'

'And he lost his purse to you, and then gambled his own mount?'

'Yes, we were playing steadily for some little while. You can ask the host of the tavern, or Agnes, the serving girl.'

'I may do so. So you say you had never met him before?'

'Yes.'

'Others say that you killed him.'

'Why should I? I had won money and a horse from him. I held no malice towards him.'

There was a loud *caw-caw* sound, and I glanced up, peering about me. It sounded just like that raven at the castle, I thought.

'Perhaps he took exception to your winning so much. He followed you outside, set upon you, giving you that bruise, but it was not enough to do more than dull your senses while he took your purse, and when you came to, you chased after him, you managed to catch him quickly and you killed him.'

'No!' Not that it should have mattered, of course. If he had attacked me and robbed me, I would have been within my rights to win it back.

'And in the process, your hat fell from you, although you did recover your purse,' he finished. He stared down at the body for a few moments, then shook his head. 'Why would you leave your hat with him? If you were there long enough, you would surely have picked that up, just as you did your purse.'

'I don't have my purse!' I protested. 'Someone stole it, as I said on the evening!'

'So you say, yes. However, how do we know to trust you? It is as likely that you retrieved your money and concealed it somewhere, and then you invented the idea of a robbery to explain away the time it took you to murder this man.'

From this you can see that Sir Geoffrey had a jaundiced view of his fellow man. I suppose it's natural in a man who spends his life viewing the victims of violent affairs, but I did not find it reassuring. His speech left me somewhat at a loss for words. I wanted to swear to my innocence, but I had a conviction that nothing I could say would sway him.

'Who else was there?'

Mal stepped forward. 'I was there. I'm the host of the tavern.'

'You saw this fellow leave to go outside?'

'Yes.'

'And the victim, here, went after him a short while later?'

'Well, he went soon enough, I reckon. I didn't keep watch on them. I was busy. All of us were. There were several folk in the—'

The Coroner seemed to ignore him, but instead walked about the figure on the ground with the look of a man who has mislaid a coin. 'Who else left your tavern?'

'No one,' Mal declared stoutly.

'Someone did. Unless you want me to believe this traveller knocked himself on his own head? Or do you mean to say that this dead man knocked out Master Passer, and strolled away a little, decided to dispose, somehow, of his stolen purse, and then took his knife and stabbed himself?'

His clerk, a wizened old man with a frayed gown of black, like a monk's, appeared to find this incredibly amusing and gave a braying, snorting laugh that terrified a wood pigeon from the tree overhead. It bucketed into the air, wings clapping, and off into the distance, leaving behind a deposit that unfortunately landed on the corpse's forehead. I tried to avoid looking at it, but the droplet of bird dung was horribly fascinating. It rested like a small piece of undercooked egg white just above his left eye. It was not a pleasant sight.

There was another *caw*, and I looked up just in time to see the raven drop into the tree, flapping its wings lazily, like an aristocrat dropping in at an execution to view proceedings. It turned its head, and I could see its beady eye on me. Or so I thought. It was more likely viewing the corpse with thoughts of an early supper uppermost in its mind. I shivered.

'Well?' the Coroner demanded.

'Well, I don't know, I—'

'Who else left the room?'

'A man or two left with him,' the tavern-keeper grumpily admitted. 'I don't know who they were.'

'What of others?'

He shrugged with a bad grace. I was reminded of a grumpy boy caught in the act of thieving apples from an orchard. Then his eye alighted on me, and I felt myself wither. There was little by way of conviviality in his look. If looks had power, I should have been shrivelled like a salted slug.

Just then Sir Geoffrey turned back to me and I was taken

through my tale once more, my words being carefully noted by
the clerk with a reed that squeaked like a slate, while the Coroner
listened most intently – as did the raven, so I thought.

At the end of my evidence, he nodded, his mouth drawn into
a bow of dour scepticism, frowning thoughtfully. 'Very well.
Let us look at the body. And someone wipe away that bird shit!'

Willing hands came forward and stripped the body until Daniell
was naked. David, I saw, turned away. I could not hold that
against him. Admittedly, were I to be presented with the dead
body of my father, I should naturally wish to see him, to make
sure the vicious old dog was truly gone – he was too determined to remain alive and make the lives of all those about
him miserable for him to go easily into his grave – but I can
understand that some fellows might feel a certain proprietary
interest in their kin, and it may affect some to see their parents
going to their rest.

'I find that there is a wound in the man's breast,' the Coroner
said, strolling to the body and staring down at it as the peasants
hauled the corpse over and over before him. 'There are the
marks of creatures of the night at his fingertips and eyes and
nose, and – lift up his arms.'

While he stared, a man lifted the arm, and the Coroner
gave a grunt. 'Aye, and he was also stabbed in the left of his
chest, a deep wound.' I turned away with distaste as the Coroner
approached and thrust his forefinger into the wound. 'At least
four inches deep, I would reckon. More likely it was five to six
inches. The blow was hard, because there are the marks of a
dagger's cross, from the look of this here. He was clearly dead
soon afterwards, for there is no actual bruise, but the flesh has
been marked. So I think this blow was very harsh indeed and
made with great vigour.'

He had picked up the dead man's shirt now and was wiping
his finger with it. Dropping the shirt, he shot me a look. I can
only say that to be pierced by those sharp eyes made me understand what a dormouse must feel when the buzzard sets his
eyes on it. It struck me suddenly that the Coroner's nose was
very akin to a beak, rather like the raven's in the tree.

'I do not suspect you of this murder,' he said at last. 'Although others might well believe you had a hand in his death, the fact that you did not know the man, that you were a stranger in this tavern, and that it was he who asked you to gamble with him and not the other way about, makes me believe your story.'

David Vowell began to stutter and protest. Now I understood why the miner had left a guard about me – he was sure that I was his father's murderer. How he could think such a thing of me was baffling. The Coroner held up his hand to stay his angry declamations and turned back to me. 'So, you went outside, you were knocked down, and when you woke, you were without hat and purse. You walked back inside and declared the robbery. Was there anything else you can tell me about the situation?'

'I think I saw a shadow moving in the hostler's chamber just before I was struck down,' I said.

'You mean the hostler might have followed you and knocked you down?'

'No,' I said thoughtfully. 'It was as I saw the shadow that someone broke my pate. Someone was behind me, at the same time as the hostler was moving about in his room.'

'So he wasn't guilty,' the Coroner nodded. He gave me a particularly intent look. 'You saw no one else in the yard as you made your way to the stables?'

I shook my head. 'If I had seen someone, I would have been more alert to the danger of a robber.'

'You had been drinking some little while? You had drunk a gallon of ale?'

'Yes, but not enough to affect my judgement.'

He looked at me then with a sort of wondering doubtfulness. I'm not sure why.

'Yes. Perhaps your judgement was unaffected,' he said, and his clerk was set off again. He was very foolish – a simpleton. Sometimes wealthy families will dispose of the more ridiculous of their inhabitants by sending them into the clergy, and I think this must have been one. I certainly couldn't see what was setting him off with this odd exhibition of mirth.

The Coroner didn't so much as glance at the old fool, but kept his eyes on me with that strangely unsettling expression. 'Enough!' he said after a few moments, while his clerk kept up his inane snorting and suppressed laughter, 'Jury, do you have any suspicions about the man who could have been guilty of this robbery and murder?'

The jurors all looked at each other, then stared at me, and suddenly there was a clear voice on the wind. It was thin and reedy, but I recognized that voice in an instant. It was the cracked old man who lived in the castle: Ned Gubbings.

'Who would win from the miner's death, Coroner, eh? Who would benefit, but his own son?'

To say that the words caused a stir would be rather an understatement.

First, David flushed and span to stare off in the direction the voice had come from, which was over towards the town itself, not that there was any sign of the man. Any impression I had once gained of his being an amiable, affable soul was discarded at the sight of him now. He was furious, and in this mood I felt he could easily have ripped a man's heart out for the slightest insult. The guard who had stayed with me last night lumbered off like an ox smelling hay, but he had no more idea than anyone else where Ned could have secreted himself. Other folk in the jury were peering after the guard with various degrees of bemusement or annoyance, in case the interruption might lead to a fresh fine on the people all about, and the Coroner himself seemed more keen to watch the jury and witnesses. Me, I was looking up at the raven, who appeared to be watching events with sardonic amusement from his high branch.

It was the men around David who appeared most affected. As well as my guard, there were three others, who all had the look of men who spent their days punching rocks for the fun of it. Their fists were scarred, their arms corded with muscles, and I had the feeling that if they were to take a dislike to anyone, that person might find his life becoming significantly shorter and more painful. They looked less like miners, more like a private army designed to intimidate and alarm others. These were not fellows who were used to hacking at the ground and digging; these were the sort of men who were more used to wielding pickaxe handles by swinging them at heads, I felt.

'What do you say to that?' the Coroner asked.

'Me?' David said. His colour was still rather plum-like, and it betrayed, so I reckoned, an unhealthily choleric temper. A man like that could all too easily be driven to wretched destruction by a chance comment from another. The rage would build and build, until his brain would burst with his fury and he would drop dead. I have heard of even minor insults being taken to heart, and a man's head actually exploding. The victim expired immediately, of course. These things are hard to believe, but I heard it from a man whose brother's friend was there and saw it. It's a terrible thing, a strong temper.

'Aye, Master Vowell, *you*! That voice just accused you of arranging for the death of your own father. What do you say to that?'

'It is a vile slur! I loved my father as a son should! I defy any man to tell me to my face that I could have had anything to do with my father's death!'

'Why would someone accuse you of this?'

'Ask that calumnious devil! How should I know why he would say such a thing? If he had an ounce of courage, he would come here and say it to my face! Did you hear that, Gubbings? If you believe this, come here and accuse me like a grown man! Don't skulk like the vile old coward you are, but come and tell me to my face!'

His bellow filled the area, and he stood on tiptoe, staring about him for his accuser, with a puce face. I moved away slightly. There was more of the lunatic in his appearance than I had seen in Ned's and I didn't want to be close in case his head popped like the fellow I mentioned earlier.

'So you think that a Gubbings could have killed your father? Why would a Gubbings come here to the town to attack you?'

'You know what they are like,' David snapped. 'Outlaws, filthy thieves and murderers who will come and attack anyone without reason, just to see what is in their pocket.'

'Do you have any evidence for that allegation?'

'The old man, Ned – ask him! He hated my father!'

'I see,' the Coroner said, peering at him thoughtfully. 'So this is likely a dispute between miners and outlaws.'

David seemed to get a grip of himself, and gradually, breathing slowly, he drew his colour back down from beetroot red to a pink that would better suit a maiden's cheek – if ever a maiden had a cheek so leathery.

'Suggesting that I could have had anything to do with my father's death is a gross slur. I accuse that man!' he added, suddenly shoving out his arm and pointing at me.

Me! I mean to say, it was bad enough that others had accused me before, but the Coroner had already confirmed it wasn't me! David continued, 'He's a foreigner, and he was clearly greedy.'

The Coroner shrugged. 'Why would he kill your father? He already had all your father's money.'

'He didn't know that! He must have wanted more! Perhaps he thought my father had more coin on him!'

'That is not true!' I said, but I confess it sounded more of a squeak than a fierce declaration of innocence. I felt the eyes of the jury on me and gave them a nervous smile. 'Ask Agnes or anyone else watching us gamble. I knew full well I'd cleaned out his purse for him! I had no reason to attack him!'

'My father was fiercely protective,' David blurted. 'Mayhap my father attacked him to take back his own money, because this *traveller*' – it sounded as if he spat the word – 'used fullams or similar dice, loaded dice, and Father realized, and wanted to take back what had been stolen from him.'

'That's—' I began, but the Coroner held up his hand to silence me.

'What evidence do you have for this?'

'Look at him! I demand you release him to me. We claim him under Stannary Law to answer to the charges in the Stannary Court!'

The Coroner lowered his head like a man-at-arms aiming his crossbow. 'This is not within the moor. Okehampton is outside the moor, and so outside the jurisdiction of the Stannaries.'

'Oh, yes, we all know why you don't want us to try him. You always hated the miners, didn't you? This is just you—'

'Be very careful, Vowell. I am an officer of the Queen. If you want to make an allegation against me, you had best be ready to defend yourself. Now, do you have any evidence for your accusation against this man?'

'I asked the host of the tavern for dice,' I protested. 'Ask him! I didn't have any dice, and I wasn't using *his*,' I added, pointing at the body.

'Is this true, Keeper?' the Coroner asked.

Mal threw a resentful glance at me, but he couldn't deny the truth of my words. 'Aye. They were my dice they used.'

'That answers that, then.'

'There's one other might have done it,' David said.

'Who?'

'Ned Gubbings. He's so soft in the head, he might have thought he had a claim.'

'Why?'

'Who can tell? The man's mazed. He's a danger to everyone.'

'Again, no evidence. The matter is closed, and so is this inquest.'

With a loud cry, the raven launched itself from the tree overhead, and I ducked instinctively. It flew away towards the castle.

I won't go into all the other details of the matter. Let it suffice for me to say that the Coroner found that one blade had probably killed the man, that the blade was worth at least one shilling and sixpence, and that the town would therefore be fined one and six as deodand. Personally, I thought they had got away lightly. I could think of several coroners in London who would have tried to fleece them for at least five shillings. But then again, knives were probably cheaper to come by down here in the wilds of the West Country.

It was after the main inquest was over that the Coroner beckoned me to him.

'You are from London.'

I had little choice but to agree. I could scarcely argue, not with my fine clothes and educated manner. 'How did you guess?' I asked suavely.

'It was obvious as soon as you opened your mouth,' the man said.

'My accent?' Of course, my refinement would have been clear even to a country yokel.

'It was more your arrogance. But never mind that for now. My interest is in that body.'

'I told you, I know nothing of it. The first time I saw that

man was in the tavern, and that was the last I saw of him. I swear, I . . .'

'Yes, I'm sure. It is interesting that someone wanted to make it perfectly clear that you were responsible for Daniell's death, don't you think?'

'Eh?'

He looked at me.

'You mean taking my hat and leaving that with him? I cannot understand why someone should do such a thing.'

'Can you not, indeed? Perhaps the reflection that someone wished to make sure that you were put to blame in order to protect someone else never struck you?'

'Well, of course it did.'

'Your presence was enormously fortunate for whoever killed him,' the Coroner mused. 'Just consider: a man from far away, a man with no local ties, no affiliations. That was enormous good fortune for someone. I often find that people who live in a town are keen to point to some stranger who was responsible for their crimes, no matter what.'

'I don't understand.'

'Really,' he said flatly. 'Surprising. If you live close by another family, and you have daughters married to their sons, sons married to their daughters, and you depend on them for shoeing your beasts, or you depend on them for hay for your horse, or you depend on them as your cobbler, or you like the quality of their alewife's brews, what, would you want to accuse one of them of committing a crime? It would mean losing your children in the arguments, it would mean your horse going unshod, unfed, you doing without new shoes, missing their ales . . . What, wouldn't you prefer to accuse a foreigner? You might even believe it was that stranger who suddenly appeared. After all, strangers could be demons sent by the Devil.'

'You think I'm—'

He waved away my interruption irritably. 'And then consider this: in a place like Okehampton, where there are daily quarrels between landowners and these damned miners – these miners who are the cause of great tension with all those who live near the moors – only a small spark could set off a conflagration here. And by chance you appear. The spark that was needed.

On the very evening that someone chooses to kill Daniell. Or did they decide to kill him *because* you appeared here? Was his death pre-decided, and it only required the arrival of a man like you to precipitate his demise?'

I confess, I did not like the direction his thoughts were taking him. It sounded as though this man was thinking that it was only because of my appearance that Daniell had been slain. I was grateful that he could not know I was employed as an assassin. That could complicate matters, I felt.

'Nay, do not fear,' he said with a sudden chuckle on seeing my face. 'I do not mean to accuse you, my friend. No, but it strikes me that it is possible that his death and your presence are not so unconnected as first might appear.'

This was not what I wished to hear. For me, it was important to remain insignificant, a mere irrelevance, a traveller who happened to be here. Even a vague notion that the killing might have been in some way connected to me was dangerous. As a professional assassin, I wished for no such fame.

I quickly attempted to put the clod straight on that, but he only gave a cheerful pat on my back and went off to talk to his clerk.

I was more keen than ever to depart this town and find my way to the coast. But first I had to retrieve my money. At least I did have my hat back. I pulled it on to my head with caution, for I had no wish to inflame the pain of the two injuries, but with my hat back on, I did feel more content. I was once more a gentleman, I felt.

The people of the town were already dispersing when I walked into the tavern. I have a reputation for courage, but I confess that the sight of my gambling companion lying on the ground in such a state had unsettled my stomach. In the tavern, I waited for some little while, but there was no sign of the serving wench. Agnes was nowhere to be seen. It was only when I wandered through the rear of the tavern that I saw her at last. She was in the doorway to the stables and appeared most reluctant to leave it.

Seeing her there, a young woman in the full flush of her youth and beauty, I was prey to a pang. She was intelligent, attractive, with a figure that could tempt the Archbishop of . . . well, to be fair, any young wench would appeal to him by the evidence of the gossips in London. Even so, Agnes had the sort of look that could make a man howl. It was something to do with her apparent disinterest, I reckoned. Just now she was standing and swinging her hips lightly like a woman listening to music. And then she darted slightly away from the door as if evading capture. Her laugh was entirely captivating, as was her expression of delight. I could not contain a grin of my own. She would be a wonderful companion in cupid's dance, I thought.

I hailed her, and instantly that look of happiness left her, to be replaced with her customary suspicious glower. It was sad to see her joy flee. I must accept that, since I still didn't have a purse, it was hardly surprising. However, I did have the two horses. I would trade the beaten little brute that Daniell had lost to me, and then perhaps there would be a couple of pennies to tempt Agnes into my room.

She made her way to me. 'What?'

'I want some wine, if it's not too much bother for you,' I said with courteous patience.

'I thought you were still with the inquest.'

'The Coroner has completed his investigation for now.'

She pulled a grimace. 'I will fetch you wine.'

'Good.'

She pushed past me as though angry, and I couldn't think why. But then I glanced at the stables where she had been standing, and saw a lithe figure moving away from the sunlight.

Inside, I took my seat at a bench near the doorway and leaned back against the wall. It was a relief to know that I was not to be accused of this murder, but it was equally worrying that someone was in the town who had killed the miner. Why should old Ned Gubbings have been accused? Admittedly, he seemed quite careless in the way he waved his knife at me, but that was different to actually stabbing a man – twice. And yet, by his own words to me, he had good reason to dislike Daniell Vowell. Maybe David was right to point the finger of suspicion in his direction.

Another thought came to me while I sat there: the two wounds in the man's torso were clearly the work of a man used to fighting and killing. You must pardon me here, but having spent much of my time in London, and some of that with the denizens of the wharfs and backstreets, I knew the difference between a death in an affray, when drunks will pull knives against each other and slash wildly, and a cleverly executed (if you will pardon the term) killing. I have rarely seen a murder so plain and unconcealed. One stab to the front of the chest, a second under the armpit, both aiming perfectly at the heart. Either would have stilled its beat, but the killer had taken no risks. He had decided to make sure of his enemy.

I felt a shiver run down my spine at that thought. For, if there was a man who had the determination and the courage to commit so plain and obvious an assassination, he would be unlikely to stop at one man. If he thought that another was likely to learn his identity, he would in all likelihood kill again.

It was from that thought only a short journey to my conclusion, which was that I had no desire to learn who was responsible for this killing. All I wanted was to be away from this foul town as swiftly as I may.

'Here.'

I looked up, startled, to see Agnes with a pot of wine. She passed me a cup and poured. When I caught her eye, she appeared apologetic again. No doubt for her rudeness earlier.

'Thank you, maid.'

'You look as though you have had a shock,' she said, unbending a little more.

I shook my head. I didn't want to admit to my thoughts about the murderer. 'It was Daniell's body. I . . . it is not common to see a man's body like that.'

'Really? London must be a boring place,' she said. 'We often have bodies here. In the winter, miners and farmers will often succumb, and then travellers passing through will sometimes be found dead. Waylaid by outlaws, knocked on the head to be robbed, stabbed by Gubbingses, or just falling prey to an accident on the roads.'

'Gubbingses? Like Ned?'

'He was one, so they say, and he took their name, but he left them.'

She told me then of the family of misfits and malcontents who lived near the moors on the road to Tavistock. They were genuine outcasts, apparently, a society of outlaws who thrived west of the moors below the town of Lydford, itself a place of infamy. In fact, everywhere in this awful county seemed to be bordering on barbaric. And the people, too. But the Gubbingses were the worst, according to Agnes. They were a separate tribe who lived in unbelievable squalor and acknowledged no master but their own, existing by robbery and thieving, leaving their hovels to capture travellers and torture or ransom them, thieving cattle and sheep from the moors, and generally making life even worse for the peasants. If that were possible. 'There are many ways men can die here in the country,' she concluded, 'but the Gubbingses make the moors hazardous for everyone.'

'London is not like that. It is a wonderful city, full of the most astonishing sights,' I said.

'Perhaps. Mayhap one day I will travel there myself,' she said in a tone of utter disinterest. 'But you should be careful. Men who are unwary can oftentimes fall victim to those who take offence.'

It struck me that she was maundering. I chose to change the subject. 'Maid, why is it that your accent is not as pronounced as that of others? I could understand you easily when I first came here.'

'I was not born here, but in Exeter,' she said. 'And when you heard me, you heard the voices of Daniell and the others from the moors. They are hard to understand at the best of times. They say that the men on the moors have their own language, some of them.'

'Why are you here, if you were born in a city?'

It seemed a sensible question to me. After all, why would a maid choose to leave a city? Even a noisome wreck like Exeter was better than this dismal place. And a young woman like her could have her pick of suitors; even in Exeter, there must be young swains with money. Why come here?

'I was married,' she said. Her face was turned away. 'I was sold to Mal.'

'Sold?'

'My father sold me.'

Now, you can call me old-fashioned if you like, but I didn't think that sort of thing still went on. Selling your daughter, I mean. It's barbaric. A child is not some chattel to be sold off. And besides, she might be worth more in a few years, if she were to get a reasonable job.

'I am astonished. To the host of this tavern?'

She looked at me with a kind of thoughtful shrug. 'He's not as bad as some, and he's at least kind. I am luckier than many of the wives here.'

'How so?'

'Have you seen the women of the town? All broken with long hours of work, hands worn out, out in their vegetable gardens, working in the fields during the harvest, washing, cooking, brewing . . . it is a hard life.'

'You work too, though.'

'Indoors, warm and dry in the winter, and happy in the summer. I am very fortunate.'

She moved away then, and I was struck by her demeanour. And by her words, for the simple fact was that she worked every bit as hard as any of the peasants in the town. She still washed clothes, made beds, cooked, gardened, as well as serving the drinkers.

Mal came out and stood at the bar, his suspicious, angry eyes fixed on me once more. I swallowed. It suddenly occurred to me that I had been thinking of bedding his wife. While many husbands in taverns would be happy to rent their wives out for a reasonable fee, I had a conviction that if I were to suggest such a convenient trade, this husband would be inclined to take umbrage.

That was when I realized that she must have been warning me. All that talk of strangers and travellers being attacked: it wasn't just chatting; she was letting me know that my life could be in danger, were I to offend her husband. Surely she was protecting me, because she liked me – but couldn't let her husband see her affection for me.

I puffed out my cheeks with relief. It was a good thing that I had not tried to enter negotiations with him for her before hearing she was married. The good Lord only knows what he might have done.

There was something about the way the host glared at me, unmoving, his eyes fixed entirely on me, that made me more than a little uncomfortable. However, I realized soon enough that it must be irritating to have a fellow like me sitting in his tavern without paying, and I had not enjoyed an opportunity to speak to him yet about the horse.

With a feeling of bonhomie that might have been the result of the wine, I beckoned him and gave him a welcoming smile.

He did not move at first. I think I saw various emotions float over his face. First, there was surprise, which was natural enough. Then a look of disbelief crossed his features, and I suppose, since he had been staring at me like a man who wanted to rip off my arm so he could belabour me about the head with it, perhaps he wasn't anticipating my inviting him to join me. Lastly, there was a kind of fierce rage, as though he believed my invitation was itself an insult. It was all most perturbing, I thought, and I was in two minds as he lumbered towards me. I was less sure that this was a good idea.

'Master Mal, I have a proposal for you,' I said.

'No!' he grated, and to my alarm I saw that both his fists were clenched so tightly his knuckles were white. I swear, if the sun had expired at that moment, his knuckles were so bright that they could have lit the entire room.

'Master, I think I have a means of paying you.'

'You want to pay in kind? I'll pay you first!' he said, and this time there was a genuine sense of vicious malevolence in his tone.

'I don't understand,' I said. 'I was going to offer you—'

'Say it – go on, say it! Soon as you do, I'll have your ballocks for candle-snuffers!'

'Why are you so angry?'

'My wife told me what you'd been saying to her.'

That stumped me. I had thought the strumpet had a brain, but clearly not. She had run straight from me to her husband and said something to him. Although *what* exactly she could have said, unless it was something to do with my expression on hearing that she had been sold to him, I did not know. Had she divined that I would willingly have invited her into my bed and told him? I recalled that first night that I might have made certain advances when she helped me to my bed – but that was days ago. Besides, he had been serving at the bar that evening. Surely he would have been aware that his wife was trying to make my tarse rise like a steeple when she sat on my lap and wriggled? He must have been aware of her value as a customer-pleaser, for why else would he allow her in his bar?

'I don't understand what you mean,' I said with complete honesty. 'I was going to offer you Daniell's horse in exchange for my board and lodging. I thought you would be able to make more use of the beast than I could.'

His mouth worked for several long seconds, and his eyes bulged like a toad about to belch. Then he swallowed, and his voice was a great deal calmer, I am glad to say. 'The pony?'

'Yes. He lost it to me in that game, so no one can complain at my disposing of it as I see fit. I thought you would like to have it as compensation for your . . . hospitality.' This last word almost choked me, but I managed to spit it out.

He swallowed again, and I was sure that there was genuine pain in his face. It was probably the unaccustomed attempt at civility. 'Aye. I mean, yes, sir. That would be very gracious. Thank you.'

'Good. Another cup of wine, if you please.'

He cast a look at me, but now there was less in the way of threat, and more a wary acceptance.

I confess, I could not bear to sit in the chamber any longer after that. As soon as he had brought me the drink, I took the cup and wandered outside once more.

Glancing at the stables, I thought I might as well walk over to there and see how my rounsey was recovering. And whether the pony had expired yet.

I walked across the courtyard, stumbling slightly on a loose cobble, and entered the stable. It was dark in there, and my eyes took a moment to adjust. When they did, I went over to the stall to see my rounsey, and was relieved to see she had perked up, and was well enough to aim a hoof at me. 'Stop that, you brute,' I said, darting out of reach. She pulled her lips back from her gums in a wicked grin. I wasn't persuaded. There are some horses that are friendly, gentle and accommodating, but this was one of the other sort, the type that would always attempt a kick or bite, just for the fun of inflicting pain. I knew because she had tried it on me plenty of times.

The other thing was still alive. Mal's payment was secure. The beast lifted his head and peered at me with that sort of sorrowful look that told of unspeakable suffering. I was persuaded. The poor brute must have had a hard time of it. Life on the moors, working for miners, could not have been enjoyable.

A sudden clatter from beyond made me spin with alarm. The bruise on my head flared. Another noise convinced me I was not about to be attacked, so I went out to discover the cause.

There, in a small chamber which was taken with all the paraphernalia of an hostler, was the groom I had seen before. He was sitting on a rough stool, smearing grease of some sort into a saddle and rubbing it in. But he had only just started his work, I could see.

'You like her, then,' I said.

He looked up, and there was a sudden cold gleam in his eye.

It was rather shocking, like seeing a favourite lap dog suddenly try to rip a finger from the hand that stroked it.

'What?' he said.

'I saw her in the doorway chatting to you. Agnes from the tavern. You know her: Mal's wife,' I added, to rub it in. I succeeded better than he with his grease.

'I know. She's lovely.'

Well, I couldn't disagree with that. 'Yes, she's a dainty little thing, isn't she?' *And very effective with a broom when she wants to prevent an innocent from escaping the town*, I added to myself.

'She's not happy.'

'Who would be, forced to live with Mal?' I enquired, I think reasonably.

'She shouldn't be bound to him,' the boy burst out. To my astonishment, he threw down his cloth and began to sob.

Now, I have been known for my sympathetic style when

it comes to women in distress, but this was a different experience. After all, it is one thing to put an arm about a young
woman who is sobbing, and something different to try to hug
another fellow. I stared at him, wondering what to do. It was
deeply disturbing, and I felt a considerable contempt for him.
A fellow does not, or should not, make such displays in
public.

'You want her, then?' was all I could manage.

'I'd do *anything* for her,' he said.

The odd thing was, as he said this, I was sure I caught a
glimpse of his eye glancing over at me. It was startling, because
it was like seeing a child discovered in a lie. He was no
more weeping than I was, I felt sure.

'I'm sure she's most grateful for the fact,' I said. 'What were
you talking about when she was here in the stable with you?'

'About Daniell, mostly. He was a hard man.'

That was a lie. Young Agnes had been swinging her hips like
an experienced trull. She wasn't talking about a corpse while
she stood there. Still, if there is one thing I have learned over
many years of living in London, it is that the best information
about people can be found from hostlers, grooms, serving
wenches and the little brats who hang around outside taverns
hoping to earn a coin for looking after a gentleman's horse
while he enters to avail himself of the bounty on offer inside.
It was no different, surely, in the country.

'Why do you say "hard"?'

'He and his men ran others off the moors if they didn't pay
him his black rent. He demanded money for their tin, and if
they didn't pay, they got beaten and had their tools stolen or
broken.'

'I heard a man say he'd had that.'

'Who?'

'He called himself Ned.'

'That old fool?'

'He didn't seem foolish to me.'

'Really?' he sneered, obviously forgetting he wanted my
sympathy. Personally, I felt Ned Gubbings was a more sympathetic man than this young gabey.

'Gubbings reckons he owns the castle,' the lad continued.

'Just because it was empty, he thinks he can claim it as his own. He's a right lurdan, he is. Hasn't the brains of a chicken.'

'But he used to work the moors?'

'Aye, right enough. He was a miner, but never found a good enough plot. He just kept digging away, and eventually he was thrown from the moors because he was doing no good to himself or anyone else. He'd have been best off digging peat.'

'But he was pushed from the moors by Daniell? That's what he said.'

'Why would a man like Daniell Vowell give a tinker's curse for a man like Ned? He was nothing, and had nothing.'

That made me frown. 'If that's the case, why did Daniell bother to throw him from his claims? Surely a man as important as Daniell would have much more important things to see to than an old peasant trying to earn his crust? Especially if there was no tin on his land?'

My words struck a chord. The lad scowled, but then his brow cleared and he shrugged. 'What of it? Daniell had his reasons. Anyway, it makes no difference to anyone. Daniell's son will take over his holdings, so Ned has lost his pitch.'

'Well, if he thinks he can claim the castle as his own, good luck to him,' I said.

'You think he'd be allowed to keep that? There are others would like to have the castle as their own. They're unlikely to let an old peasant like him keep it.'

'Who would want to keep the castle?'

The hostler laid a finger alongside his nose in a sign of conspiracy. 'That's for me to know.'

I bridled at that. It was tempting to draw my pistol or my sword, but then I reflected that I had neither with me.

'Perhaps,' I said, 'for now. Of course, that might well change.'

'You think?'

'Yes. If it were to become known that Mal's wife was enjoying a game of hide the sausage with the hostler, I think you might regret not sharing things with me,' I said lightly.

I have been surprised, on occasion, by the speed of other people's reactions when they have need. Some who appear entirely dull and without the intellect to know which hand to use for a spoon can nonetheless sometimes shock a fellow with their swiftness. Now, I would not like to give the wrong impression of my own abilities, but I think those who have read my memoirs will understand that I have a very pronounced understanding of my fellow man. In this hostler's case, it was clear that I had him over a barrel, as it were, and that he should instantly tell me what he thought was such a serious secret.

However, sometimes even a fellow as fog-witted as this could surprise me. I had just fitted an easy smile to my lips when he changed from a mild-mannered servant to the travelling class into a raging demon. He hurled his saddle and cloth at my face, driving me backwards so I almost fell, and then startled me by leaping over the small table, pinning me against a wall and holding what felt like an extremely sharp implement at my throat.

Having your head thrust hard against a wall is unpleasant. Being held with a forearm across the neck, a knife or similar blade pricking you, and having a very angry young man's face two inches from your own are all experiences to avoid, in my view. Especially since he had been eating garlic only recently.

I tried to swallow, but with his arm in the way it was not easy. And I could feel the blade's point slipping into my throat. It made me try to stop swallowing halfway, and that was enough to make me begin to choke.

'You think you can scare me, just because you come down here with your smart clothes and your smart manners and your smart comments, eh? You don't know what you're doing, *Master*! You aren't in London now, and if you try pulling clever little tricks, you'll find we down here have a few of our own.'

The keen point of his blade pushed, it seemed, even closer, and I could feel the blood – God's bones, he was going to kill me! – start to drip down my throat. As it was, the choking was increasing as he pushed his forearm harder, and I saw sparks of red and blue pass across my vision. Then, as suddenly as it had happened, it was over.

I fell to my knees, gasping for breath, anxiously putting a hand to my throat, while he stood over me, eyeing me with apparent contempt, before returning to his seat.

'See what you've made me do?' he spat, picking up the

saddle and greasy cloth. 'I've scuffed the edge of the seat now. I'll have to smooth that before I can get back to work.'

And apparently that was that. He ignored me as I tried to clamber to my feet, coughing and trying not to spew in case it upset him. I reached the door before he spoke again, in a quietly conversational tone.

'Don't forget what I said, Master. You try mentioning me and little Agnes to Mal or anyone, and I'll feed your liver to the pigs.'

You may well imagine that it was a pensive Jack who stumbled from the stable and leaned with his back against the wall, his hand thoughtfully held at his neck. It was some little while before I dared look at my fingers. I knew that they were drenched in my blood, and if there is one thing I cannot bear, it is the sight of my own life's blood.

Steeling myself, I stared at my fingers. There was moisture on them, but no blood. When I began to feel the wounded area more urgently, all I could find was a surfeit of sweat. Which was a great comfort, naturally. Heaving a sigh of relief, I levered myself up from the wall and stood undecided. There was the open door to the tavern, which held the possibility of conversation with Mal the tavern-keeper; there was the stable door behind me with the opportunity of extending my chat with the stableman. The field's gate had a view of a bullock, who was peering at me with the sort of look I imagine he would have worn had he learned that I had recently eaten parts of his mother, and the other way held the road and the walk back to the castle.

It also offered a turn to the right, however, and that would take me to the town itself. Anything was better than remaining here, I decided, and set off.

'Oi! Where are you going?'

I felt my shoulders sag. It was, of course, the guard set to watch me by David Vowell. I had forgotten the bovine since the inquest, but now he appeared, truculently moving down the road towards me. His face had the look of a man who was capable of only the one thought. He had caught hold of that – the fact that he was supposed to be watching me, I suppose

– and now that single theme sent his legs in motion. I stood waiting while he walked to me.

'Well?' he demanded. 'Where are you going?'

'Why? You heard the Coroner. I am free. There is no reason to delay me.'

'My master told me to watch you, so I will.'

'I have no need of your company, and whatever your master wants is nothing to me. Just now I don't desire your company, nor any other's. If, however, you wish to join me walking to the town, you may. Just keep away from me and don't interrupt my thoughts,' I said. I was past caring about this fellow. My personal terrors were still fixed on the lad in the stable and the feel of that dagger at my throat. I felt again, to make sure that there was no effusion of blood, but it was still only sweat.

'Eh?' he said, his fist clenching, but with a doubtful expression in his large eyes. He reminded me of a dog which, having brought a joyous present to his master, is struck with the suspicion that this leather boot perhaps should not have been chewed with such enthusiasm.

There are some fists I have seen that look like a small purse filled with nails, and others which are like a bolster. His put me more in mind of a maul, and I was eyeing them with some perturbation when I saw the confusion in his face. It did not register anger: his fists were clenching more for something to do, while his brain tried to catch up with the conversation.

I suppose my lack of concern had disconcerted the poor fellow. He found it difficult to maintain any thoughts for more than a few moments at a time, and my insouciance was debilitating. He was not the sort of man who had been raised to consider deep and meaningful concepts. Rather, he was a block of muscle designed for digging or hitting things with a large hammer. When confronted with my disinterest, he was at a loss. I should by now have been a quivering wreck. My indifference left him confused.

'Come!' I said, 'you can join me. I have nothing to hide, after all, and you have no right to follow or threaten me, so let's go together as companions.'

If my lack of fear was unsettling, my suggestion that we might walk as companions was still worse. He scowled with a

face as black as a coal pit, but in his eyes I could see only
anxiety. That was enough to allay any concerns I might have
held.

It has to be said that a muscle-bound companion with a little
brain rattling about in his skull is a boon when a man has a lot
of thinking to do. We had walked along the lane to the main
road through the town, and when we had walked from one end
of the town to the other, we turned and walked back, all the
while in silence.

At the rivers, which met at the foot of a small hill, I turned
back and walked towards the moors. In truth, I paid little
attention to the direction – I merely wished to avoid stepping
through the ford and getting my boots wet unnecessarily.

'What is your name?' I said after a while.

We had reached a flattish plain of some ten acres or more,
bounded by a river on our right, with a hill climbing away
steeply. It seemed to me that every hill in Devon should have
had 'steeply' added to it. I eyed it unenthusiastically before
continuing onward around its base.

'I'm Nye Turner.'

'What are you, Nye? A miner? A bodyguard?'

'I work for Master Vowell,' he said with evident pride and
satisfaction.

'Now the old one's dead, you work for the younger, then?'

'Aye. David will keep me.'

'So you are a miner?'

He cast a look at me as though wondering whether to answer
my questions, but it was a pleasant day, and I think he was an
amiable enough fellow when not instructed to pull a man's head
from his body, so he continued happily enough.

'I was a miner. I had a plot up near Wistman's Wood, but
my scraping didn't work, and soon I'd lost all my money with
nowt to show for it. So when Master Vowell came to me and
said I could work for him, it were easy.'

'What sort of work?'

'You saw Master. He was a hard worker. He had grit in his
soul, as well as under his nails. He was the sort of man would
help any other in trouble, but cross him, and you had an enemy
for life.'

'He liked to gamble.'

'Oh, aye.'

'So he was in the tavern to gamble? He wouldn't let me go without a game.'

'Aye, well' – the man had an itch in his hosen, or felt guilt, more likely – 'he did have special dice. He always used them when he could and I never seed him lose.'

'You mean he had fullams?'

'Don't know about that, but his dice were lucky.'

That was something to muse over. Nye was plainly embarrassed at having to confess this, but if he knew that the dice were loaded, then so did others in the tavern that night. If a man comes and regularly wins with his own dice, people tend to notice. I suddenly felt gratitude for Mal and the use of his dice. He must have known Vowell had rigged dice, and would have known Vowell would be unhappy with his providing other dice for us to use, but he let me have them anyway.

'So he was there to gamble?'

'No, that was making up time. He was meeting a man.'

'Who?'

'Don't know. But he said to me, "Nye, you come with me. I don't want him getting no ideas. He might try to knock me on th' 'aid." I said, "Master Daniell, you sure you want to see 'un? Wouldn't it be best to leave 'un till another time?"'

'What did he say to that?'

'Only that there was only the one man he was seeing, and Master had me and two others. He'd be safe against the fellow. But I was to watch behind him.'

'But you didn't.'

'I tried,' he said, turning mournful eyes to me. A spaniel pup couldn't have looked more appealing. 'I did try, Master. But you went out, and I was watching the others in the room, and when he walked out, I thought it was only to go and have a piss – it didn't occur to me that . . . I thought he was going to knock you down and get his money back, so I waited in the tavern, kept all them inside . . .'

He broke off and stared at the water in the river. 'He saved me, you see. He saved me from starving up there on the moors. And I deserted him when he needed me.'

'You realize I didn't kill him, don't you.' I didn't need to ask. It was a statement.

'No, I don't think you could. If you'd tried to fight Master Vowell, he'd have broken your haid for 'un.'

I bridled a little at that, but I didn't want to point out that I was a paid assassin. If this fellow was convinced of my innocence, it would be better not to place suspicion in his skull. Soon my mind was whirring.

'If you saw him leave the room, was it long after I walked out?'

'No, only a little while.' He shot me a look. 'See, I'd thought he'd gone to knock you down and take your purse. Then, when you came in and whined about being struck down, I thought he must have done it. Didn't occur to me he was dead.'

'Did anyone else leave the room after us?'

'No. All stayed inside. Only you two walked out.'

'In that case, did you know of anyone outside?'

'No. But there must have been the man he was seeing.'

'You think this other man, the man he was there to see, you think he killed Vowell?'

'Yes.'

'But you don't know who it was?'

'Only it was something to help us get more money from the mining.'

It gave me much to think about: a man who had not been in the tavern, a man who had arranged an assignation with Master Vowell, a man who came across him in the dark and slew him.

'Are you absolutely sure you have no idea who it was?'

'He wouldn't tell me.'

'But he did want you with him when he saw whoever this man was?'

'Yes.'

'I see.'

I have always been quick to see the way through the trees. Give me a problem and I will soon give you the answer, and here the answer was plain enough: Vowell had wanted his guard with him when he saw this other fellow. But he walked from the tavern just after me and didn't want his guard with him. He might have been going out to empty his bladder, but equally he might have been going out to meet his companion – except why would he do so without his guards? He brought them for that express purpose. No, it seemed obvious to me that he had followed me to steal my money. Then, on his way back to the tavern, he had been met by his murderer, a professional man, who had stabbed him under the armpit and then in the breast. This 'stranger', perhaps. Or was it Ned? Was Ned mad enough to kill like that? Perhaps. Either way, it had paid Vowell in kind. He wanted to knock me down to take the money I had won from him, and when he had done so, he was attacked in his place.

Yes, it served him right. Justice was seen to be done, to my mind.

'Do you know where the Coroner is staying this evening?' I said.

Sir Geoffrey had taken up residence in a pleasant enough inn at the eastern edge of the town. Nye and I crossed over the main road, took the ford and made our way to the inn with feet squelching in sodden boots. The river water here was brown, and I didn't want to think what was in it.

'So you think this stranger may have had something to do with Vowell's death?' the Coroner asked when I had finished my tale.

'It makes sense, doesn't it? This man was his guard, but Vowell left him behind. He was clearly following me to steal my purse.'

'Your winnings. And whose dice did you use?'

'The tavern's,' I said stoutly. 'I told you that, and Mal did, too. I refused to use Vowell's dice because he was so keen. They had to have been unfair in some way.'

'Yes. So you said. And you think he followed you and knocked you down, and then he was knocked down in his turn.'

'How else to explain the matter?'

'I can see several different options just now. First, he was, as his guard thought, on his way to empty his bladder. You killed him, but then you were knocked down by a thief who took your purse; second, he went out, witnessed you being knocked down and robbed, tried to catch the thief and was murdered; third, a man decided to knock you down, thinking you were him, and when the assailant saw you were not him, he robbed you and took your purse and left your hat on his victim; fourth, that—'

I held up my hands in defeat. 'I see.'

And I did. I truly did. This Coroner was a man who still believed I could be guilty of murder. He didn't believe even the guard set to protect Vowell, because he distrusted everyone. I rose, but he waved me back into my seat, leaning forward and gazing at me with a sudden intensity. 'You think you might have reason to believe someone else was out there that evening. Who?'

'I have no idea. I don't know any of the people in this town. I come from London.'

'But if you have any suspicions, you must tell me.'

'My suspicion is that Vowell followed me outside and struck me down, and . . .'

'Before you were hit: think! Did you see anything or anyone who could have had nefarious reasons for being there?'

'All I know is . . .' I said, and then I hesitated.

'Well?'

I glanced at Nye, who was standing at the wall giving his famous impression of a moorstone block, but he didn't seem to notice me. 'When I was there, in the stable, just before I was struck, I could have sworn that there was a movement at the far side of the stable. I told you that. It would have been in the hostler's little room.'

'So you think the hostler hit you?'

'Of course not! That's the point – he was in his chamber, so someone else hit me. But if he was there, he surely should have heard or seen something? There must have been someone else there, yet he didn't speak out at the inquest. It struck me as strange.'

'Yes. I see what you mean,' the Coroner said. He glanced up at Nye as well, and clearly took the same view as me, that speaking to him was worse than pointless. Looking at me again, he said, 'Perhaps you could take me and one or two others to meet this man.'

I had no desire to reacquaint myself with the fellow, but when a coroner gives an instruction, it is best to obey him, I have learned. And the fact that it would be him, me and two men from the town, constables armed with stout staves and knives, meant that the risk I was taking was greatly reduced. In short, I didn't mind if I did join this little party, because it would give me the chance of seeing the rascal's face when he was confronted by me with three strong, armed men at my side.

The Coroner collected two men, and soon we were marching back to the tavern. We splashed through the ford and strode on up the road to the tavern. Once there, I led the way to the stables. The door to the hostler's room was open, and I pointed towards it. The Coroner nodded and indicated that I should lead the way. I looked at it, then back at him and shook my head. I had no intention of being first in there, not after the hostler's attack earlier. The Coroner glanced at the two men behind me and jerked his head. I think he was trying to show that he would appreciate their taking part, ideally in walking into the chamber and seeing if the hostler was there, but the man on my right clearly felt that could be dangerous, and rather preferred to see someone else entering. Having experienced the hostler's welcome before, I could easily understand his reluctance.

In the end, the Coroner rolled his eyes contemptuously and stepped forward, but before he had reached the door, there was a clattering behind us. Turning, I saw the hostler glaring fiercely at us at the main stable doorway. I gave a sharp yelp on seeing him, but I don't think anyone else noticed, because we were all startled.

The hostler was first to recover. I have to admit, I was impressed. He took one look at us, turned and sprinted away. I could admire his presence of mind.

For a moment, the men with me were too stunned to move. Then the one man who didn't have to worry about bringing his brain into focus, since it was never fully engaged – Nye, that is – lumbered into action.

To my surprise, he actually moved quite swiftly. Perhaps it was all those hours with no thoughts passing through his moor-stone block of a brain that meant his muscles were ready to act at a moment's notice, but for whatever reason, he was outside the stable after the hostler before the rest of us had begun to move. Second after him was the Coroner, and the two others with him joined the pursuit.

Personally, the idea of a chase through the town was unappealing, but the reflection that if he were to escape his pursuers, he may well return here to the tavern where he had seen me with the Coroner, and decide to take some form of revenge on me, spurred me into action. If I were to see this man again, I wanted to have other fellows around me.

I bolted out from the stable, only to see the last of the town's men out in the road. Hurtling along in his wake, I soon saw the Coroner and Nye farther along the way towards the castle. The thought that the hostler could have hurried away, concealed himself and doubled back lent wings to my feet, and I fairly flew along that muddy lane until I had overtaken the rearmost man and was gaining on the second. To my mind, remaining at the rear could make me easy prey to the man if he had hidden himself. I was far happier in the middle.

The route Nye was taking took us almost all the way to the castle, and thence, splashing wildly through the ford at the foot of the barbican, we sped onwards. I groaned at the sight before me. I must have mentioned before in this memoir that the most obvious and outstanding aspect of Dartmoor was the hills. There must have been a different route, I am sure, but just now the only way to keep myself secure from the threat of the hostler's knife was to keep with the Coroner and his merry men, and that meant continuing up the steep slope of this first hill. I stared at it, all the while trying to stop my heart from leaping from my mouth – it appeared to have broken free of its moorings and was attempting its own escape, perhaps because of the sight of the hill.

But Nye was already out of sight in among the trees, and the Coroner was charging in after him. I glanced at the first of the men from the town, and the look he gave me told me, as clearly as speech, that he had little desire to continue. However, he was an officer of the law and didn't want to be the recipient of the Coroner's ire, so he closed his eyes, pulled a grimace and set off at a slow trot once more. The other man was some yards behind me, leaning on his staff like a man about to vomit, so I quickly set a pace that would carry me before the constable and place me between him and the Coroner. I still had no wish to be last in the column.

This path took us through the woods. Where there were small streams, slabs of moorstone had been set over them. This must have been a popular route for someone to have taken such efforts. I hurried on, glad to see glimpses of the Coroner, my legs growing more and more tired as I went, the breath stinging my lungs, and when I finally came to reach the Coroner and Nye, who stood panting slightly as if he had merely taken a bracing walk, the grassy slope led away up to a high ridge.

Of the hostler there was no sign.

I waved my hand at the hill, attempting to speak, but no words came. Nye gazed at me with an expression of faint interest, and the Coroner himself scowled up at the hill.

'He is there somewhere. He cannot have made it all the way to the top of that hill. He must have ducked down behind the furze or into a dip.'

I was impressed. The Coroner sounded as though he had hardly exerted himself at all. He rested his fist on his thigh and stared up at the hill with a fierce gaze that should have scorched the bushes and reduced them to charcoal.

'There is one thing for certain, Master Passer,' he said at last. 'That man obviously has guilt on his mind, for why else would he run from me? That being so, I think I have to be reassured that your own involvement is less likely.' He mused again, frowning deeply. 'I am still more inclined to the view that you may be innocent.'

'I am glad to hear you say it,' I said, with a faint hint of hauteur entering my voice. After all, he had been accusing me of being a murderer.

'This felon has to be discovered. He is clearly a dangerous man,' the Coroner said, 'and must be hunted with all the vigour possible. Constable?' This was to the first of the two, who had now come puffing and huffing like a pot set on the fire to boil.

'Yes?'

'You will run back to town and raise the hue and cry. I want the town's posse up here with horses urgently. Make sure that my own horse is brought, and this gentleman's, too.'

'Mine?' I said, as coolly as I knew how. Still, it has to be admitted that my voice had risen somewhat. I was not entirely in favour of hunting a felon over these moors.

'You will join us, of course, to remove any final stain on your character,' the Coroner said with a nasty little smile.

I didn't like the man, I confess.

We continued up the hill as soon as the constable had been sent back to fetch help, and I had taken his staff. It struck me forcibly that up here on the moors it could be quite easy for a desperate man to leap on an innocent fellow like me and do him some injury. That was not an appealing reflection.

'We shall continue up this hill,' the Coroner said, and we toiled up it, spread out over some tens of yards.

No one should have been able to hide himself in so desolate a place. On we went, with me stumbling every so often on the thick tussocks of grass which concealed deep clefts between them, once falling flat on my face when I tripped over a stone and was forced to lie, wincing with the pain from my jarred head. All the way, I continually searched in every direction for any sign of the hostler. I did not want to come across him alone. I gripped the staff firmly and tried to keep a scowl of ferocity on my face at all times, although after a few moments it invariably slid into a mask of terror.

'He were here,' Nye bellowed.

We all hurried to him, where he stood pointing at the ground. 'See? It is a boot print, and I saw this boot three places on the way up the path. It's him.'

'How can you tell?' I demanded. I was weary, and the idea that a man could tell one print from another, one man's foot mark from the rest of humanity, struck me as fanciful in the extreme.

Nye looked at me with a serious frown puckering his brow. 'At the stable. Clem's boots were plain enough.'

'Clem?' I said.

'Aye. That's the name of the hostler. There's a bar across the sole of his left boot. He stood on a burning rod once. You can see it here – look.'

I looked. He was not wrong. The imprint of a shoe with a line straight across the sole was absolutely clear. If it had been a nobleman's seal, it could not have been more plain. 'You mean to tell me that you noted his shoe print there in the stable?' I said, dumbfounded.

'Didn't you?' he asked, with every indication of surprise.

'He is sure enough,' the Coroner said. 'On!'

He continued climbing the hill, Nye occasionally pointing out the footprints and persuading us to move to the left or right, but to be fair, there was little need of his aid. The steps stood out in the midst of a great collection of similar boot and barefoot steps that led up the hillside. There were men, and many of them, who used this path, and not only men.

As we went, we became aware of a man coming towards us, an elderly fellow, with a filthy, sweat-stained cap on his head, a leather jerkin over his shoulders. He led a pony that looked, if anything, even closer to expiring than the pony Daniell Vowell had given me. It was walking slowly, a cart behind that threatened to push it all the way to Okehampton and beyond. Nye nodded towards him. 'We can ask Arold. He knows this part of the moor.'

'Have you seen a young man heading up the hill?' the Coroner asked when the man was in range.

'What sort o' 'un?'

I gave an accurate description of the man. It was easy. I would be unlikely to forget the sight of Clem's snarling face inches from my own, nor the casual ease with which he leapt across the table at me. He was a sight to drive terror into the heart of St George himself.

'Not up here, no,' the man said after a long, considering pause. 'Why?'

'We are hunting him. I suspect he is guilty of murder,' the Coroner said.

'Hmm. No, not here,' the old man said. He pulled his cap off and wiped his brow with it. Pulling it back on, he set off once more.

I glanced into the cart as he passed. It was full of turves and cartwheels.

Nye saw my look. 'He is fetching peat. But so many miners

have their wheels break up here, he always brings spares to sell. Old Arold makes a pretty penny from them.'

I looked about me at the rolling moors. 'He's welcome to all the pennies he can make.'

The landscape was as desolate as any I have ever seen. Thick tufts of grass stood all about, interspersed with tortured clumps of the yellow-flowered bushes they called *furze*, boulders of grey moorstone, and glistening rivulets of water that glittered like silver under the sun as it passed to the west. We stood at the top of the first rise and looked about us, desperate for a glimpse of the hostler, but there was nothing to see up here. Only an occasional sheep and a few cattle.

'We should wait here, I think,' the Coroner said at last. He looked quite disconsolate. I wanted to remind him that it was not his life that had been threatened by the hostler, but mine. That thought was enough to send another shiver running down my spine. Here, on the open moors, I could all too easily see the hostler living a feral life, perhaps chasing innocents like me, slaying them and robbing them. As he surely had with me. Apart from the slaying, obviously.

He must have had an accomplice who waited in his chamber, while Clem himself used my head as a drum. Or he waited in his room while his friend struck me down. Either way, it was surely him, or why would he run?

The Coroner picked a plot of rock and settled himself on it. 'What do you think?'

'Me?' I said.

'Yes. If you were up here, where would you go?'

Nye answered for me. 'He'll try to find a way to the miners. There are some parts, up near Benjy's Pool and others, where there are plenty of miners and peat-cutters. They may shelter him.'

'Not if we get to them and find him.'

Nye looked at him. 'This is the moor, Coroner. Your law doesn't hold sway in a miner's court. Here it's the law of the tin miners, and no one else matters.'

'I will have that man.'

Nye shrugged.

'How far is it to the nearest camp?' I asked. The idea of
lawless miners was giving me that sour taste in my mouth again.
I have known many unwelcoming people in my time, but the
idea of walking into a miners' camp was one to fill me with
concern. I had seen Nye, Daniell and David, and none filled
me with a sense of friendliness and compassion. More, they
gave me the certainty that if they could see any profit in my
death, it would take no time for them to attempt my murder.

'Only a short distance. You can see their smoke over there,'
Nye said, pointing.

'Perhaps we should reconsider,' I said, but already the Coroner
was blathering on about the miners with Nye.

I had no interest in their discussion. My sole interest had
lain in the thought of briefly making the hostler's life unpleasant
before he was captured and taken to the town's gaol, but now
it looked as though it was likely I would be stuck up here on
the moor all night. I had no desire for that. Especially since I
had neither powder, shot, pistol nor sword with me. I hated the
feeling of nakedness that I was now experiencing. Having no
means of defence was terrifying.

Sulkily, I sat on a rock and studied the ground. Grass, as far
as the eye could see. An occasional bush, all too often bent and
twisted, leaned to the east, as if the Devil himself had blown
his brimstone breath at them. I could have wept. I had only just
agreed to let Mal take Daniell's horse, guaranteeing me an
actual bed for the night, and now here I was, on a cold, desolate
moor, without food or water to sustain me, let alone a bed or
Mal's wife.

She was a pretty little thing, that was certain. I would welcome
the chance to snuggle with her in my bed, but not while her
husband lived. He was a terrifying ogre at the best of times. I
could still remember the sight of him with that club in his hand
on the day I returned to the tavern after stirring from my assault.
My head throbbed in sympathy with the memory.

And yet the silly chit was enjoying an affair with the hostler
in preference to the vile tavern-keeper she was married to. It
struck me that it was a case of picking a fresh foolishness over
the mistake she had already made. But if the picture of her
in the doorway to the stable was anything to go by, she was

keen on the boy. She must have seen something about him that was different to the view I had been given. All I could see was the violence lurking beneath the surface.

'Nye, you know the boy well?' I asked when the others were quiet for a moment or two.

'Everyone knows Clem. He was born up here and had a good reputation. He was a strong lad, but stuck to the rules and was a decent fellow.'

'In what way was he "decent"?' I said, trying, and failing, to keep the sarcasm from my tone.

'If a man had a problem needed fixing, Clem would be one of the first men he would approach. He would always help any man and never owed a debt. If you needed an assistant, you would go to him.'

'And he was a thief.'

'Not that I've heard,' Nye said.

'He robbed me of my purse,' I pointed out. 'And he struck me to get it, before murdering Daniell.'

The Coroner nodded. 'There you have the right of it.'

Nye grumbled to himself a bit on hearing that, and then he glared at me as though it was my fault I had been attacked. 'He's a good man for all that,' he said.

It was almost dusk when five riders appeared, climbing the slope before us, one leading a riderless mount. There was no sign of my own brute.

'Did you not bring a spare one for Master Passer?' the Coroner said somewhat irritably.

'Mal didn't let us, Master,' one of the men said nervously. 'He said he was owed for his board and lodging, and until he paid up, his horse was forfeit.'

'Did he! How's he going to join us?' the Coroner demanded. 'He can't walk on while we ride!'

A second man, who appeared to be the leader of the party, shrugged, unconcerned. He scratched at his jaw.

'You carry on, Coroner,' I said. 'I will walk back with Nye and the constable.'

'I may need you to identify this fellow Clem,' the Coroner said. He looked at the man scratching. 'You will have to lend him your beast.'

For the first time, the man appeared to pay attention. It was a grim-faced and angry bailiff who stood watching us as we rode away.

Thus it was that within a few minutes of the posse arriving, I was off and riding with them further to the centre of the moors.

It was a mess. A chimney stood against the skyline, belching fumes at the sky. Below, it was lit with an unearthly glow from the fires. The ground was dug up and churned into a filthy black mud, and the men in the camp were all stained with it. Bearded, thickset, with grime ingrained into every crease and wrinkle, they were the picture of demons from the deeps. If a commander had come out with a cheery smile, shaking hands, with horns, goat's feet and a tail, I would not have been surprised – nor, if he had, would I have been more fearful than I was at the sight of these.

'We are looking for a man who may have come this way,' the Coroner called.

'What's his name?' a man asked.

'He is known as Clem.'

'Don't know him,' 'Haven't seen him,' 'Who?' came from all sides. The men were wielding pickaxes and shovels like men who didn't realize they were not weapons of war.

'What has he done?' a familiar voice called. When I peered over the heads of the other men all about, I saw David Vowell. He stood a little apart from the rest of the men, thumbs in his belt, smiling broadly as if this was all a tremendous joke for his benefit. It struck me, not for the first time, that he did not appear to be greatly distressed at losing his father – but it wasn't incongruous. I knew what it was to be fathered by a brute.

Even when the Coroner explained why Clem was being hunted, David appeared unconcerned.

'What of it, Coroner? This is not a crime committed here on the moors, so he is free to come here unmolested, if he wants.'

'You would harbour your father's murderer?' I cried.

He looked at me, and I felt his gaze like a sack of snakes deposited on my head.

'Do not presume to think of me as one of your London pretty

boys!' he rasped, stalking towards me. 'But I will not have the laws of the miners ignored for any man. You come here to our blowing house and demand to know whether my father's murderer is here? I can tell you, no. He is not. But if he were, I would not release him into your hands. This is Dartmoor, and the law of the miners holds sway. Now, be gone! You have no authority up here.'

The tavern was quiet when I finally returned. I left my fresh mount with one of the other members of the posse and walked to the entrance. There were noises of buckets and water from the stables, so I guessed that a fresh hostler had been found, and my mount was being well enough looked after.

Inside, there was a fire smoking badly on the hearth, but only a couple of drinkers. The ride back had warmed me, but it had been damp, and a shower in the twilight had left me feeling chill. I needed to sit near the fire. Not that it would throw out a lot of heat with all that smoke rising. The wood must have been young and damp. No, not wood; it was more turves.

There was another man already there. He sat on the settle with his legs outstretched. He was wearing a heavy-looking leather jerkin of a strange cut, and a cloak lay neatly rolled up beside him. His face was strong and square, and he had a thick, gingerish stubble covering his jaw and lank hair under his cap. He smiled at me when I motioned to the seat opposite him. That was when I heard his accent – it was the strongest I had so far heard in Devon.

'*Ja*, nature-ly,' he said, waving a hand towards the bench opposite him. I nodded, took the poker and stabbed at the fire a few times optimistically. It had an immediate effect. The smoke ceased and the fire died.

'What are you doing?' Mal bellowed from the bar.

'I was only trying to make the fire work better,' I said in defence.

'Does it look better? You've killed it!' the infuriated landlord roared.

'Mein host, bitte. Let me,' my companion said, and was soon on his knees with a flint and steel. After three attempts, he had a small flame from a piece of tinder. Soon a pyramid of sticks was alight, and he began to set larger sticks about them. The flames were a welcome sight, and I sat back as he worked.

I was contentedly closing my eyes when he rose and seated himself.

'I am glad, my friend. The fire was doing little more than smoke. I was waiting for the excuse to rebuild it, yes?'

'You are not from here?' I said.

'No, do I look like a local man?' he asked with a smile.

He didn't, now he mentioned it. Although he wore clothing of a similar style to that of a stolid yeoman, there was rather more flamboyance about him. His sword, in particular, I thought, was different from the modern style in London. There, sword masters were tending to move towards the thinner Spanish or Italian rapiers, but this man had a heavy-bladed sword of an older form.

'I am from Nuremberg in Franconia,' he said.

'You are a long way from home,' I hazarded. I had heard of Nuremberg, but it was not a city I could place on a map with any conviction.

'*Ja*, a good way. But here there are opportunities, yes? For men who can help with the mining.'

'You are a miner?'

'Ha! Yes, and also not yes,' he said, his eyes twinkling. 'I am a diviner. I find the things that miners want. If they seek coal, I can find it. If they seek lead, tin, iron, I can discover it for them.'

'How?'

He paused a moment. 'I think of the thing I want to find, and it calls to me, if it is there.'

'I should beware of doing that around here. The people are so backward, you would be likely to be accused of wizardry and burned at the stake.'

'They do such things here?' he said, suddenly perturbed.

'They do that and more,' I said. It was good to see his anxiety.

I was about to expand on the dangers of his actions when the room was invaded.

A harpy ran in, shrieking some of the filthiest language I have ever heard, and in an instant I was beaten about the head with the board she used as a tray.

'What? What are you doing?' I demanded. 'Get off me!'

'You told them, didn't you?' Agnes spat, hitting me repeatedly with her tray. 'You told them about him, you made him run! It's all your fault!'

There are few more uncivilized positions for a man of my sensibilities to endure than a prolonged attack by a woman. Of course, a gentleman like me cannot respond in kind, and although a punch would have ended her tirade in a moment, it was better to suffer her to continue, while covering my head as best I might. However, when she clipped again the side of my pate where the first blow of my visit to Okehampton had been struck, I confess I saw red. I took both her hands in mine, and said, 'Maid, stop!' – or some such similar injunction.

She snatched her wrists away and leaned down to me, snarling from a mouth that was curled into the most perfect sneer I have ever seen.

'You betrayed him, didn't you? You told the Coroner, and you had him chased away. Well, don't think you can get away with that. He'll be back, and he'll be looking for you!'

That, I confess, was not appealing news. She raised her tray once more, and I flinched – unsurprisingly – at which she tossed her head and stormed away.

'This maid, she is angry with you?' my companion asked after a moment.

It was not the most perceptive question.

At that moment, I was in no position to respond. I was running my fingers through my hair, bemoaning my renewed injuries and wondering how the mad bitch had got to hear about the hunt for Clem, and how she realized I was responsible. I felt as though someone had written a board and hung it from my back, saying, *Hit me*.

In the midst of her onslaught, my hat had flown from my head, and I searched for it on the floor. Too late, I saw that it was on the hearth, very close to the flames, and it had begun to smoulder. I quickly retrieved it, but with a sense of the inevitable unfairness of life, I saw that it was dreadfully scorched all along one side. The glorious feather which had decorated it was now a shrivelled and ruined wreck, which reeked – if you have ever burned a feather, you will be able to imagine how foul it was. I slapped it against my thigh a couple of times to dispose of the worst of the odour, and the feather's remains disintegrated. Sombrely, I pulled it on to my head. I would not be able to replace it any time soon. There were no decent hatters between London and Paris, as far as I was concerned. I made a moue at the smell of burned hair and feather, and shook my head. 'She is very upset,' I said.

'Upset? *Ja!* I should dislike to see her truly angry,' the man said. He held out his hand. 'My name is Frantz Lippert.'

I introduced myself in my turn, and we fell to talking about other matters.

Master Lippert, I soon learned, was a famous man in his own lands, where his skills were valuable. Here, though, he had not realized that there would be such a difference.

'I was told to come. Your miners wish to find more metal. I find metal for them.'

'Who called you here?'

He became coy at that. 'Ah, it was a gentleman who wished to have his thinking secret, you understand?'

'No.'

He leaned forward. 'I am often called to see places. Here there is much metal, yes? I have been called to find it.'

It was easy enough to understand that, if this fellow was as good as he appeared to think himself. A man who could look into the ground and see where the metal lay would be a very useful resource in his own right. 'And you had a message to come here and look for tin very recently?'

'*Ja.* I came here, and for four weeks I have been at Exeter. Yesterday, I received a message, and I came. It took me all day to reach this town.'

He looked about him with the same disgust that I felt.

It made sense, as I say. There were plenty, like Ned Gubbings, who toiled fruitlessly on the moors. A man who could show them where to dig would be worth a fortune. After all, much of a miner's life, I guessed, must involve hunting for the right spot to dig, because until you lifted the soil, how would you know where to start? Any number of miners would be willing to pay for the services of a man like this. Especially someone like Vowell – the father or the son.

'So now I may go to the moors and dowse for the metals, and then return home.'

'How do you dowse for metal?'

'It is the same as divining for anything else. I take a hazel branch with a fork, and hold it so, with the branch pointing forward, and the two twigs of the fork in my hands,' he explained, showing how the twigs rested over his forefingers, gripped by his thumbs. He mimed walking, his head moving from side to side, his feet stomping on the floor, until he imitated surprise and the imaginary stick suddenly shot downwards. 'And then we mark the place, and the men dig, and they find what they seek.'

'So you just find where there is metal?' I said.

'No, no. I find metal, or water, or gold. I find what you tell me to find. I imagine it, and the stick finds it. The stick will find whatever you want it to find. It is easy, once you have been properly trained.'

'So you could find money, or a purse?' I asked.

'*Ja!* Whatever you wish,' he said. 'The stick is just a pointer.'

An idea, you see, had occurred to me.

'It sounds as though the stick is possessed by a demon. The demon makes it work. Have you—'

The second interruption was no less startling than the first. I had been about to ask whether Lippert had signed a pact with a traveller at any time, thinking the fool must have given his soul to the Devil for a bewitched stick, when there was a sudden bellow, and I shrank back against the wall.

This time it was the landlord himself who appeared before me. A fist reached out and grabbed my shirtfront. I was hauled to my feet, trying not to gibber and making a very poor show of it, and shortly afterwards I had my second interview with a man with his nose and bawling mouth only a couple of inches from my face.

I do not recommend such interviews.

'You whining cur, you dumpling! You cloth-headed, cloth-eared lumpkin, you . . .'

There was rather a lot more. To be honest, I was quite impressed that the tavern's landlord had such a fund of abuse, because I had not considered him to be a man of many words, but I suppose it is innate in one who spends all his waking hours in a tavern that he should be filled with a surfeit of choice, descriptive and insulting language. Some was really very good, but I won't bore you with it here.

I averted my face from the flying spittle and winced. 'What is the matter, landlord?'

'You *know* what the matter is, you bitch whoreson whelp, you shite-brained puppy, you . . .'

'I don't know what you are talking about,' I said firmly.

'I have a stable with horses, and you have managed to chase my hostler away, haven't you? Fine gentleman that you are, you would have to pay for a new groom, but you have no money, do you?' he sneered. 'So I have to find someone to muck out the stables and feed the mounts in there. While you're doing it, you can at least guarantee how well your own beast fares, can't you? But you need to look to the others as well!'

'I have paid you already, with that fine . . .'

'You have done *nothing*! You offer me a horse that a dead man left in my stable. It's mine now, but it needs feeding and so does yours! I've fed and watered them today, but you'll get outside now and see to them tonight, and you'll see to them tomorrow and the day after as well, until I find a new hostler!'

Every eye in the tavern was fixed upon us, and I could tell that all those with horses in the stable were much on his side. After all, the alternative to Mal's finding a helpful groom might involve them having to do the work themselves, and no traveller at the end of a long day's ride particularly wants to have to check his mount for injuries, rub the beast down and spend any longer than entirely necessary dealing with the many little problems that a horse might have. Far better, in their minds, to have some other lurdan get on with it. And if it happens to be a fly cove like me, so much the better. They would be happy to see me wander outside and deal with their beasts while I shivered and slaved, no doubt.

It was tempting to point out that by driving away the hostler I had saved him from wearing the cuckold's horns, but just now that did not seem a sensible matter to be raising while he was in such a stew.

Still, I was not prepared to take any nonsense about having to work. I bravely stood up to him. 'Now, look, this isn't right,' I said.

'Shut up!' he bawled, right in my face. It felt as though a wash that evening wouldn't be necessary. I was already smothered in the spume from his mouth.

'Master, surely this is not right?' I heard Lippert say, and felt the grip on my shirt loosen.

To my astonishment, Lippert had not risen from his seat, but he was gripping his sword – and I was right: it was a good, broad blade, not a clever, slim rapier – and the point was on the tavern-keeper's back. Later, I saw a small red dot on Mal's shirt, which indicated that he had been pricked already. At that moment, all I knew was that it had caught his attention.

'Master Lipp – um – this doesn't concern you. Put up your sword, or I'll attend to you in a moment.'

'You are treating your customer there like a dog. Please to put him down.'

'I am having words with him,' Mal snarled.

'Master, you will put him down.'

'Or what?'

'Or I will tell your friend Master David that you were most discourteous to me.'

That was an interesting one. I could see the anguish in Mal's face. He was enjoying the thought of beating me to a pulpy mess, and the idea of stopping was pure torture.

'Master Lipp – er, Lipping,' he protested.

'Mein name is Lip-pert, Master, and I think you should remember that, yes? I am a guest of your tavern, no? Now, please put my friend down and listen like a gentleman, yes?'

'Who do you think you are, eh? Be damned, you foreigner, and keep out of my business!' I felt the fist at my breast clench again.

To my astonishment, the expression of raw, murderous fury on his face suddenly changed. He relinquished his grip on me and stood very still. When I glanced at Lippert, I wondered whether he had some other form of magic to use, not only to find metal underground but to see into a man's heart and change his humours. But then I saw that Lippert was holding his sword higher. Its point was between Mal's shoulders at the base of his neck.

'Master Mal, I am a foreigner in these parts, yes, but I have friends who would not take kindly to hearing you describe me so, you understand? You know the miners, I think? Hey? They will be most disappointed to hear that you have treated me with such rudeness. Or that you treat a friend of mine in such a manner. Now, go, fetch us more wine, and when you have poured it, I think you will wish to see us drink your health. Yes? And then you can go and leave us in peace.'

As a man in a nightmare, Mal turned away from us and walked – or staggered – away.

I watched him closely, as you can imagine, suspecting that he might well be reaching for a club behind his bar, but when he reached it, although I saw him cast a surreptitious glance down, he threw a quick look at Lippert and clearly changed his mind. I don't know whether it was the broadsword or the thought of David being displeased, but the idea of punching Lippert, while appealing to him, was clearly less appealing when set against the likelihood of David and his miners appearing and remonstrating in a moderately physical manner.

He left the room.

Lippert leaned back and slipped his sword back in its scabbard. 'My apologies for that. Now, tell me, what does that fellow have against you?'

FOUR

Friday 31st July

There are times, on waking, when a man feels a need for the simple things in life. A warm fire, a jug of something kind to the stomach, the soft kisses of a lover.

On this occasion, what I needed was a bucket.

You know those days when a kindly workman has taken a leaden maul to the inside of your skull? When he is presently enjoying attacking you with that and a large chisel, while his best friend is at his side scraping chalk down a never-ending slate? A day when every joint is as fragile as glass, and every muscle aches? When all you ate yesterday was converted to acid in your stomach, when every breath threatens a burp, and every burp threatens a violent bout of spewing?

This was one of those days.

It took a while to open my eye. I say eye, because I dared not open both together in case the world's spinning became even more pronounced, and my ability to hold down my supper from the previous evening became still more precarious.

In short, I was the victim of one of the worst hangovers of my life.

It is peculiar, because in London I was known to be a man with a sound head and stomach for drink. When a group met about a mess table, I would be first to the sack or claret, and I would still be there when others had left or were snoring under the table. I have the belly and head for strong drink; I always have had. But today was different. I could only think that the damp, cold air of Devon was affecting me strangely.

There was a horrible noise. I didn't want to shake my head in case something fell out, and it didn't sound as if it was in my ear. It was oddly penetrating and seemed to come from behind me. Glancing about me, I could see that my room was the same as before, with one exception: when I peered over my shoulder, there was a companion in the farther side of my bed. I cast my one eye over the figure. From the look of the hair, it was not Agnes, which was itself a relief. The previous day, I was incapable of defending myself from the landlord. Were he to come into my room now and find me snuggled up with his wife, I would be entirely at his mercy in my present state.

A soft snore made the windows tremble and the floorboards quiver. More to the point, it made my stomach begin to clench, and that was not a sensation I could afford with any safety. I slid my legs from the blankets and rested there a moment while I acclimatized myself to the new sensation. It was not good. I pulled the coverings from me and tried to sit upright. Lifting my head to the vertical caused ripples of nausea to roll from side to side from my head all the way down to my bowels, with a short portage from my ballocks to my liver en route, like a ship of misery rolling on the stormy waves of anguish. I felt more wretched than ever before. Everything felt grim.

Standing at the side of the mattress, quaking, I searched about me for a piss-pot. There was nothing. Cursing the backwardness of this uncivilized locality, I was forced to go to the window. It was closed, and I had to pull the rope to let down the wooden shutter, and then stuck my head out into the cool, fresh air. For a moment, the noise of the snoring was gone, and I could enjoy a little peace, with a false conviction that the immediate threat of vomiting was past me. The air outside was clean, chill and refreshing on my face. It smelled pure, and the faint soft breezes cooled the sweat on my brow and throat. I leaned on the window sill with my eyes closed, just enjoying the sensation.

And then the first convulsion gripped me.

You will, I am sure, have seen those humorous fellows who will fill a pig's bladder with water or some similar liquid (I will not go into the more gross fillings employed by apprentices when they are allowed off the leash and have consumed too much ale), point the open end in a direction best suited to causing hurt or offence, and then firmly squeeze the bladder? The ensuing jet of liquid is itself more than enough to cause extreme anguish in even the most amiable of persons when it strikes them in the body or face.

However, my first thoughts were not for the reaction of another person. No, it was more the sensation in my belly.

It was as if a giant had taken my stomach in his grip, one hand on either side, and now squeezed the two together with all his might. A sudden, tumultuous eruption of vomit was forced up my throat and out through my mouth and nostrils.

Word cannot convey the vile sensation and stinging pain. If I had been overtaken by a demon who was now enjoying himself at my expense, the feeling could not have been worse. My nose smarted, my throat felt as though someone had taken a scrubbing brush to it, and all I knew was an overwhelming revulsion and feeling of languishing. I was convinced I must have been fed poison. Perhaps Mal had so adulterated my food the previous evening that I was succumbing.

The irony! Here I was, an innocent man, and because of the harpy he had married, I was dying. She had told him it was my fault the hostler had left, forgetting to mention the matter of her affair with him, and now he was determined to kill me. I had run here for safety, and yet without realizing, I had hurtled head first to my doom. Fate had a sense of humour.

Those were my initial thoughts, but soon something else came to me. Over the snoring, I was sure I could discern something else. It made me frown, even as I felt my stomach convulse again. I leaned out further, and soon the expected inundation arrived. And again there was something that caught at my attention: a strange, mewling noise, as if a cat was being strangled.

I opened my eyes, and when I looked beneath me, I discovered the source of the sound.

Below, covering an area some three yards across, there was a layer of vomit. Unfortunately, almost in the centre of this space there stood a figure shaking with incandescent fury: Agnes.

There have been times when I have been minding my own business, when something has startled me into a sudden appreciation of the nearness of death. Once was when flying through the air after being thrown by a horse; another happened when I was knocked on the head; a third when I came to after being struck down. The similarity was, in each case, I seemed to see not my whole life flash before me but certain highlights –

although it would be more fair to call them lowlights. They all involved the very worst situations in which I had found myself over a life that had been all too eventful. The most embarrassing, the most painful, the most unpleasant, all came to me as a series of images to remind me, you might think, that no matter what happened next, it could hardly be as bad as this.

Except that just now I could envisage nothing so bad and so painful as what was likely to come. It quite took my breath away and had the beneficial result that I lost all thoughts of throwing up further.

There are many people over whom I would not wish to empty my stomach. Chief among these would be, I suppose, the Queen, her chancellor, my sub-contractor Humfrie, or the landlord of this tavern.

With good fortune, I had not hit any of these. However, I had succeeded in hitting poor Agnes full on. And that was cause for some speculation as to what her husband's reaction might be when he heard of the mishap that had befallen her.

Suddenly, I felt the nausea returning.

It is rare that I am at a complete loss for words. After all, my trademark was my easy confident manner with others. Usually, I could be relied upon to bring a witty remark to an otherwise dull evening. However, it is one thing to sit in elegant company and make a comment deriding another's dress sense or manner of comportment to the amusement of others; it is quite another to be confronted with a woman who has just been beslobbered with your vomit.

If I was nonplussed and at a loss for words, at least I could appreciate the situation from her perspective. She was, just now, incoherent with rage. In her face, I could see that indignation, offence and horror were vying for release, but at that moment she was incapable of making a reasoned choice as to which she should vent first. I can honestly say that I have never before or since seen a woman in quite such a state of inarticulation. She stood bespattered, drenched, and stared up at me with an expression of such loathing, such abhorrence, that I chose, sensibly, to withdraw my head. I could hear a little squeak, then some squawking, like a chicken clearing her throat for some serious comments about the indignity of egg-laying, and then there was a merciful slammed door.

Merciful from the point of view that she was not about to scream at me from the yard, but not at all pleasant, because the inevitable result would be that she would go to her husband and lay the facts before him. I had not enjoyed the experience of having his fists at my throat the night before. I felt sure that I would not enjoy meeting him today. He would be likely to deprecate my offence against his wife. I had a notion that he might consider my throwing up over her to be a grave affront to her dignity. And to his. From his reaction the previous evening, I reckoned this might be a good time to think about escaping the town and making myself scarce.

I wiped my mouth and hurried to my clothing. Pulling on hosen and jack, I scurried to the door. There was no sound outside, so I pulled it wide and ran along the passageway to the stairs. Here, I hurtled down as best I could, desperate just to be away from this terrible tavern.

Once in the yard, I ran swiftly over the vomit-smothered stones and out to the roadway. I dared not return to the moors, for who knew might be up there already? In preference, I turned right towards the town. At least there I should find somewhere to rest without fearing the sudden appearance of an enraged tavern-keeper.

Without thinking, I found myself outside the inn where I had met Sir Geoffrey. I hesitated but, glancing behind me, I knew I had no choice: I must enter and ensure that I was always in front of other men, if I was to protect myself from Mal's justifiable anger. Not many men could bear to see their wives bear the full brunt of another man's puking.

The Coroner was sitting at a table with a trencher full of meat and cheese, and was apparently making the best he could of present circumstances. Looking up as I walked in, he beckoned me and motioned to the seat opposite him.

Now, it is an odd thing, but since being unwell all over Agnes, I had acted with the utmost clarity of purpose and single-mindedness. I had wanted to be away from the scene of the crime, as it were. To do that, I had run, and in all the journey

I had not been aware of a desire to be unwell again. Yet the fact is, as soon as I sat in the heat of the inn's chamber and saw this gross man sitting and licking his fingers, burping softly and taking a great gulp of wine, suddenly I was assailed by the threat of another multi-coloured hiccup.

'Well?' the Coroner said. 'Have ye something to tell me?'

He speared a large lump of meat. It glistened unpleasantly on his knife, and I could not help but stare. He set it near his mouth and bit into it, a little blood trickling down from the corner of his mouth into his beard.

I was transfixed by that little dribble of blood. I am usually a calm man who sets much store by good food, and for me, a good cut of beef or pork should be pleasantly darkened. I am not one of those who likes to hear a cow moo in pain when I stab a steak; I prefer not to taste just blood. And just at the moment, I was aware that my stomach was rumbling in an increasingly unpleasant manner. It was not only the blood, but also the warmth in the room – was it only me who felt that the fire was too hot? – the noise and the closeness. There was little air, so it felt.

'Are you all right?' the Coroner asked. He was looking at me in a peculiar manner, as if I were a felon who had confessed to regicide.

'I am fine,' I said, stuttering. And suddenly I knew I wasn't. I rose from the seat and flung myself towards the door. As I reached it, a man was coming in. I drew the door wide and tried to escape, but I struck the unfortunate visitor with my elbow, and he gave a gasp as I winded him. Still, I made it to the roadway before I was forced to crouch with hands on thighs and empty my stomach all over again.

Again done, I rose slowly to the vertical, puffing and blowing. There were three children opposite who appeared to be laughing at something, and a dog sat nearby with his head tilted enquiringly as he stared at me.

I wiped my mouth and returned to the tavern.

'You feeling better?' the Coroner asked, and I tried to nod, but my head moved in the negative.

He laughed and ordered me a weak ale.

*   *   *

'How do you feel now?'

I was, at last, able to smile. 'I'm fine.'

'Are you sure?'

'Never better,' I said. And it was mostly true. A quart and a half of ale had taken away the feeling of incipient vomiting and left me feeling alert, capable and ready for anything. I felt well enough to chuckle at the memory of the appalled Agnes staring up at me, and just now I could even smile at the thought of Mal and how he would react to the sight of his wife. In short, three pints of ale had made the whole world look considerably more rosy.

It was all the more appealing when the Coroner had his servant go to his room and return to me my sword and gun. I slipped the straps over my head with a ready appreciation and gave him a grin of gratitude. He was a delightful fellow, this Coroner. I felt sure that we would become firm friends.

'You should go and put your head down,' he said to me.

'No, no. I'm fine now,' I assured him. 'And I have to be getting on with my journey to Plymouth.'

'You intend to continue on your way?'

'Yes, after I have searched the stable for my money. There's nothing to keep me here, once I have found my purse,' I said. 'I only need to fetch my belongings from the tavern, and I can be off.'

I took my leave of him shortly afterwards. As matters stood, I felt sure that I had a means to find my money. After all, my companion of the previous night's festivities was a capable dowser, so he said. He had told me of dowsing for metal. What could be more natural than that he might dowse for my purse? It seemed perfectly logical to me. The man may be driven by a demon, but if the demon found my money for me, that would be fine. It was welcome to Lippert's soul.

After one last ale with the affable Coroner, I walked along the roadway with a cloud of happiness enveloping me. The weather was fine, I had my weapons, and soon I would have my money and could continue on my way to the coast. All was well in my world. Nothing could distract me from my course.

*   *   *

The sense that something might be amiss began to strike me as I drew closer to the tavern. A small but niggling doubt was making itself felt.

What, I wondered, if Mal didn't quite see the situation in the roseate hue by which I viewed it? What if he took a more mean-spirited attitude and chose to take offence at my treatment of his wife, accident though it might have been? What if, in short, he was waiting for me at the tavern ready to pull out my liver and kidneys with his bare hands?

This was indeed a consideration. I found my pace slowed as I approached the tavern, and when I reached the entrance of the yard, I peered in with every nerve tense.

Perhaps the courage I had felt before was only due to the ale I had drunk. But now I was wary enough to continue, although with caution.

I listened. There was no sound in the yard, apart from a whinny or two from the stables. There was no clattering of pans from the kitchen, and I could see no one in the house or the stables. There was, however, a rather rancid odour about the place. I chose to ignore that and slipped about the entranceway, searching for a sight of the Nuremberger. I had hoped to see him sitting on a bench outside the tavern, but there was no sign of him. Perhaps he was inside? Surely he would not still be abed? I edged nearer to the tavern itself and took a quick peep through the open window. There was no sign of him. Was he still in our bedchamber? I looked up at the window overhead, and as I did so, I realized he must have left. He had mentioned that he wanted to get out early, for he had to meet with the miners. Perhaps they had sent a messenger to collect him, and he had been off as soon as I left? That was a cause for irritation, for it meant I would have to wait here to see him again, and who could tell how long that might be?

I was about to turn and make my way back to the Coroner's inn when I heard one of those sounds that makes my scalp try to flee my body and run. It was a footstep, approaching quickly.

In my considerable experience, steps approaching at speed from behind seldom spell anything good.

I have one foolproof method of defence in such situations, which is to immediately sprint away from the footsteps. This has the advantage that I cannot be alarmed by whoever the assailant might be (and it invariably tends to be an assailant), which might cause me to hesitate and thus become embroiled in a contest that I might well lose. It also means that I save valuable time: rather than turning, seeing an opponent and wasting moments in being terrified by a henchman as he all the while gains on me, I am instead already haring away at full speed, which is all too often considerably faster than those who try to capture me. It is an approach that has worked in the past on numerous occasions. However, this time there was a considerable handicap.

I was facing the wall.

Trying to stifle my bleat of terror, I tried to dart to the right and evade any attempt at capture, but even as I made my manoeuvre, a hand thudded heavily on my shoulder. I gave a little cry of alarm, just as a horrible sound came to me. It was the hiss of a riding crop flying through the air, and it landed most painfully on my other shoulder. I gave a whimper of pain and tried to break free from his grip, but the fact is, he had a grip like iron. It was like being held by a blacksmith, and when a smith lays hold of your shoulder, you don't escape unless he wants you to.

That riding crop came down furiously, beating me with a determined malice. I felt it on my shoulder, back, rump, flank, then my head and neck, and all the while the man said nothing. It was a silent, bitter anger that drove this man. And I could not break free. Instead, I let out a high keening sound that rather surprised even me, and suddenly I was hauled around to face my attacker.

'What are you doing?' I said.

You see, I had been fully expecting to find myself confronted by an enraged tavern-keeper. Instead, I found myself face to face with Clem, the hostler.

'Looks like I'm punishing the vile little man who did so much to try to hurt my Agnes,' he said, and raised his switch again.

I was staggered. I mean, it is rare to find a man who will willingly risk his neck just to see the local tavern wench, but this was the same fellow who had robbed me, killed David's father *and* had been shown to be overly keen on the tavern-keeper's wife. None of the three was conducive to a long and healthy life.

'I've done nothing!' I protested.

'You threw up all over her!' he shouted.

'Yes, but that was an accident. I had no idea she was there, let alone that she was right beneath me when I had to . . .'

'You threw up all over her. She was smothered in your vomit.'

There was a sort of wondering tone to his voice, as though he was struggling to contain a certain admiration for my accuracy, which was competing with his proprietorial sense of injustice at the way his inamorata had been treated. Which was understandable. The injustice, I mean.

Now I could, I suppose, have called for help, but were I to do so, and Mal came running, I venture to consider that my life would be curtailed rather more swiftly. As it was, I felt sure that a little swift talking and careful suggestions of danger for him would soon have me running.

I attempted a smile, which was a mistake, because the last thing I saw was his fist accelerating towards my face just before I appeared to be hit by a slab of grey moorstone.

Do you ever have the dream in which you fall into a tunnel of blackness that opens in the mattress where you sleep? A sense of tumbling through an unimaginable depth, in unutterable blackness, knowing that when you land, it will be painful?

I went backwards, and fell, and then the ground seemed to open at my feet, and just as in the dream, suddenly I was swallowed up by the darkness.

Being struck on the head or face is not recommended. All the well-being I had felt before had left me by the time I came to once more.

I have said already that I have had experience of waking after a number of blows. This, however, was a novel waking even for me.

My stomach was compressed. That was the first thought that came to me. My belly was being punched, softly, but relent-lessly. The smell told me I had been sick again. I tried to sit up, but couldn't, because my hands were bound before me, and when I tried to move them, a cord about my ankles tightened.

I opened my eyes.

It appeared that I was hanging upside down over a moving roadway. My hands were bound, and I was hanging from something that moved slowly and deliberately. From the odour, I realized I was thrown over the back of a horse, and that it was bearing me up a lane. I was bound hand and foot, a strap under the beast's belly binding wrists to ankles. I could no more move than fly.

'Help!' I cried.

'Shut up,' Clem said, and hit me with his riding crop.

I hurriedly obeyed, and we continued on our way. When I glanced ahead, it was obvious that I was on my own horse. That, I felt, was the height of bad manners. Using my own horse to lead me to my death was intolerable. But then I reflected that the more important aspect of this was the fact that I was being taken to a place of execution. And when I looked around, I could see where he was taking me – up to the moors. The desolate wastes about us were uninhabited so far as I could see. Every so often, we entered long, gloomy tunnels of green, trees reaching out overhead and joining branches with their companions on the opposite side of the lane. The walls were smothered in mosses and thick with brambles and nettles. Everywhere was abundant vegetation. I longed for the safety and security of a decent alley in Holborn or near the Tower.

'What are you going to do with me?' I asked. I don't mind admitting that my voice was tremulous.

'Shut up!' he said.

We kept climbing the flank of a long hill. Soon we had left the shrouding trees behind and were on the high moor, a grim vista if ever I saw one. Yellowish grasses stuck up in thick tufts, a long, dark pool reflected the sky and clouds, and, in the distance, hills rose and fell, each with a cluster of grey moorstone rocks at their summit. All about there were larger or smaller rocks, with one or two stunted, ill-favoured and wind-swept bushes clinging desperately to the soil. I got a crick in my neck from glancing all about me, trying to see where we were heading, where I could try to elicit some help. Not that I had much hope. After all, the only people scraping a living up here on the moors were the miners, and I hadn't found them to be particularly helpful.

I thought I saw some men working on a hillside, but they were too far away to hear my cries. Smoke rose from the farther side of a hill, but there was no one on this side to help me. A cart appeared up ahead of us, and I thought I recognized Arold, the purveyor of peat and cartwheels, but as my horse plodded on, Arold continued on his way around a hill and out of sight. I let my head fall. It felt an impossible weight when I was trying to lift it and see the route ahead. In any case, what was the point? There was no one here to save me from whatever this fool of an hostler was going to do to me. He had knocked me down twice, killed old Daniell, and now he was going to put paid to me as well.

An overwhelming despair smothered me. I was as insipid as a drunken slug. There was no energy in me. My doom was come upon me, and there was nothing I could do about it. I was forced merely to endure this journey and wait for Clem to pick a spot. No doubt he would stab me and then drop me into a mire so no one would ever find me again. I would just be a disappearance, perhaps a cause of annoyance to Mal and Agnes, because I had not fully settled up – although they had Daniell's horse. This one, apparently, was not going to remain with them, but they could not have expected it. Clem had clearly taken my horse as his own. And I was being carried to my death.

I began to weep.

'Stop your snivelling,' he said.

It did not ease my concerns. In fact, I began to wail, bemoaning my fate and his cruelty, until he stopped the horse and began to belabour me with his whip.

I shouted and protested, but he slashed at me with a vigour I hadn't seen him demonstrate before. Soon I was smarting afresh from each new cut of the whip, and it was seriously painful.

And then, mercifully, it stopped and I saw him jerked backwards, as Nye took hold of his whip arm and snatched it from his hand.

*   *   *

'What are you doing with 'un?' Nye grated. He took the riding crop from Clem's hand and broke it in two in front of his face.

I could have wept for sheer relief, seeing a – well, not exactly a friendly face, but at least one that was less unfriendly than Clem's.

'Get off me! I'm takin' 'ee to Vowell's.'

'Vowell tol' me to see to 'un.'

''E tol' me to bring 'un.'

Clem was game, I'll give him that. He stood with his chest puffed out as far as it would go, almost as though he would be prepared to enter a ring to fight the miner. Personally, I would have been happy to watch such a bout, but would sincerely have deprecated entering a match against either of them.

The two appeared to come to some kind of conclusion, and before long we had set off once more. This time, there was less in the way of physical violence towards me, yet my journey was still deeply uncomfortable. I don't know whether you have ever been forced to lie atop a horse, but I can assure you that it is not a comfortable mode of travel. The belly suffers discomfort from the rolling gait of the brute, the ankles and wrists chafe from the cords binding them, and the neck suffers untold pain, aching from trying to look up and see ahead. The alternative, having it dangle, means every jolt leads to a painful bump either against the horse's chest or, mostly worse, an up and down jerking of the neck. Either was dreadful, and I began to long for the end of this journey, no matter what the outcome might be for me.

And then, mercifully, it was over. I think I must have been knocked partly into a daze. With the number of injuries that my head had endured in the last days, it would not be a surprise were I to have fainted away. Be that as it may, I was suddenly aware of even more pain at my wrists, and then they were suddenly free, and I felt someone grab my shin and lift it. Still a little confused with pain and befuddlement, I could not make out what was happening. I felt the back of the horse, which apparently rolled itself along my belly to my thighs, and then there was a momentary weightlessness and once more that dream-like feeling of falling through a mattress, which was this time suddenly curtailed by reason of my head hitting the ground.

'Ow!'

'You should be glad,' a familiar voice said. 'If it were not so wet and soft, you might have hurt yourself.'

At that, there was a general, sycophantic chuckling all about me. Looking up, rubbing my head, I realized I was surrounded by some of the roughest-looking men I have seen outside of a butcher's shop. Broad, heavy-shouldered men, few of whom still had all their teeth, or all their fingers for that matter. Capped, clad in a mixture of rough, thick clothing and leather, they all appeared to clench their fists around more or less heavy tools, or, as I was forced to consider them, weapons of slow and hideous murder.

I attempted to climb to my feet, but the lack of feeling in arms and legs was problematic. Yet, where there is a desire, even the most battered body can manage it. In my case, the incentive came from the sight of one man I had hoped not to see again for a long while.

It was David Vowell.

He stood before me thoughtfully, an apologetic little smile playing at the sides of his mouth. In his hands he held a ballock dagger.

'Welcome to the parish of Lydford,' he said.

Those words took a few moments to sink in. Mostly, I spent them gazing at him with some perturbation and confusion. 'Eh?'

His smile broadened, but there was a sort of bemused wrinkling at his brow. 'I find it rather difficult to believe that you can be quite so foolish as you make out. After all, I think people have mentioned Lydford to you already.'

'Aye,' I said, and suddenly I was nervous. 'Lydford Law, you mean? It is the justice in these parts, I understand?'

'It is the justice of the moors. You see, fellows here tend not to believe a great deal in the mercy of far-off Keepers, Coroners or Justices. We know it takes all too long to go and ask for one of them to come and discuss complaints or claims. So we tend to hold our own courts. We have our own parliament, and we have our own laws, so we keep to our own courts. It is all perfectly logical.'

It must have been the knocks to my head that did it. I still could not make out what he was driving at. As far as I was concerned, this was all of only academic interest to me. And I was no academic.

'I see. Well, yes, of course. And now, thank you for rescuing me from that hostler. He has treated me abominably, with his cuts from a whip, knocking me down, binding me hand and foot, and wasting my time by bringing me up here. I hope your "Lydford Law" will punish him.'

Suddenly, the smile was gone, and in David's place there stood a demon from the pit. It was almost instant, and it was very alarming to see the transformation. When I first met the man, I was sure that he was a pleasant, apologetic character, and now here was this.

'You continue to treat us all like country fools, don't you? Are you laughing at me? Do you think I am so stupid as to find your words helpful? I could cut your tongue out now for your insolence!'

I cast a look around me. Truth be known, I was looking for any support or indication of sympathy, but even as I glanced about me at the circle of miners, I saw that not a one showed any signs of leaping to my defence. Rather, they appeared to be more of a mind with David Vowell. They were without exception grim and determined-looking men, without a single compassionate look between them.

'I . . . er . . .'

'Yes, you will feel the full force of the law here on the moors. We will take you to the gaol and court, and see you hang.'

'That's not right,' I protested. 'You have to give me a trial!'

'This is Lydford Law. We don't have time for all that folderol. We'll give you a fair trial later.'

And I think that was when the true impact hit me. Because it was perfectly obvious from the look in his eyes and the tone of his voice that this was no idle comment or pleasantry. He was in earnest.

Thus it was that shortly after being cut from my horse, I was tied with a long rope to her saddle, and while the miners jeered and laughed at me, three men, one of them Nye, set off with me to go to the gaol.

At least they had not executed me on the spot. Not that it would have been easy, there being a lack of trees of sufficient height. I suppose, being miners, they would have had capable carpenters with them, but I dare say David would not have wished to waste perfectly good timber to break my neck. Easier to send me to the gaol and make use of one of the trees there.

It was a long walk, and while some of my guards indulged in a light, bantering conversation, I did not try to join in. For one thing, I could scarce understand any of them, and for another, I was petrified with fear for my future.

Other men, who live in enlightened areas like London, would be dragged to their execution on a cart or hurdle, and would at least enjoy a last view of an elegant city on their way. But for me, all I was granted was the unutterably dreary and dismal sight of the moors. Was there ever a view more designed to numb the senses and bring to a man the true horror and brutality of existence as he prepared for his doom?

Rocks, grass, the yellow-flowered furze with leaves like needles, and occasional bushes – I cannot call them trees – so malformed and blighted that they resembled less the oaks from near London and more the tortured branches in a charcoal-burner's clamp. This was not a place for men to live. It was a foul, tormented land, and from all I could see, David and his men were welcome to it.

All I wanted was to be away from here.

I don't know how long it took for us to reach the gaol. All I know is that it was dark as I stumbled down the long track into the town of Lydford and caught my first glimpse of the horror that was Lydford gaol.

It was a huge block of moorstone that stood on its own mound. Bleak, grey and square, it looked more daunting than any vision I had held of the Tower in London. At least at the Tower there were usually signs of pleasant life: there were flags fluttering merrily in the breeze, and while you could hear the screams of the damned, at least there were cheery taverns in the courtyard, and wenches who could be available at the right price.

Here, there was little of that nature. No women, just a straggle of peasant houses with occasional children playing, who all went silent as we approached. I had the impression that they didn't often see elegantly clad men like me. I almost expected to receive a stone in the back after we had passed them. These fellows looked as if they were backward enough to want to assault any visitor to their town.

But it was the castle that took my eye rather than the folk.

It was set upon a little mound a short way outside the town itself. Our path took us round to the rear, where there was a grim doorway. It was opened, and I was thrust inside.

I felt I was being shoved into the deepest pit of hell.

In my time, I have had some experiences that I never wish to recall. This, however, was to become the key and primary event to forget.

I don't know if you have ever been pushed into a small gaol in a provincial town like Okehampton, but from personal experience, the life of the gaoler is usually quite pleasant. He has a good brazier or similar fire, plenty of firewood or coals, and usually a skin of wine or small barrel of ale to pass the time. What the prisoner tends to find is that they are slung into a cold, wet, vile little cell with a small window high in the wall, and no creature comforts.

This was no exception in that regard. I could see that at a glance. There was one larger room here, and two smaller to the left. There was no need to peer into the cells to see how I would be treated, and that was because I could see how the gaoler himself was viewed by the flickering light of a few rushlights set in holders. When the people about can't be persuaded to allow the gaoler a candle or two, you know he's not viewed with any great sympathy.

He was a shrivelled hulk of a man. Once he had been tall, but now he stooped; once he had been broadly built, from the look of him, but now his belly had deflated and decreased and hung over the top of his belt. He had jowls like a mastiff's, and beneath his chin he had flesh dangling like a cockerel's. Watery eyes spoke of the cold and misery. There was no fire, no cheery glowing brazier, and no ale or wine. If the people here were to treat him so inconsiderately, it did not bode well for me as an inmate.

The other thing that did not seem to imply that I would get a friendly reception was the way in which Nye kicked me in the small of my back and sent me sprawling on the wooden boards of the floor.

'Ow!'

My head was still hurting from the various beatings it had received, and after my march over the moors, my legs were as weak as a fresh-born foal's. Were I to try to stand again, I was certain that I would only fall. So I didn't bother to try, but instead attempted to roll over to see what was happening. But while I had the idea, the old gaoler suddenly sat on my back.

If you have ever had a fear of being waylaid, this was much like it. I was assailed by a quickening terror. In many ways, it was like being in a dream. I could feel a tight-fitting cord being wound about my wrists, and then a man was sitting on my ankles too, and I was utterly incapacitated. I wriggled and tried to break free, but then stopped, and my eyes widened.

I know that dowsers and others claim to have supernatural gifts that allow them to take part in their chosen trades. I have no idea how many are truth speakers and how many are char-latans, but I can tell you that I can sense when a razor-sharp knife is approaching my throat. There is a kind of prickle that comes first, rather as though a block of ice was coming close. I've always found that knives at my throat tend to be very cold. Odd that. Still, as I lay there, suddenly I was aware that there was something of incredible coldness near my neck and, without looking, I knew it was a dagger with an amazingly sharp blade. At once, several things happened. First was I stopped struggling, preferring instead to concentrate on this new threat; second was that my hackles all rose, and I felt the tingle from behind my ears all the way down my neck to my shoulders; third, my throat dried as if all the moisture was desperate to escape that keen edge; fourth, I became aware of the gaoler's voice in my ear, saying all sorts of things in his broad accent. Most slipped past me, since I was in a complete funk about the idea of that knife being wielded by an ancient old fool like him, but the gist, I think, was that if I was to keep buffeting him, he would give me more than a little twinge. I would be, so I understood, marked significantly for life. So I should keep still.

There was a quick stinging sensation, and I gave a sharp cry, while the man chuckled nastily. 'Any more trouble, an' you'll get more of that, boy.'

I was persuaded. In short order, I was taken to a trap in the floor, and forced to descend a ladder, which was no easy task with my hands tied behind my back, and as I went down, the gaoler demonstrated his famous, I suppose, sense of humour. He took the top of the ladder and jerked it violently forwards and back. Without the use of my hands, I could not maintain my grip or try to balance. I was flung from the ladder and thrown bodily to the ground, which happened to be largely rock, mud and a mixture of unpleasant additional remnants no doubt left here by past occupants.

That was, I think, the most vile, noisome cell in which I have ever been held. It was wet, it smelled, and it was horribly uncomfortable. There was no blanket, let alone a mattress or bed frame. Just a small chamber hewn into the rock, and when the ladder had been pulled up and the trapdoor dropped, I could tell there was no window either. The only light that would penetrate my dungeon was that which filtered through the floorboards overhead. I peered up, looking at the yellow glow from the rushlights fighting its way through the cracks.

There was rough laughter, and then the slam of the door, and I could see that the gaoler was still there, stomping about the place. I called to ask that my hands be unbound. They were so tightly tied that I could not feel my fingers already. After a short pause, the trap opened once more and the ladder was let down. The gaoler clambered down it, glowering at me. He indicated that I should stand before him, and he slit the cords that bound me. Later, I found that he had also sliced into my wrist, but at the time I couldn't feel it. I was just glad to be released, and turned to thank him, but he was already more than halfway up the ladder. As I watched, he turned at the top and grinned.

'Sleep comfy, boy. Tomorrow you'll be sleeping with the Devil!'

And the trap slammed.

FIVE

Saturday 1st August

I would like to be able to say that I passed a comfortable evening, that I was given ale, bread and cheese, and that I woke to the sound of birdsong and the cheery voices of the town's maidens singing or at play. I would like to be able to say that I didn't wake with the damp freezing my bones, that the floor didn't seem to be comprised solely of stones and bits and pieces of gravel, each curiously designed to be all sharp edges, or that as soon as the gaoler deigned to wake, which was somewhat later than me, it has to be said, his walking about in the chamber above me did not lead to great drizzles of fine dust and dirt showering me from between the cracks of the planks overhead.

Yes, I would like to be able to say all this, but the fact is that I spent my night huddled with my arms about myself, shivering in the cold and wet with moisture seeping into my hosen, my jack losing any ability to keep me warm. Yes, I did try to lie down, but there was only one place that did not smell as though the last hundred prisoners had died there, and left their bodies' fluids to mature for a year or more. In the end, I found the least wet, least noisome area and tried to make myself as comfortable as I could. I was not overly successful, and it was not only the lack of any creature comforts.

The wind howled about the place. All night, it was like listening to the howling of demented, tortured souls. There were words in that wind, and it was cursing and damning all those who broke up the soil on the moors. Not that many would want to be there. The poor fools who tried to make some sort of a living out there in the wildlands were not there for the joy of their labours – most would be constantly screaming for escape, I'd imagine. It would take a civilized person only moments to realize that a place like that, with the mud, foul weather, vicious wind and general feeling of utter decay and revulsion, was no place for a man of sensitivity. Any man who was unsure of the fact need only look at the features and bodies of those who lived there: the peasants and miners.

Or, of course, the gaoler.

My first sight of him that morning reminded me of nothing less than a particularly unhealthy bull at the baiting. You see them, sometimes, scraggy old beasts so ancient you know that even strenuous exercise cannot tenderize their meat, and which look about with grumpy ferocity.

This man was like one of those old bulls. His frame was dissipated and shrunken, but his eyes held the same malevolence. I have seen many a dangerous felon in my time, and they all tend to have that same, flat, uninterested look in their eyes. They see a human being like themselves, but without caring or any form of compassion. This fellow had light-grey eyes and grizzled hair that was more shades of white rather than black, and he looked at me like a farmer spying a rat in his grain store. There was only vicious disgust there.

He stared down at me like the brother of the prodigal son watching his spendthrift sibling return after blowing his pelf on high living while he had been spending his time at home looking after the farm. It was not a look to inspire confidence. When he stood upright, and his hand went to his cods, I was convinced he was going to urinate on me, and scrambled out of the way, but he just bared his teeth like a terrier spying a new ankle to bite, and disappeared.

A few moments later, the ladder materialized and slid slowly down into the hole. I studied it warily. I am a man who has experienced almost every form of betrayal and I eyed the ladder like a man in a well staring at a rope and wondering whether climbing it would lead to his escape and freedom, or whether it would bring a heavy bucket on to his head. After all, I had not heard anything good about this gaol, and no gaol gets a dreadful reputation when the gaoler is a kindly, Christian type. If I were to climb up to the daylight, I doubted that I would be offered a feast. More likely, I would be stabbed or beaten, if I was any judge of character.

I was still there, torn with indecision, when there was a

sudden noise, which I *almost* recognized. It was a familiar, dull sound, one that I thought I had heard before in a different environment entirely, but I could not for the life of me remember where or when. It was the sort of sound with which I was well acquainted, and yet in some way was curiously unknown. And it was deeply unpleasant. Like a reminder, if you follow me, in the same way that the sight or smell of a drink in the morning can remind a fellow of the drinking session he had the day before and bring back memories of spewing. It was that sort of recollection – foul, and somehow distant.

And then, much to my surprise, a face appeared at the trapdoor. It was the peasant woman I had spoken to before seeing Ned that day, the woman in her garden.

'You plannin' on staying till dinner time?' she asked peevishly, 'or are you getting out?'

If she was there, I was sure that the gaoler must have left for some reason. I needed no urging. Stiffly, because of the cold, I took hold of the ladder and made my way to the top. It was a long climb in my condition.

'Tek yer time,' she said when I was halfway up, peering down at me with a face as expressionless as an oak's bark. 'Nothin' to hurry for, 'ceptin' David Vowell and his friends coming here to see you swing.'

That gave my sore muscles and weary legs the incentive they needed. I tried to hurry up the last rungs, and at the top would have toppled back into the depths, but for her strong arm grabbing my jerkin and helping me over the trapdoor's lip.

It was a chastened and panting Jack Blackjack who finally fell to the floorboards and lay there panting, staring at her with confusion.

The source of the noise was instantly obvious. It was one of those sounds with which I was indeed well acquainted from personal experience: it had been the crack of a cudgel against the gaoler's head. He now lay, snoring with the sound of an elephant breaking wind, only a few paces from me. I stared at him with revulsion, although just now he looked less like a dangerous, evil tormenter of innocent travellers. Strange how sleep makes any face become more innocent. At present he looked like an ancient who was ready for his coffin.

I was happy to help him on his way, and once I managed to stand, I swung my foot at that part of him which would be least used but most sensitive, even for an old man like him. No one likes to hit a person when they're down, but, cold, hungry and thirsty as I was, I was prepared to make an exception in his case.

The peasant woman grabbed my arm as I tried to kick a second time, and pulled me from him. In my weakened state, I was all but unbalanced and tottered some steps. 'Do you want to escape?' she snapped. 'Then come with us! The miners will be here before long.'

So saying, she strode out through the door, leading me around the building to the main road. Here, to my surprise, I found Ned Gubbings. So she was not alone in rescuing me. I had thought that my rescuer was the woman, because if a man has chiselled features like mine, well, it is never to be commented upon when she is smitten with love. It happens to me all the time.

'What are you doing here?' I managed, but then I found both arms grabbed, and I was being pulled away from the castle at speed. Overhead, Ned's damned raven flew, giving a regular *caw* that sounded like a cackle of sardonic amusement at the sight of me being pulled along. Actually, I thought it sounded like a pet demon.

'What the—' I began, but then I had to concentrate. There was a lane which headed roughly south-westwards, away from the town itself, and soon we were hurrying along it, I with an arm in the grip each of Ned and the woman. They pulled me along like a recalcitrant puppy, and several times I was almost dragged off my feet, until I was forced to protest.

'Hold! I cannot go so fast! I am weary and have not broken my fast!'

'Aye, you're right,' Ned said. His scrawny figure belied his strength, and he stopped and looked up at the sky. 'He's right, Joan. What's the need to hurry, eh, when there are fifteen or more men coming to put a rope about his neck, eh? They'll be gentle, won't they, Joan, when they see he treated one of their number with such kindness? The gaoler is one of theirs, isn't he, Joan? I think he's father of one of David Vowell's henchmen.

They'll want to chat about that, I suppose, not that it is terribly serious. What is that small matter, or the fact they think you killed their leader's father? They will be understanding, I am persuaded.'

'I didn't kill anyone,' I said firmly.

'That's good. You can tell them that. Don't forget to repeat it often as they drag you to the hanging tree. Did you see it? It's the oak up near the crossroads t'other side of the village. I've no doubt your words will be repeated in court when they hold your trial. That will be in a few weeks, of course, and you'll already be in a grave, but it'll ease your passing to know, I'm sure, that they might find you innocent.'

'They can't hang me until the Justices have spoken,' I said.

He gave me a long, withering look. 'This is Lydford. Lydford Law don't countenance delay. What, spend their treasure feeding a man who's going to hang anyway? What would be the point?'

'I am a gentleman from London,' I pointed out. 'They would not treat me in so contemptible a fashion.'

'You remember that man from London, Joan?' Ned said to his companion. She nodded. 'He was a Member of the London Parliament, weren't he? They still threw him into gaol.' He turned to me again, snarling, 'You don't understand it yet, do you? This isn't your soft, safe land. This is *Dartmoor*, this is *Lydford*, and these men are miners who think you've killed one of their own. They're coming to hang you, now, here, *today*. If you bide awhile, you won't be leaving. Ever. Do you understand me?'

I nodded, dumbfounded. I felt like a child who, on waking, finds that his nightmare is continuing.

His raven fluttered down and landed on his shoulder, cocking his head at me and giving a muted *caw*, as if reinforcing Ned's words.

'Then, hurry!'

We hurried along the road, and, after a few yards, it turned down a track that was even more grassy than the unused lanes here in Devon.

I have to say, when I mentioned earlier in this chronicle that all civilization ended at Exeter, I should have made mention of the roads. They were unfailingly awful. The majority were little better than grassy clearings between trees or, occasionally, fields. There was scarce enough traffic to create a rut or pothole, and for the most part they must have been unusable in winter. In summer, the grass, weeds and brambles overtook the surface, such as it was. Worse even than that was the way that they led, invariably, along the top of ridges and spurs of land, so that the traveller wishing, say, to visit a farmstead or huddle of farm buildings in a valley, or to take a different road, must turn off the higher road and descend a steep hillside to do so. There were some roads that accommodated the traveller by running alongside rivers, but for the most part these were dangerous trails that could take a fellow into bogs or marshes.

'I should thank you both,' I said after a distance. 'I am very grateful for your rescue. I had no idea that the miners would be so treacherous to a poor traveller.'

'You talk a lot.'

'I just wanted to make you aware . . .'

Just now, a scant hundred yards from the gaol, the two stopped. Ned scowled, which was, after all, his common expression, and stared ahead. Looking back the way we had come, he muttered something that sounded deeply impolite, and then began to set off again, but this time it was to the right, down a steep slope.

I was not content with the look of this path. It was narrower even than the lane past the gaol, and I was sure that no horse could have pulled a cart up that slope.

'Wait!' I protested naturally enough. 'Where are you going? That's a steep path – why not go a little further? Why are you—'

'Listen!' Joan said urgently.

'Why, there is nothing but . . .' Then I heard it. The sound of a strong party of men tramping along together. I swallowed. 'Come along, hurry! Be quick!' I urged, and hurried ahead of them both in my desire to be away from that place and any possible discovery by David and his men.

The path was difficult to navigate. Stones of greater or lesser size seemed to offer sound footholds, only to roll or slide away as soon as a boot was set on them. Patches of grass slipped away as easily as a badly fitted wig, threatening to send a man tumbling, and even when I tried to grab a branch or two, they had short but foully sharp thorns that could drive into a hand as easily as a Spanish sword into . . . well, into a hand.

As is my wont, I was careful and maintained a dignified silence as we scrambled down the slope, although I might have given a short curse when the second thorn attacked me.

'Hold your tongue!' Ned hissed, helping me to my feet once more, 'Or we'll leave you to them!'

I am sure that it was an empty comment, and more a proof of his desire to keep moving than a genuine threat, but it served to keep me hurrying.

It was when we were a little more than halfway down the hillside that I heard a high-pitched cry. It was a hunting call, I was sure, and there were words, but what with the distance, the incomprehensibility of the accent and the noise of the blood pounding in my ears, I could make out little. What I could see was the expression of horror on the face of Joan as she turned to look at Ned. Both appeared to hold a brief conversation, although no words passed their lips, and then Ned took hold of my arm and hauled. At the same time, Joan pushed my back, and in no time, I was rolling and bumping down the steepest part of the hill, jolted and bruised, trying to utter curses as I went, against Devon, against men who dwelt in castles, treacherous old men, and especially hillsides.

As I went, there was a loud roaring in my ears that grew and grew. At first, I thought it only the bellow of my own rage and anger at being so duped, but then, as I fetched up against a rock, all the breath knocked from me, I could hear it still. I lay there panting, counting the abrasions and welts, listening to the scuffling of the other two, and as a couple of stones came bouncing down the slope, I rose to my feet before another stone could brain me.

Walking towards the noise, I realized it was a narrow, swift-moving stream in a deep gully cut from the rocks that seemed to be in an extraordinary rush to be away from Dartmoor – not that I could blame it. The waters seemed to me to be demonstrating an excellent common sense. I only wished I could join them.

At one point, there was a gap in the rock wall, and I could

peer down into the stream itself. It was filled with clear, refreshing-looking water that bubbled and chuckled, but when I glanced to my left, I saw a horrible slit in the rocks, from which the waters whirled and span, bursting down into the valley in a torrent. It was a truly terrifying sight, as if the waters had been inhabited by some demon of the moors, and it was being forced to dash itself against the rocks in an effort to destroy itself.

There was more detritus coming down the slope behind me, and it struck me that perhaps the miners might come across Ned and Joan, and decide to take their frustrations out on the two of them. If that was the case, I had an excellent opportunity now to escape this hideous place. I could hurry south to the coast, and . . .

But I had no money. With that sinking, desperate feeling I was growing to recognize so well, I knew I had to return to Okehampton.

Oh, but that was a cause for wild rage! I could have danced on the spot and raved about the unfairness of the matter. After London, Okehampton was the one place I had no desire ever to see again. The grim, grey buildings, the accusations of the miners, the suspicion in the face of the Coroner, the look of hatred on Mal's face, and on that of his wife – all left me eager to be on my way. Yet if I were to make it to the coast, what then? Without money, I would merely be another vagrant sleeping at the shore, waiting for someone to take pity on me.

Not that anyone would, I noted bitterly, looking at my scuffed and muddied clothing. Once I had been the picture of elegance and style in London, and now I was reduced to the appearance of a pauper. It was enough to make a man want to scream fit to burst.

There were more stones, and it suddenly occurred to me that these may not be those caused by Joan or Ned's headlong flight, but that they could have been captured, and these were dislodged by our pursuers.

Or *my* pursuers!

I turned to flee, darting between trees, under low branches, stumbling and almost tripping where a bramble caught my shin, and then hurtling on, all the while running parallel to the river,

until by chance a small gap between stones caught my
foot, and I was sent flying. It was all I could do to keep from
giving a loud cry as I tumbled, and then I closed my eyes firmly
as I clutched my twisted ankle to me, cursing the day I had
thought to cross through this benighted county. I rolled from
side to side on my back, trying to hold back my whimpers,
eyes screwed tight shut as the pain stabbed. It was excruciating,
and I stayed there without murmuring anything while the
moisture seeped into my clothing once more.

It was some moments before I opened my eyes again, and
then my mouth.

Before me were three men, and one was holding a dagger at
me in a distinctly threatening manner. It was an all too familiar
stance, to be fair.

There are times when polite introductions are the order of the
day, times when a more cautious approach seems more suitable,
and certain occasions when running is by far and away the
best and safest option. The way behind me was, for all I knew,
filled with miners eager to pull my intestines out through my
nose, and while these could have been miners, from the way
that the nearer of the trio was pointing his dagger at me, there
was something about them that didn't seem right for miners.

Admittedly, they were as filthy and scruffy a group as the
men who spent their lives digging in the filthy soil of the moors;
they were bearded and had clothes that bore the hallmarks of
decades of sitting in mud. Their hosen were worn and frayed,
with stains at knees and buttocks, yet still there was something
different. I think it was a faint aura of authority.

It was most evident in the knife-wielding man, but the others
had it, too. The miners, many of them, appeared to be cowed
by David and his henchmen, but this trio . . . well, it would be
hard to think of anyone cowing them.

Meanwhile, even if I had wished to flee, there was an issue
with my ankle, which felt as though someone had inserted a
ballock knife into the joint and turned it. No, I could not run
away from them. With both my legs functioning, it might have
been possible, say, to run through and past them. Yes, it would
have been feasible were I hale and healthy, but today it was

obvious that I would not make it far. Noticing that the fellow on my right carried a particularly ancient-looking and worn bow, I was forced to reflect that a bow that well used meant that its bearer was likely to be perfectly competent at striking me down.

'Hello,' I said, and tried one of my more winning smiles.

'What are you doing on our land?'

This was the middle fellow speaking. He was a middling-height man who looked as if he was in his twenties, but the older side of me. He had a vaguely familiar face, but bright, kindly eyes that twinkled as he spoke, as if this was all a tremendous joke, and wouldn't we laugh about it later. Or he would, anyway. There was still a little edge to his smile, as though, were I not to find the situation as amusing as him, there was the option of a rather more serious end to our meeting. Not that it would prevent his laughing later, of course. It was just that my own circumstances might be a little more precarious.

His face broke into a grin. It was the sort of grin I'd expect to see on a really drunk executioner just before turning his victim off from the ladder.

'Um,' I said.

I know, I was not at my most loquacious. In my defence, consider this: in my time, I have come across a fair number of complete lunatics.

There were the ordinary, everyday idiots that everyone gets to meet, from the draw-latch and purse-dipper who think they will never be caught, to the fellow with the glint in his eye who believes he has a special task from God and is destined for great things. Then there are the political madmen, like the fool pretender who reckoned he was Earl of Devonshire and Lady Elizabeth's bedmate, who consider themselves superior to all others, and clever enough to take power without running the risk of being spotted and stretched by an unsympathetic monarch who *really* wants to understand what makes them tick – I've known too many of them – and the crazed fools who know that by pulling out a sword and yelling, 'Follow me!' as they run towards guns, they will persuade more thoughtful and considerate men like me to follow them. It doesn't work, of course – even though, sometimes, they make it to the enemy lines and take the guns themselves against all the odds. Not that it helps them. They soon get cut down by their enemy.

So you can take it from me that when I met Roger Rowle for the first time, I knew I was in the presence of the true, the genuine, unadulterated essence of Jack of Bedlam. This was a man who could look into a whirlpool and argue it was flat calm. He knew only one law, and that was his own – but he made it up as it pleased him. There was no logic to him or his thinking, only the simple fact of his mastery of his people and their lands.

Of course, I wouldn't learn all this until a little later. All I knew at first was that this man held my life in his hands, and I had no idea how to persuade him to help me. Because shortly a posse of irritable miners would appear, and then my life would be forfeit.

So no, I was not at my best that day. I had a certain amount on my mind, and although '*Um*' may not strike you as the ideal introduction, I could not tell whether this man was a friend, enemy, or interested witness to my demise.

There were some crashing noises behind me, and I turned to see who was causing them, and when I turned back, the three were nowhere to be seen. They had all disappeared.

It is not as if I am often at a loss. Any impartial reader of my story will know that I am inventive, sharp and intelligent, and yet just now it seemed to me that they had leapt into the sky or been swallowed up by the ground. I accordingly looked up and then down, but there was no sign of them. It was impossible to see how they had achieved their feat and disappeared so entirely.

I was, I confess, utterly confused.

More noise from behind distracted me, and I tried to climb to my feet, but my ankle was still in a terrible condition, and I yelped when I put it to the ground. There came a loud hiss, and I turned my head this way and that to see whence it came, but before I could do more than gaze with nervous consternation, there were more crashes and lumberings behind me, and I turned to see a pair of miner types appear.

Both stared at me in terror, which I found ironic, bearing in mind these men had come to see *me* swing. I would have run, naturally, but there was no pleasure in the thought of putting my foot to the ground at that moment. Instead, I gave them a sickly grin, which only seemed to petrify the two still further, and then the man to the left gave a little gasp, his eyes rolled up, and he sort of sagged to the side, making a sad little thudding sound when his head hit a nearby rock.

At that sight, the second man gave a bleating sound like a lamb with its tail caught in a barn door, and he made as though to leap at me. I gave a similar cry, and as he approached me, I tried to move away, but it was no good. His fist caught my jack, and I was sent flying once more, but this time when I landed, it was with all his weight on top of me, and a sharp, jagged lump of rock sticking in my back in a highly uncomfortable manner.

'What are you doing?' I demanded as forcefully as I could with all the air in my lungs driven out by him.

He didn't reply, but sighed in a languishing manner, and I was forced to pull a face and turn away, his breath was so rank. Still, he didn't speak, but he shivered and coughed a few times, spattering me with his spittle, as I thought. And then his eyes ceased to focus on me, and I realized he was dead.

Have you ever been in a situation like that? A dead body is astonishingly difficult to remove when it lies on top of you, and you are not in the best of condition already, as I wasn't.

The night before, I had slept very little, since I was shivering and wet through; I still hadn't eaten, and I had injuries to head and ankle, not to mention the pain at the wrists and ankles where I had been bound to the blasted horse. And now I had a dead weight . . . my apologies, but he was clearly dead, and he was a great weight. In my current condition, it was difficult to move at all. I tried to rock him, and roll from underneath, but the body proved singularly unhelpful. All I won for my efforts was drool from his slack lips that fell on my cheek. It was repulsive.

I could at least see what had caused his sudden collapse and that of his companion. As I continued to try to remove him, I saw a pale feather in his back. He had been struck by an arrow or bolt. From the thickness of the shaft and its length, I assumed it was a bowman's arrow, and even as I had the idea, my grinning idiot reappeared, and I recalled his friend's well-used bow. I stopped squirming as the thought struck me.

'My name,' he said conversationally as he crouched at my side, casting an approving eye over the dead man holding me captive, 'is Roger Rowle. I am by way of being the lord of all these lands about here, and you seem to be trespassing. Now, I was asking you what you were doing here, before these unpleasant churls came hunting you, but I suppose I can assume you were escaping from them. Is that fair enough?'

From this close, I could see that his eyes were bright and shining with happiness. It was like looking into the face of a child. He really looked as innocent as a saint as he chatted to me over the corpse of the man.

'I think they were going to try to kill me,' I said. 'Um, I don't suppose you could help me and remove this . . .?'

'Were they miners?' he said without moving a muscle to pull the body from me.

'I think so.'

'They must dislike you if they wanted to kill you.'

'I suppose so.'

'Why?'

I gazed up at him, unsure how to proceed with this line of questioning. 'Well, one of their friends was murdered, and they wanted someone to blame, and I was just travelling by when it happened, so they blamed me, and . . .'

'So they say you killed Daniell Vowell?'

'Um . . . yes.'

His face had grown serious. 'Killing a man is a serious business.'

'Yes, I . . .'

'You have to make sure you are killing the right man for good reasons. You cannot just kill someone for no reason.'

'No, I . . .'

'I mean, if I were a violent man, I could just kill you here now, couldn't I? But would that be right?'

'Yes . . . No, I mean no!'

'But this man,' he continued, taking my weight's chin in his

hand and studying the face, 'why should he take such a dislike
to you, eh? Did he see you kill Vowell? Of course not. You
wouldn't be so foolish as to murder him in broad daylight,
would you? Besides, I rather like your face. You don't look like
a murderer to me. So, why should he try to hurt you? It makes
little sense. That was why I decided to stop him. It didn't seem
to me that he was being reasonable.'

'And I am very grateful to you,' I said. It felt like the old
torture of *peine forte et dure*, lying there with the man pressing
down on my chest and belly. I swallowed. 'Could you please
remove this fellow? I can hardly breathe.'

'Him?' Roger let his gaze move along the body without much
interest. 'Oh, I suppose so.'

He must have beckoned the other two, because they were
suddenly with us, and with them pulling on an arm and a leg
each, suddenly I was able to take a deep breath. I sat up and
felt my ankle. The pain had dissipated considerably. I have been
told by a very eminent physician that a man can only cope with
one severe pain at a time. He demonstrated the fact by stabbing
me with a needle and then stamping on my foot, and he triumph-
antly informed me that the reason I could not feel the stab any
more was proof of his theory. I punched him on the nose and
asked whether he wanted me to hurt him more to test his concept
further, but he was reluctant to be so informed.

However, it did occur to me today that I might be best advised
not to try to bolt quite yet. The ankle may have felt better
because I had other things on my mind – a dead body squashing
me and the opportunity of instant death from a crazed outlaw,
for example, because I considered Roger Rowle to be both quite
mad and an outlaw. Not many men who are not felons themselves would wander about with bow and arrow and slaughter
people.

'Are you well?' he asked now, and I nodded. 'Good. Then I
think you should come with us. It would be safer for you, after
all.'

There are times when a man makes an offer when you just
know that he is in earnest, and other times, like this, when the
actual offer being made sounds rather more like a threat. It

mattered little. I had seen the three disappear in the blink of an eye, and then return having killed two men without hesitation or compunction. If they had wanted to murder me, they could easily have done so already. And I couldn't run on my ankle. That was brought home to me as soon as I put some weight on it. I didn't think it was broken, but it was definitely sprained.

The bowman grunted something or other when he saw my pain, and went in among the trees. He soon returned with a heavy knife in one hand and a long, slender ash stick in the other. He slashed with his knife and the twigs and branches were soon sliced away, and he presented me with a staff. It was a little thin and bouncy, being so fresh, but it made my hobbling considerably faster, and before long I found that my ankle was coming back to life again.

Our route took us, so far as I was concerned, in the wrong direction, away from Okehampton – but it was at least away from Dartmoor as well, which was good. Not that the country-side was inspiring. It was all rocks, green slime and mud. And then we came to a place they called the Devil's Cauldron, which was a hollow in the rocks. A stream flowed in at the top, and whirled about in the 'cauldron' like a drunken hound chasing its tail, round and round, faster and faster, but the water never tired or fell. It was a terrifying sight. I imagine any man falling into that would be drowned. There could be no escape with the smooth rocks and the rush of water. It was horrible.

We followed the line of the stream, with a steep slope rising on our right, and the chuckle and hiss of the waters on our left. Soon the narrow gorge began to open up, and we continued, crossing over to the southern side of the stream where there was a fork in the valley. Here we continued up another steep-sided gorge to a sudden bowl in the ground, where we stopped, Roger Rowle giving a sharp whistle. There was an answering whistle from ahead, and suddenly we were not alone.

All around us, vegetation moved, and we were in the midst of a small throng. I learned later that this hillside was a maze of little caves and tunnels, and the folk merely pulled mats of growing brambles, creepers and ivy over their entrances to conceal them. They were easy to push out of the way as soon as they wanted to leave, but for the most part, they could remain in their hollows and watch any visitors. The odd unfortunate was likely to find himself stabbed with a dozen arrows before he knew he was in the land of the Gubbingses.

That was the uncouth name they had given themselves – the same as Ned in the castle. The Gubbingses were nothing more than a group of felons who had so far escaped the rope, who lived by their own laws and rules, and who answered to no higher authority than Roger Rowle. They had little by the way of possessions, and did not seem to care. They had their homes and hearths, and they had the bounty of the area, with deer aplenty, as well as pork and mutton stolen from the local peasants. The farmers must have cursed them, but I confess I found them, for the most part, a wild but decent collection of misfits and vandals. They were cheerful without exception, and had a childlike quality in the way they looked to their leader for their every need. And Roger Rowle returned their trust with a capricious honour. He was not beyond a murderous rage on occasion, but he tended to treat them as an older brother might his younger siblings, with an affectionate tolerance.

'Welcome to my home,' he said with a beaming smile, taking in the whole area with a theatrical gesture. 'Here, you are under our protection. You are safe with us.'

I smiled and looked around me with a sense of mild wonder. It struck me that these people were all outlaws, and were I to be discovered in their midst, I would also be viewed as a man who might be executed. Still, the miners intended to kill me anyway, so it made little difference. For now, all I needed was a place to sit and rest my ankle, and perhaps to eat a little food. I was hopeful that there must be some food here.

There was food aplenty. And terror, too.

Before long, I was sitting in front of a fire of good logs, a rough wooden trencher filled with roasted pork and a slab of bread on my lap, and a large pot of cider at my side. It felt as near to heaven as I could imagine after the last few days, and I was happy to tell my host so. 'This is the best meal I have had in Devon,' I said.

'You were staying at Okehampton?'

'Yes, in the tavern.'

'Did you meet anyone there?'

'Lots,' I said.

'Who?'

'David Vowell, Mal, the innkeeper, Nye, the Coroner . . .'

'What did you think of the man in the castle?'

'Ned?' I smiled. 'The King? He was a very striking fellow, with the best of homes. You know him?'

'Everyone knows Ned,' Rowle said proudly.

'More than that, he is the man who saved me this morning. He came to the gaol and freed me. Otherwise, those miners would have taken me to the gallows this morning.'

'It was all him? So you like him?'

There was an edge to his voice that sounded a little strange to me, but I put it down to the man being permanently ill at ease in the presence of a man like me, who was clearly his superior in so many ways. After all, he was only a peasant who had taken the decision to break the law and live outside it. I was a man of quality from London.

'How could I not like a man who saved my life?' I asked reasonably. 'He and the woman with him liberated me, and for that I must be ever grateful.'

'What happened to them after they freed you?'

'They were up the slope, and pushed me down the steeper part to help me escape capture.'

'So you didn't see them?'

'The miners had no argument with them, I suppose. If they were found, they would have been ignored. It was me whom the miners sought.'

'Possibly. I am glad you like the King and Joan, though. They are good people.'

'Certainly. Unlike David Vowell and his miners. They kidnapped me from Okehampton and took me to the moors, and then brought me hence, even though the Coroner determined that I was innocent.'

'Ah, the Crowner; now he's another I wouldn't trust.'

'Really? He seemed a good fellow to me,' I said without thinking.

It is always worth considering your words when you are in the home of a relative stranger. Who can say but that the next person you meet is by nature a fellow like Roger Rowle and disinclined to honour those who uphold laws he disapproves of?

In any case, I was soon given cause to regret my words, for with a snarl he launched himself at me. My trencher flew from my lap, the cider was upended, and I landed on my back, wide-eyed, staring over his blade at a furious Roger Rowle who was now sitting on my breast.

'Say that again,' he hissed.

'He was good to me,' I said defensively.

Roger Rowle leaned down until his nose was a scant inch from my own, his eyes almost perfectly round and enraged, and then he gave a chuckle. 'Well, of course, and why shouldn't you? He was kind to you, and he would see in you a friend and ally.'

'Um . . . yes,' I said, climbing to my feet and picking up my bread before a lean-looking wolfish hound could take it. The brute stared at me while he reached down and gulped my pork in one swift movement. I sat again, holding my bread close to me.

Rowle sat again, somehow sheathing his knife in the process. It merely disappeared, as he himself had in the woods. 'You have to understand that the Crowner is determined to see me hang. And all my friends here. And we do not wish to see him entertained in that fashion. He is an evil man.'

I would soon learn that almost everyone who was not a Gubbings was, by definition, an evil man in Rowle's perception. He was a man with a simple philosophy, which was that all those in the world were divided into two parties: those who were with the Gubbingses and did not condemn them for acquiring animals, clothes or other items as they required them, and the rest of the world who did. However, there were apparent levels of disapproval. Rowle and his followers deprecated the miners more than others, because the miners had driven them from their homes, and had tried to attack them here in their hideaway.

'The Crowner, he doesn't mind things so badly. He would capture us if he could and he'd have us in front of his Justices; Vowell and his like would have us in Lydford and see us hang without a trial.'

It comes to something when your life can be summed up by

gradations of how badly other men want to see you dead. In my experience, such a position can only lead to problems. I have had a lot of such experience, after all. In my short term as an employee of Master John Blount, I have been unfortunate enough to be forced to sit between the Queen, Lady Elizabeth, the French, the Spanish, and all manner of others in the middle. It is not a comfortable position to inhabit.

'I think the Crowner can tell when a man is innocent, and seeks to serve justice, whereas the miners seek only to enrich themselves at the expense of any who stand in their way,' I said.

'The miners are enemies of all,' he agreed. His quick fury had gone completely and now he was affability itself. He smiled at me. 'I think you could be my brother,' he said.

I smiled back. It was easy to smile at him. The alternative was to send him into a quivering rage, as I had seen. Smiling is preferable to having a knife in the belly.

SIX

Sunday 2nd August

I remained with Roger Rowle all that day and most of the following. In that time, my ankle healed nicely, although I maintained a limp, just because it doesn't do to show people that you have recovered when you don't know whether you will have to flee them before long.

The crazed rage that simmered below the surface was always there for a man to see, were he to look. Rowle was a cauldron of boiling pottage, and every so often the board laid over the top would be thrust aside, and the furious liquid would burst forth and scorch those nearby.

The first sign I saw of it was that first evening. A group of the Gubbingses had been off on a 'collecting' which, as far as I could make out, was a raid conducted by groups on the small farms nearby. This time, it involved robbing a small farm on the western border of the moors, where a man had beaten a Gubbings before, and now the men wanted to punish him. So the party, on their return, brought with them the man himself. He had been captured, and I could hear him as they half dragged him to the Gubbingses' camp. At the same time, Roger Rowle stood from the fire where he had been resting, and wandered over to meet the men.

They had with them some five sheep, herded by one of the lads, and these were led straight away to a little pound which the clan had built of wattles. Their owner was less fortunate.

'You are Jack of Forder, aren't you?' Rowle began. His entire manner was amiable, his voice low and almost cheery. He stood, arms akimbo before the man, and turned to his audience with a beaming smile as the farmer confirmed his name.

'Aye, that be me. And you are the murderer and thief.'

'Me? Thief? All I do, I do for my family. We have to live.'

'Then work. Stop robbing the poor farmers on the moor.'

'You call me "thief"? I am no thief. What I take, I give to my people. I am like Robin Hood: I take from them as can afford it and give to the poor who need it.'

'You are a thief and felon. You'll hang one day soon.'

Suddenly, the mood changed.

'Me? You say I'll hang? For looking after my friends?'

The amiable, affable leader had disappeared and now was replaced by a vengeful fury with glittering eyes and a thrusting head. He sprang forward, and there was a sudden stillness in the camp. Roger Rowle was in front of the farmer for a moment, concealing the fellow from me, and then, as I watched, I saw the farmer's head jerk upwards, a startled cry breaking from his throat, and he stiffened like a man being bled. He remained like that before slumping slowly to the ground, and his foot tapped against a stone a few times. Only then did I realize that he was dead.

Roger Rowle turned slowly, his hand red with the farmer's gore, his dagger gleaming evilly. 'Don't let no one ever call us felons, thieves, nor nothing else. Me? Hang? For protecting you? You're my family, and I'll protect you howsomever I can! Them as say we're breaking the law, we say we *hold* our laws! And those coming past here, they can go rot!'

I am courageous by nature, as you will already know, but I confess, seeing my host with his hand and forearm coated in another man's blood, I was disturbed. As the evening progressed, I spent much of my time watching Roger Rowle and his heathen companions. The mutton was slaughtered and cooked on sticks over the various campfires, and I ate because I was starving, and yet I could not forget the casual murder of the farmer, nor the sudden explosion of anger in Roger's face as he launched himself and held his knife at me as though he was about to kill me, too.

In my life, I have lived with danger. In my earlier days, living with dippers and thieves, living only for the moment, for no one could tell what might happen the following day, I was happy. Yet perhaps that was because there was little to lose. What, a life? When a man has nothing in his purse, when his stomach grumbles all the while, and his last coin was spent a day or more ago, the extension of life means little. It is easier to think of the present moment, to the exclusion of all else, when all else involves slow starvation, death by the cold or death in a brawl. At such times in a man's life, a longer existence is the least of his concerns.

But this was different. Roger Rowle seemed to believe that he alone had the right of life and death not only over his own clan, which was perhaps reasonable, but also over the folk who lived in the area, and even travellers who were only passing near his camp. It left me feeling a cold chill every time I turned and saw his eyes light upon me. And the truly terrifying aspect was, he seemed genuinely to like me, as though he thought me a kindred spirit. Even though I was relieved that he considered me a friend, it was terrifying. After all, this was a man who could slaughter another in cold blood without thinking. Today he had killed some miners chasing me, and then a local farmer. Tomorrow, it could be me.

Later that night, it could be me.

So is it any surprise that, when I finally made it to my bed, I was less sleepy than I should have expected after the last two days. Even after the lack of sleep in the gaol, after all my adventures, I was still constantly alive to the risk of a dagger in the dark. That evening, taking my rest on a bed of heather and ferns in the open, it was cold: very cold. I had thought that a gaol cell would be uncomfortable and even sleeping in the open air would be preferable. All I can say is, I was wrong. I was not comfortable. Exhausted as I was, I hardly slept a wink, and when I did, visions of Roger Rowle slipped into my mind, his arms besmottered with gore, telling me, 'You're next, Blackjack!'

When I decided to try to rest, some helpful woman gave me a cloak, which smelled as though it had contained an entire flock of dead sheep for the past year, and another gave me a blanket that was so wet as to be useless against the cold. Yet I huddled into both, desperate for the comfort that they hinted at.

But when the sun allowed her rays to pass along the gorge and light the camp, I was miraculously still alive. The clattering of men and women preparing pots and pans, clothing themselves and preparing for the day ahead was deafening, and I was nothing loath to rise. My first act was to test my ankle and see whether it was working still, and to my immense relief it was. There was a little soreness, but nothing to give me trouble, and I determined that today I must escape from my friendly murderer.

Which should have been moderately easy. I saw others moving in among the trees and making their ways from the camp, and began to sidle idly towards the dangerous area of the stream while no one was observing me.

But my new damnable fiend of a friend spotted me.

'You're up early! Good, I like a man who makes the most of the day,' he welcomed me effusively. 'There are many who prefer to stay abed when there is much to be done.'

'Yes,' I said.

'I had thought you would remain sleeping after your experiences in the gaol. That must have been terrible. Those miners have no respect for others. They held a Member of Parliament in the gaol, it's said. It was a while ago, when . . . well, before I took over here.'

'How did you do that?'

He suddenly looked shifty. 'Ah, well, there comes a time when the past leader has to admit that he can no longer claim the full support of his friends and colleagues, and then it becomes necessary to . . . weed out the dead wood. My father was a good leader in his time, but we had a falling out, and he left. Now he lives in Okehampton, and I visit him when I have time. He appreciates some of our little gifts.'

This was merely proof, had I needed it, that this fellow was a ruthless, vindictive devil, who would overthrow his predecessor, even his own father, no doubt without bothering to attempt subtlety or charm, but rather by ensuring some form of ruthless deposition. Still, it was at least better than slipping a dagger into his father's heart, as he had with the farmer.

I nodded. In my life, I have learned the skill of keeping my thoughts to myself. In situations like this, it is important not to betray any concern or lack of calm. For some reason, he shot me a look like a man who witnessed a friend swallow a bee. 'Are you quite well?'

'Yes,' I said quickly. My voice sounded high and squeaky even to me, so I tried to moderate my tone as I continued, 'Yes, I have never felt better!'

'Good,' he said, giving me a look that seemed questioning rather than suspicious. 'Well, today we shall enjoy giving the miners a bloody nose,' he said with satisfaction. 'We shall lead my men to the miners' camp and drive them away from it.'

'But they'll only go and gather more of their men,' I pointed out.

'Ah, yes, but by then we'll have taken their stores of tin,' he grinned.

'Ah,' I said. So the revenge on the miners was in truth a simple robbery.

'We can take their food and drink, of course.'

'I see.'

He gave me a curious look. 'To feed the poor and needy,' he said, as though offended by my lack of enthusiasm.

I nodded. He thought himself and his merry gang were all poor and needy, of course. To him, this all made perfect sense, no doubt.

While he stalked about, issuing commands like a small Caesar, I kept my eyes open, ready for any opportunity to escape this madness, but there were few enough. Roger Rowle had his men as organized and drilled as London's volunteers during the mayhem of the Wyatt rebellion, which means their training was non-existent. Men and their women milled about – some coming, some going – and it was not clear to me what was happening until Roger Rowle called me to his side, and we began to follow the stream back the way we had come the day before. And that was when I realized that a lot of the apparent disorganization was, in fact, very organized indeed. The men had all spread themselves up in among the trees, so that as we made our way along the stream's banks, the other members of the group were high on the hills at either side. Not that they could cling to the lower ground as the valley grew steeper and steeper. Now the men on the left were high up the hillside, those on the right spread more thinly, with numbers of the men making their way to the higher ground, while we made the best we could of the narrow way beside the waters.

I found myself considering the distance to be covered before we could reach the miners' camp. Once we left this deep cleft in the rock and had to climb, we must still have a good few miles to cover. Perhaps an entire morning's walk. And then there would be a fight, and we would take what we could and make our way back to the Gubbingses' hovels, where no doubt there would be more mutton cooked over the fires, and perhaps some ale or cider taken from the miners. Not much, I hoped. The thought of these foul felons being plied with vast amounts of drink was too horrible to contemplate. Drink leads to bickering and fights, and I wanted nothing to do with that kind of danger.

'What will the miners do?' I said as we went. This was the other point that concerned me. A camp filled with brawny and fit miners seemed to me to be certain to take a dim view of Roger Rowle's appearance and intentions to rob them.

'They never do anything,' he said.

'You've done this before?'

He flashed his teeth at me like a schoolboy discussing raiding the neighbour's orchard. It was all glorious fun to the murderous brute. 'We do it every few months. But this time, of course, it's to punish them for their treatment of you, because you're our friend.'

A merry jest, that. Perhaps he thought I was as simple as his colleagues – but I was not. I had lived in London, and I knew every form of knavery known to man, and quite a few that most Londoners had themselves forgotten. He was perfectly capable of pulling the wool over the eyes of his friends and companions here, no doubt, but for all his boasting and cleverness, I felt sure that he would fare badly in London, were he to make his way there and try to do the same with any of my friends. I was not so innocent as to believe his protestations that he was doing all this for me. For one thing, I was quite certain that he had not suddenly planned this raid. He must have been considering it for weeks. I was merely the spark to the powder keg.

We made our way stealthily (for the most part) to the steep part of the gorge, and just before we got to the horrible, swirling monstrosity that was the Devil's Cauldron, we began to climb up the right-hand hill. At first it was a scramble, but then we were forced to clamber up the rocky face.

It was a foul, dangerous place, that. A huge thundering was heard to our left, and the rocks were beslimed and slippery with green excrescences that lay thickly all about: mosses, weeds, all sorts of green stuff designed to send a man tumbling down to his death. I was fain to leave, to head west and forget all about miners, my money, and especially these creatures. They lived here in such foul conditions it was hard to believe they were human. Who would want to live in an ancient wood with water all about them? Apart from the nuisance they posed to travellers and farmers with their incessant thieving, there was little to begrudge them. They were in so mean a place that no one else would want it.

But, of course, no one who lived near to them could think of leaving them to their own devices. Their entire existence was based on theft and nothing more.

We eventually climbed out of the deep gorge, and I hurried away from the cleft in the ground. One glance down told me all I wished to know about the place. It was not pleasant.

'Don't 'ee like the cleave?' a man asked me. There were two or three of Roger Rowle's men about me, grinning to see the Londoner leave the depths behind.

'I've seen worse,' I lied, and set off eastwards at a trot after Roger himself.

It was a miserable, bleak sight when we came to the open land beyond Lydford's woods. There, ahead of us, were the moors.

I don't know what it was about them, but I shivered at the sight. The hills were grey and rolling, with an occasional outcrop of the moorstone at their peaks. Silvery gleams showed where more rocks were scattered about their flanks, and the hills looked as if they were ancient monsters crouching and ready to spring at us. I am not superstitious, of course, but the sight did make me feel just how far I was from London and the security of civilization once more. There, in the alleys and streets, the most a man had to fear was a rent collector or a mad hound. Here – well, the dangers could not be underestimated.

I looked about me at my companions, and the sight was not one to fill a man with confidence. If I were to gather together the dregs of all society, if I were to scrape from their villages all the realm's idiots, I could scarcely have collected a more unappealing accumulation of misfits and the plain stupid. Oh, for the sight of a London mob, the apprentices all a-bellow, the merchants waving fists, the butchers with their cleavers – that was a sight to rouse a man. These fellows looked as though half would not know which was the pointed end of a dagger. Roger Rowle might think these would strike fear into the hearts of the miners, but I felt they wouldn't concern my Lady Elizabeth's ladies-in-waiting. They were more like a gathering for a festival than a dangerous army bent on mayhem.

I was concerned. If these were to come across the miners, surely the miners would trounce them. And that must mean that I would also be trounced. With that thought came the inevitable conclusion: I must get away from these fools.

It was a grey day, full of the threat of rain and misery, with clouds charging across the sky. The moors were themselves obscured on occasion, at first momentarily and then for longer and longer, as mists swept past.

I recalled the journey from the walk in the opposite direction, but somehow it didn't seem so foul when I was heading west. Now, returning to the grim hills with their heathers and soggy grasses, the pools and brown waters, the constant risk of breaking an ankle on the thick tussocks of grass or a small boulder, or just falling into one of the mires that the folk seemed to revere, filled me with horror.

The way we took led us over a series of pastures and thence on to the beginning of the moors. Several times farmers would appear and stand and watch as we passed, leaning on shovels or rakes or whatever it is that men of their profession use in their daily grind, but Roger Rowle would not allow his men to attack them.

'No, they'm our neighbours,' he declared several times, always loud enough to be heard by the men in their fields. He was keen to make them know that he was their friend, I suppose. And until he felt that they might have betrayed or cheated him, he would keep talking to them as if they were all his friends – no, more as though they were his especially protected children, who must rely utterly on him, and him alone, for their security. In his world, they were his wards.

You will understand that I had no wish to be included in his mad escapades, and that, to me, included the risk of being involved in a fight on the moors. He may well believe that the miners would merely turn and run when he attacked their camp, but I had a memory of David's men, of Nye, of the three others who had boxed me in at the tavern's yard, and I had the strong opinion that they would be less likely to submit than Roger Rowle believed. He struck me as one of those fools who can quickly persuade himself that black is white by a simple process of repetition. It did not convince me.

As we began to leave the pasturelands and started to climb the hills, I was quickly struck by the length of the way before us.

You may be assured that I kept my eyes open for the remotest possibility of escape, but as we approached the moors, opportunities for fleeing were remote. All I could do was keep on with the main group. To the left and right, the view was clear, with grassy slopes and occasional rocks breaking the soft aspect. If I were to run, they would be able to see me for over a mile, and I had already seen how deadly one at least was with his bow.

Naturally, while being dragged the other way, to Lydford, I was thinking more of the welcome that awaited me in that hideous gaol than the actual journey itself, and the decline did not strike me very forcibly. Now, with my path leading in the opposite direction, I was much more given to thinking about the way that the hill rose before me. And not only the one, because it seemed that every time a summit appeared close, it was only an illusion, for as soon as we breasted that hillock, it became obvious that the true height was beyond it. Every time that I thought I was reaching the top, a fresh peak rose beyond as though mocking my hope of a rest.

And so we climbed, my hopes rising with each apparent peak, and at last we came to a spot where I saw something most peculiar.

Here, there was a great mound of rock at the peak, and it appeared that we were all to go about this and continue behind it to the moors. Roger Rowle and his fellow-felons were all making their way with much panting and ballyhoo to the left of this mound as if it was some form of secure post, but with my military experience, I found myself eyeing it with suspicion. After all, a great heap of rocks like that would be sufficient, I thought, to hide me and a considerable number of others. Perhaps it was my innate perception, perhaps an anxiety about being so close to a place that would offer such possibilities for a daring raid (my purse-cutting days had taught me the art of quick actions and seizing opportunities as they presented themselves), but whatever the reason, I suddenly felt sure that I saw a rock shift.

Now, you can call me foolish or superstitious, but I had heard so many stories about piskies, that I all but expected to see the rocks move. What, was this: a spirit of the moors, ready to come and strike fear into the hearts of poor folk like me? Was it the Devil himself, coming to try to steal our souls? At the thought, my cods quailed. But there was no doubt in my mind that the rocks were moving. It was hard to see, for a mist was falling upon us, and there were swirls and thickenings in the air that made me mistrust my own eyes, but then there was a sudden breeze, and with a quick clarity, I saw what my senses had been trying to warn me of.

It was a great number of men. We were not the hunters. We were the hunted!

There are times when I have had trouble communicating with others. Rarely, it is true, but every so often I lose my ability to explain myself. This was one such moment.

I rushed forward to see Roger Rowle, but when I got near, three wizened idiots tried to hold me back. All the Gubbingses seemed malnourished, but these three were the worst of the lot I had seen, and even as I attempted to push my way through them, they blockaded their commander and spiritual leader. The addle-pated sons of . . . I don't know what!

'Roger, Roger!' I cried, but although he glanced in my direction, he took no notice at first. He was so used to the adulation of his friends, I think, that he thought me just one more of a similar type.

When I shot a look behind me at the rocks, I could see that the figures I had seen were now out of sight behind a fresh bank of mists. I stared, trying to pierce the swirling mists, but I might as well have tried to look through the rocks themselves.

And now the swirling, weird haziness was not merely above and behind us, but all around. For me, it made little difference, because I knew nothing about this land, but I could see that others among us were finding this particularly difficult. It is one thing to feel brash and bold in country where no one else knew the land as well as them, in a wood where the trees protected and concealed them; here, in the broad, wide expanse of open moorland, they felt threatened. Now, when they depended on seeing their enemy, they were blinded by the mists. Their usual method of attack was to assault the enemy while being concealed. Now, they were trying to creep up on an enemy that could be anywhere. They were in the same position as those who had tried to assail them in their forest fastness. It gave me a certain pleasure to think that they might be prey to the same fears that they had inspired in others.

Of course, there was one issue with this. I was here with them, and that meant that if there was an attack against them, I would be very likely to be treated as one of them myself. And if my experiences with the miners before had given me any insight, I felt sure that I could expect short shrift from them.

That led to some very quick calculations.

As the mists thickened, I began to move towards the left of the group. Soon swirls began to conceal those who were further from me, like gauzy veils blown by the wind. I continued forward, frowning as though determined to see a way through the mists to the miners' camp, while simultaneously making a path further and further to the left, away from the main body. And then, when a thickening fog concealed me from the rest, I dropped down into a hollow in the grasses.

I don't know who was the more shocked: me or the face that welcomed me with a glare.

Giving a maddened bleat, I sprang up, and the sheep, which had been lying in the shallow scrape of the peat, bucketed upwards and away from me. I heard a bellow, then shouts and a short scream, followed by still more maddened blaring from the sheep – or, perhaps, other sheep – before a gale of laughter as the Gubbingses realized that the source of their alarm was only mutton.

At the sound, I dropped down and rolled to peer over the grasses, but mercifully the fog still hid the rest of the Gubbingses. I say 'mercifully', because now a sequence of noises began to reach me. There were a series of sharp, wet sounds, rather like damp cloth being slapped against a body, or perhaps like a man cutting forcefully into a cabbage. It was at once quite a common-place sound and yet simultaneously terrifyingly repellent. And then the truly petrifying sound came to me of a man crying out, and then a shriek, and I realized that this was the perfect time for me to be somewhere else.

I began to crawl away. And if you have any understanding, you will appreciate that the main key to this was that word 'away'. I wanted to be away from there as quickly as I could be.

First rolling, then crawling, I added some more stains to my already ruined jack and hosen, before at last fetching up at the far side of a group of rocks. From there, I listened as the Gubbingses or the miners were massacred.

To be honest, it was very difficult to tell which side was coming out the worst. Whether it was the men who had set off with me that morning with such high spirits or the men they had intended to attack, I could not tell. All was a terrible confusion of noise, and the main aspect for me was that the action, so to speak, was all out of sight. I could see occasional struggles in the mists, sudden flashes of men grappling with men. At one time, a figure collapsed, and I saw another standing over him, lifting something long and heavy in his hands before a swirl of fog hid them from view, but not from hearing. The man on the ground gave a gasp that was, in its quiet, seemingly natural commonplaceness, more shocking than all the signs of violence I had so far seen.

I ran.

Not that I had any idea where I was running to. This was

not my usual bolting from danger, when I was merely evading capture; this was a panic-filled hurtling over rocks and grasses with no thought of the consequences, only to preserve my life. For I was convinced that if I were to be found by either the miners or the Gubbingses, I would surely die.

Once, high on a hill, I saw a sheep being chased by a hound. The creature bounced from rock to rock as she made her escape. That day, the sheep would have been jealous of my skills as I sprang from one boulder to another, from slippery, muddy patches of bog to grassed tussocks. All the while, I was aware of the hot breath of the men behind me, less because they were chasing me, but because their blood was up, and they would all have been content to stab or beat me to death.

'Hold, friend,' a voice called, and I slowed. Vaguely, in front of me, I could see shapes in the pale mists. I slowed anxiously, staring. It looked like a great crowd of men in the mists, and then I was struck with relief, realizing it was only rocks.

'Dowser! It's you!' I cried. Truly, seeing Frantz Lippert's friendly face, I could have sobbed with relief. After all my tribulations, the knocks on my head, being thrust into the gaol, rescued by bloodthirsty murderers, and just now thinking that I was surrounded by even more peasants, it was refreshing to see a face I knew I could trust. Especially since, if anyone *were* to have chased after me, they would come across this sturdy fellow, and I could continue to make good my escape while Frantz tackled them. What I had taken to be other men was no more than a scattering of rocks behind him, I realized.

I fell forward to Frantz Lippert, my legs barely capable of supporting my weight, my face breaking into a smile of pure joy. 'Frantz, what are you doing up here? Are you' – sudden concern stabbed at me – 'are you with the miners?' It occurred to me that he was supposed to be meeting with the moorland workers, and might even now be here in company with other miners who would be keen to see me returned to David's justice.

'No, I was asked to come here by the good fellows of Okehampton,' he said easily, and as he did so, the mists cleared behind him. Yes, it was my German friend, but behind him there were no rocks such as I had been accustomed to seeing up here on the moors. This was no tor of moorstone – it was another band of men. But these were not armed with spades and pickaxes. These bore staffs, spears and swords.

And suspicious, grim expressions.

One thing for which I am well known is my ability to explain myself quickly and succinctly when in danger. My friends in London will all vouch for my skill in diversion and deflection, sending those who could bring disaster upon me in entirely the wrong direction. I once persuaded a London mob, which had been going to capture me and surrender me to some foreign gentlemen in order that they could castrate me, to instead take a stand against the foreign foe. Only recently, I convinced a hangman not to take revenge for my selling him a very poor grade of black powder . . . although that did not end with quite such a gratifying outcome.

In any case, I am known for my ability to use words to best effect, and in the past this skill has saved me many times.

Thus, naturally, you would assume that I would merely point behind me and indicate that the present company should hurry back the way I had come. But I couldn't. Partly because I was so out of breath that I could do little more than pant, but also because the group was staring at me with little favour.

I was acutely aware that I was not popular with these people, the townsfolk of Okehampton. There, close behind my friend the dowser, stood Clem – what was he doing with the townsfolk? – who was glaring at me with vitriolic hatred; at his side was Mal, who was swinging his large club into his left palm in a manner that left me in little doubt what – or whom – he would like to bludgeon with it. There were many other men there, all of them more or less familiar from the tavern or the inquest.

Only two were likely to be trustworthy, I felt. The dowser himself, and the man on horseback, who was now leaning forward, his forearms on his horse's withers and peering at me with a look of quizzical interest.

'Ah, Master Peter. I am very glad to see you again. I believe you disappeared the last time we were going to meet. No doubt you will welcome the opportunity to explain why you took that opportunity to flee?'

*   *   *

It was the Coroner.

In my long and troubled life, I have had a number of experiences designed to petrify and bring me to my knees. This, however, for sheer baffling unfairness, left me totally confused. I gaped.

I stared at him, then back at the dowser. Other men were familiar, too. I found myself meeting the unforgiving glowers of men whom I recognized. That was enough to make me return my gaze to the Coroner again.

'Um,' I said.

The simple fact was, I could not think of a single useful comment I could make that would not bring me to even more trouble. As matters stood, most of the men before me still thought me a murderer, and would use any opportunity to harm me. If I were to speak, they would assume I was trying to deceive them in order to escape once more. Which was fair: I would, if it were possible. But it did leave me with more than a little difficulty.

'I thought so,' the Coroner said.

'Flee? What do you mean, *flee*?' I said.

'You ran. It was as clear a sign of guilt as I've heard. Clem caught you and took you to the miners for justice. It was a mistake on his part, for he should have brought you to me, but it was excusable in the circumstances.'

'I did not run! After I saw you that morning, he knocked me down, bound me to a horse and took me away to hide his guilt!'

'What guilt?'

I was about to answer when there came a shriek from behind me. A loud thud, then a sort of soggy slapping sound, like a man being struck with a wet shirt – or a belly being stabbed and opened by a broad blade. It was enough to make my stomach heave, and I pointed behind me. My mouth opened and closed a few times, but I could not utter a coherent sentence for a while. 'Miners . . . Gubbingses . . . battle . . .' was my best attempt, but the only response I received was the loud clap of Mal's cudgel striking his cupped hand. He had the habit of doing so, I was coming to realize, whenever he managed to catch a stray, random thought that involved damaging bits of me. But then again, since my unfortunate accident, vomiting over his wife, I suppose he had good reason to view me less askance and more in a kind of unsympathetic and unfriendly fashion. I suppose it was natural, especially since his stableman was rather close to her. He had a lot to be bitter about.

The Coroner eyed me with a degree of amusement as I flailed about for an explanation, but nothing was forthcoming. In the end, I just closed my mouth and returned Clem's glare with every ounce of bile I could.

'You and you, take this miscreant back to Okehampton,' the Coroner said, pointing to Clem and Mal. 'This time don't lose him. I want to see him when we return.'

'What if he tries to escape?' Clem said.

'Restrain him. But don't kill him. If you do, I will have you in court.'

'Coroner, this is wrong!' I protested. 'I am only here because he knocked me down and dragged me here! He wanted to see me killed by the miners because then . . .'

'You were here with the miners?'

'No, with the Gubbingses—'

'You were consorting with outlaws?'

'Well . . . The miners wanted to kill me.'

'I wonder why,' the Coroner said drily.

'But I didn't try to escape from you! Clem knocked me down and brought me here! Ask Arold – he saw me on the moors, he saw me tied to Clem's horse!'

'Yes, Arold told us. Not that it matters,' the Coroner said. 'Clem says he saw you kill Daniell, and that was why he was so fearful for his life that he ran to the moors to hide with the miners. But he saw you on the road trying to escape justice, so he captured you and took you to the miners for their justice, before returning to the town and confessing his cowardice.'

'What? But he knocked me down in the tavern's yard!'

'And then we heard you had escaped. And now we learn from you that you joined the Gubbingses. That makes you an outlaw. Take the scum away!' he added contemptuously.

'But, but . . . I had nothing to do with the Gubbingses, beyond them feeding me! I'm innocent!'

'Tell that to the Justice of gaol delivery and the Judge.'

A sudden inspiration struck me, and I stood and pointed an

accusing finger at Clem. 'That man is the murderer! He must be! He was determined to see me dead. Not because he thought I had anything to do with the death of Daniell, but because he wanted to still my mouth!'

'I can at least understand that incentive,' the Coroner remarked in what I could only think of as an unnecessarily cynical tone of voice. 'Take him away!'

'Wait! Why do you think he wanted me dead? He had no feeling for Daniell, did he? He wanted me out of the way because I knew something.'

The Coroner gave a low sigh. 'Very well. What did you know that was so important?'

'Um.'

'Please: enlighten us! What marvellous news could you bring that would explain his wanting to see you dead?'

My mouth opened and shut several times, and I saw him begin to turn away. Almost unintentionally, I blurted, 'His affair with the tavern-keeper's wife!'

And I waited for the passion and rage. Except, there was none. I had thought that Mal would turn on Clem, but he remained staring at me, his club slapping into his hand in a distinctly unfriendly manner.

I looked at Mal, disconcerted. He seemed to have no interest in my words. I would almost have said that he could not have heard me. And as for Clem – well, he was smirking in a twisted, nasty manner. Frantz just looked rather embarrassed.

It left me with a strange, hollow, nervous feeling. I could feel the sweat breaking out down my spine.

If my news did not work, that must mean that Mal already knew of his wife's infidelity and cared little about it. In which case, my last opportunity for defence was lost. But I had thought him devoted to her. How could I have been so wrong?

'Really?' said the Coroner, glancing at Mal and Clem.

Mal shook his head. 'He's making it up. My wife told me this piece of dung had tried to pay her to whore for him, but she told him off and slapped his face for him. And now he tries to put the blame on Clem? I ought to beat him black and blue!'

'There's still time,' Clem said pointedly.

*　　*　　*

There are times in everyone's life, I suppose, when things just don't seem to go right, and this was one of those. I can recall once successfully taking another man's purse, only to find that the well-filled interior was actually full of wooden tokens and no money at all. That gave me a similar feeling of injustice.

After all, I mean, I'd seen the wench with Clem; I'd had his knife at my neck when I mentioned it. And now the hussy had apparently told her husband that I had tried to fondle her, just in order to defend herself from a justice that was only too well deserved! It was so unreasonable that I could only goggle at Clem. That the man was dangerous was obvious, from my experience with his dagger, but that he was also this devious – well, that was a surprise. I had not expected that.

The posse trotted off up the hill a short while later, seeking any Gubbingses or miners they could beat up, while I was bound and pulled with Clem and Mal. Soon enough the sound of shouting and screams increased as, I assumed, the townsfolk met with the miners and Gubbingses. It was enough to make me peer fearfully over my shoulder in case a fresh pursuit came after us.

Mal and Clem, the two men whom I would seriously have preferred never to have seen again, were in charge of me now. A length of rope ran from my bound wrists to Clem's fist. He jerked it regularly, just to add to my misery, trying to pull me off balance and sniggering nastily as he did so.

It was a horrible journey. Only a short while after we set off, the skies opened and God threw buckets of water over us without even a *gardez-loo* as warning. The only thing that made me feel slightly less threatened was the sudden appearance of a large black raven ahead of us. It landed in a squat bush of furze and gave a loud cry. It made me look about, hoping that Ned might be somewhere near, but there was no sign of him.

You already know my opinion of the moors. They are a hideous, wet, mud-filled series of hills, and where there are not rocks to turn your ankle, the grass itself is so thick and lumped together that it feels like rocks underfoot. Make a misstep, and you can break an ankle on either. If the ground is flat and safe, it is only because there is a bog beneath you, ready to swallow you whole.

There are places where I have travelled which have been worse, but just now I cannot call any to mind. The moors were horrible: miserable, wet, grey and constantly trying to destroy a man. And if anything could make them worse, it was the company I had with me. As I tried to keep up with Clem, all the while I could hear the sound of Mal's stout cudgel slapping into the palm of his hand. He kept up that rhythmical effort all the way as we made our way back to the town.

The ground was particularly treacherous when we came down towards the ford at the bottom of the hill. Before we could venture to the river, Clem led us over a flat, smooth expanse of grass, and as we went, I found the grass oddly springy. The ground felt like a partly deflated pig's bladder rather than soil and stone, and I suddenly felt dizzy. It was rather like being drunk: ahead of me I imagined I could see the grass rising and falling before us like ripples on a pond. It was most peculiar, and I peered at it as we went, until I heard a sudden gasp from Mal. At last his tapping ceased, and he gave a strangled cry of 'Clem!'

The lad before us turned with a frown. 'What?'

'It's a bog, you fool! Don't you feel it?'

Now, if you have heard this before, skip this bit, but apparently there are places where the soil beneath the grass is so sodden that if you step on to it, only the grass holds the surface together. If a man steps too harshly on the grass, it will split like a paper stabbed with a knife, and the unfortunate traveller will slide through it and under, to drown in the mud and horror of the peaty soil.

It would be pleasant to be able to tell you that the fools both perished in this bog, and that I was able to slip away. For one moment, I thought I would be fortunate. Clem, a light fellow, cautiously made his way back past me and returned to firm ground without problem, but it was different for Mal. I watched him pace backwards, carefully retracing his steps while I made my own way at an angle, thinking to avoid the areas where he had placed his feet. And then I saw his brows rise in the middle, and a low moan of terror broke from his lips. There was a sort of wet tearing sound, like shears cutting thick grass, I suppose, and then his feet sank.

He gave a loud roar which sounded like *Woohoar*! and burst into a gallop, lurching like a bullock, lumbering and rocking with each step as he gave louder and louder bellows of terror, each time his legs disappearing into the foul, brown slime. Honestly, if I hadn't been so anxious about my own safety, I would have roared with laughter to see him. But as it was, I was much more concerned about my own feet. The ground was appallingly wet and slippery, and I could feel the grass moving under my own feet as the fool bounded from one foot to the other, his face wide-eyed and despairing, and I was forced to spring like a young deer to reach the safety of a small collection of rocks.

Mal reached safety shortly after me, and fell on all fours, head hanging and panting like a bull in the baiting pits, finally rolling over with a grunt and lying on his back, mouth agape, staring at the sky. He had believed himself to be about to die, and he was entirely incapacitated for some time, while I sat on a rock and tried to shelter from the rain that was pelting down. Clem stood a short distance away, eyeing me suspiciously, until Mal had gathered himself. He stood and then gave an oath. There, where he had first sunk into the mire, I could see his cudgel protruding from the ground. It was a source of great loss to the fool, as if it was some family heirloom or a prized reward.

I didn't like Mal.

Clem pushed me in the small of my back, and we were off again. This time, we made our way considerably more warily, keeping an eye on the ground. We did not encounter any more marshes or mires, but I did injure myself.

It was at the roadway approaching the ford. There was a track that was clearly marked for miners and peat-cutters here, but the way was thick with glutinous mud, and I had no desire to put my foot into the middle of it. My London-made boots were losing their polish as it was, and I saw no need to speed their deterioration. Instead, I picked my way at the side of the road on the verges, where there was thick grass. Placing my foot on a tuft, I believed I was safe. Yet in Devon even the grasses can be deadly.

As I put my foot down, I heard a sudden loud *caw* overhead. Shooting a look up, I was just in time to see that raven again. But my footing was not secure; as I put my weight on my foot, the grass parted company with the mud, giving a little squelch of protest – or amusement – and my foot flew off ahead of me, forcing my leg – the leg I injured at Lydford – to twist almost about as I fell vertically. I heard a loud crack from my knee or ankle – I don't know which, for both hurt abominably – and I fell on my rump. I heard another *caw*, which sounded like a sardonic chuckle.

Sometimes, when a fellow hurts himself, he will realize immediately that he has done damage. On other occasions, he will rise without understanding what he has done. This was the case for me now. I had slipped sideways into the muddy track, and incidentally into a pile of manure from the last horse to pass this way. On my arse, I could feel the sogginess seeping through my hosen and into my rump, and immediately struggled to clamber to my feet, but there was a problem. As I tried to rise, an agonizing pain shafted through my ankle and knee.

'Ouch!'

'Get up, you puny, misbegotten lurdan!' Mal spat, which I thought was a bit rich, coming from the man who'd had to swim, almost, to safety, and then lay moaning and panting like a half-drowned hog.

'I can't!'

'You will if I . . .' at that moment he appeared to recall his cudgel was still in the mire up the hill, and went mournfully silent, until another thought loitering about in his skull held up a hand for attention '. . . if I kick you!'

'I've broken something in my leg,' I snarled, and yes, I did actually snarl. My leg hurt, and this inferior creature was not going to make me move with oaths and threats. 'I can't get up.'

And it was true. Before, when I had fallen at the feet of Roger Rowle, I had been in considerable pain, but this was entirely different. My knee was swelling – I could see it – and my ankle felt as though someone had thrust a dagger into the joint. Every time I moved it, the dagger's point seemed to press into the nerves between the bones. 'I can't go anywhere!' I said forcefully.

'You'll have to crawl, then,' Mal said nastily, and he lifted his boot to kick me, but even as he did, I heard a welcome voice.

'You stop right there, Mal Keeper! You kick him and I'll kick you myself.'

'He's just pretending. He don't want to be taken to the gaol.'

'Pretending, eh?'

It was Joan, Ned's woman. She walked to me and stared down at my leg. 'His ankle is twice its usual size,' she commented. 'And his knee: look at that! He's badly injured. You'd best bring him to my cottage.'

'He's a prisoner, Joan,' Mal said sharply. 'He's going to the gaol.'

'He's going to my house, and you're going to help me put him there, Mal Keeper, and if you don't watch your tongue with me, you'll get such a slap you'll wish you were back at home with your father beating you. I said he'll stay a while in my cottage, and you're both going to take him there. Help him up, now. Arms about your necks, and you two hold him up, too. And if you drop him, Mal, or you, Clem, I'll be the one to learn you how to carry a body. You won't like my lessons. Well? Come on, then!'

To my astonishment the two men, after her hectoring, helped me to my foot with something approaching civility and gentleness. I found myself half carried, hopping carefully on my good leg, while my two escorts gripped me about the ribs and scowled at Joan.

The ford was up and the water freezing. At one point in the middle of the river, I caught my foot on a rock, and felt my eyes widen as I began to plummet. At a snapped command from Joan, both caught tighter hold of me, and I was halted in my dive and then gathered up by the two.

This woman must have had a hold over the men in the area, I thought. She was not terrifying to me, obviously, but these two peasants were entirely cowed by her in a way that not even the Coroner had managed. I suppose it is the natural way of things, that a woman with a certain degree of authority will often be able to browbeat men with less intelligence and courage. It wouldn't work on me, of course, since I was from London, but I could understand how those of feeble intellect might succumb.

'In here,' she said, and the two men hobbled along between her raised beds of greens and beans, and in at her door. She motioned them towards a stool at the rear wall, and the two carefully deposited me on it before stepping away a couple of paces.

'I'll leave Clem here, mistress, and go to fetch—'

'You'll do no such thing. You'll both leave now. You can return with a small barrel of ale, Mal Keeper, and you'll be quick about it. The men are all up on the moors – who do you expect to find to come here? Besides, there's no need of a guard. He won't be running any time soon, not with that leg.'

There was a good deal more, mostly from the two men who seemed determined to have someone stay there and keep an eye on me. Not that they needed concern themselves: as she said, I could not move that leg, and I had no desire to walk anywhere. I glared at them in my turn, and eventually the two left, grumbling as they did so, and set off back to the town.

'Mistress, I am very glad you were there,' I said.

There was a tap, and when I looked over, there was a raven at the window, tapping against the wooden bars. Joan walked to him, collecting a strip of fat from a dish on her way and passing it to the bird, who took it in his beak, gave me a dark stare, then flicked his head up and swallowed it in one gulp. He returned to studying me like a metal smith peering at a particularly interesting piece of carving.

'So you came back eventually,' Ned said as he entered the room from behind me.

If my leg had been working, that shock would have sent me through the door and out to the road at speed. I would have been halfway to Plymouth before my heart had stopped thundering.

'What are you doing here?' I demanded, a hand at my breast. Honestly, if the sight of that damned bird of ill-omen had not been there, perhaps I would not have been so alarmed, but to be concentrating on the black beast, and then to have a voice behind me, and me all the while fretting that the men would

return at any time to try to drag me to a gaol – or gallows –
well, I ask you, is it any surprise I should spring halfway to
my feet with a sharp cry of alarm, or that I should yelp with
pain before falling back against the wall, with a fine sheen of
sweat bedewing my brow?

Ned eyed me with some of the same elderly suspicion with
which he had viewed me on the day I first met him in the castle.
'What have you been doing?'

'Eh?'

'We saved you from one gaol, sent you down to our boy
Roger and his companions, thinking you would escape the
danger, and now here you are, returned to the town. What did
you do? They say you have started a war between the miners,
Gubbingses and the townsfolk!'

'No, I haven't! The Gubbingses decided to attack the miners,
but the townspeople learned of this, and decided to go up there
themselves! It's nothing to do with me!'

'Aye, mayhap it isn't. You don't seem the sort of man to
have too much ability when it comes to deviousness,' he said.

Which, I confess, I was a little annoyed to hear. After all, the
fellow was denigrating my abilities. Not that I wanted people
to think me a devious fellow, but still . . . his words jarred. They
were hurtful to a fellow of sensibility and intelligence.

'Why would you think I was responsible?'

'You go there, you speak to Roger, and a day later you've
gone with him to pick a fight with the miners. What would you
think?'

'Roger Rowle? You can hardly find anything he does
surprising! He is a madman! You must know he regularly attacks
the miners in their camp, takes their food and tin, and I suppose
sells it on. He is a thief and a murderer.'

'Yes, I know.'

'The first night I was there, he murdered a farmer! Right in
front of me!'

'Yes.'

'He stabbed the fellow,' I said, somewhat deflated by the
casual lack of interest displayed by the other two.

'Yes,' Joan said.

'I mean, for all I know, he cut out the man's heart and ate

it,' I said. He didn't, of course, but I wanted to see some form of reaction from the two of them.

'Are you saying he's a cannibal?' Ned snapped.

Suddenly, I was more than satisfied with his response, as he drew his knife in a flash and sprang forward to hold it under my chin. I was very still for a moment, peering with some agitation into his eyes, which were only a matter of two or three inches from mine. 'No. Not a cannibal,' I said with great care. 'No, he was very kind to me. But I was just saying that, for all I know, he was capable of such an act. Or maybe not,' I added quickly as the pressure from that damned blade increased. 'No, in fact I'm sure he would never think of such a thing! He was too kind and generous to me for him to think of anything like that!'

The face was withdrawn. A heartbeat or three later, the knife was also withdrawn, and at last I could breathe.

'You don't understand, do you?' Ned said. 'When you insult him, you insult us.'

'No, I am sure I—'

Joan went to Ned and slipped her hand in at his elbow, her other hand going to his cheek. 'He doesn't understand much, Ned,' she said with a calm smile.

I confess, I had no idea what they were saying.

'You see, Master Passer, Roger may be all those things, but he is our son,' she said.

'I . . . Your son?'

Ned shrugged. 'What of it?'

'But . . . you are a Gubbings, and his name is Rowle?'

'He's a Gubbings, too. My name was Rowle when I was a miner. When I left and joined the Gubbingses, I took their name.'

'Oh?' I tried to sound interested. In reality, I was thinking more along the lines of a large brandy to help take away the pain of my knee and ankle. 'I recall you said you had been a miner.'

'Aye, until the thieving scrotes decided to steal my land and take my tin,' he snarled. 'That was Daniell Vowell for you. A villain who would steal the ring from your finger when he shook your hand, or cut your finger off to steal it, who would stab a friend for the price of a penny – that was what Daniell was like. A foul, devious, lying—'

'Ned!' Joan said sternly.

'Oh, very well! Anyhow, once I had a good claim. That was how he worked: he waited until someone like me had proved a good spot to dig, and then he would appear and try to take it. He beat me, because I wouldn't pay his black rent. He demanded money to protect us, and if we didn't pay, he showed us how dangerous it was. The black rent was to see we were protected from him. I refused, and two days later, I was attacked and beaten.'

'I found him,' Joan said. 'He looked nigh to death, the poor fellow. I saw to him, saw to his wounds, fed him and helped him, but it was no good. Daniell forced us to run.'

'Couldn't you have told the Justice? The Coroner or Sheriff?'

Ned shook his head. 'The Justice? It's the moor, Passer. The moor answers only to Lydford Law and the Miners' Parliament. And Daniell was the leading man there. The others owed him – and he owned them. There was no justice up there. No, so I had to leave my little plot, and made my way down the hill. Joan helped me, took me down past Lydford, and there we met with the Gubbingses.'

'You did?'

'And he became their leader,' Joan said, smiling at him with such pride it almost warmed my heart, until I recalled she was telling me that this wizened old fellow had been a leading outlaw and felon in the area.

'It wasn't hard. They were desperate for someone with a brain to rule them,' Ned said. 'So we stayed there for many years, and it was a good life. But two years ago, we thought of a cottage with a hearth, and a roof, and no longer to listen to the constant drip-drip of water on a cave wall, and no longer to worry about miners or a posse coming to attack us, and it appealed to us. So we spoke to the others, and named my son to be the ruler in my place, and he's there now. Roger Rowle, son of Ned Rowle, the leader of the Gubbingses.'

'But don't the people of the town here know? Are you safe here?'

'Oh, yes. We don't do anything to upset the local folk. And they know that if anything was to happen to us, Roger would be down here faster'n goose fat through a hound, and he'd take revenge for us. So it's a good balance.'

'What now, though?' I said.

'Now?' Joan said.

'If the miners and the posse have managed to destroy the Gubbingses, there will be no more protection for you. If they're gone, the locals may well attack you.'

Ned curled his lip at that. 'You have no idea who you're talking about. The Gubbingses are a strong force here. Anyone attacking us would regret it.'

'As long as they survive.'

Joan rolled her eyes. 'Do you know how often they have attacked the miners?'

'How often have the miners known they were coming and ambushed them? And then had the townsfolk join in against them?' I asked.

Ned gave a *pah!* of contempt for my presumption in questioning the might of the Gubbingses, but when I glanced at Joan, I could see the concern flaring in her eyes.

'You have no idea,' Ned said. 'You don't know these people as I do.'

'No, I don't,' I said. 'But I have seen the miners and the townspeople and what they can do. And while I admire the fighting ability of Roger Rowle and his friends . . .' I said no more. I didn't need to.

Ned's mouth had fallen open. 'You think the miners and townspeople would join against the Gubbingses?'

I said nothing.

'Ned, if that happens—' Joan began tentatively.

'Quiet, woman!' he snapped. He turned from us and stared out at the castle, then turned back to me. 'Can you walk?'

'This leg is—'

'Because if we leave you here, and the people come back to get you, best you can hope for is you'll be thrown in the town gaol.'

The raven at the window turned his head as though questioning me, too.

'I can't move quickly,' I said, but I knew that he was right. I tried to lift myself.

'Stop!' Joan said. She looked at my knee and ankle. 'He can't, Ned. He's badly injured; you can see that.'

'Then we'll have to leave him here,' Ned said uncompromisingly. 'We have to help Roger.'

'What can you do up there on the moors?' I said disbelievingly. 'There are only two of you! If they have caught him, there's nothing you two can do against all the townspeople and the miners together, is there?'

Ned threw me the sort of look that a father would give a child just seen digging a hole in the house's wall with a knife. Then, 'He's right.'

Ned was plainly worried, but to be quite honest, his fears were no concern of mine. After all, he was facing the threat of men coming to injure him, but he still had both legs and no injuries to his head such as I had received. Yes, he was old – but that only meant he had already enjoyed a long life. I, on the other hand, had my life stretching ahead of me. And I didn't want to see it ended by stretching my neck on Okehampton's town gibbet.

So no, my sympathies were not fully engaged on his behalf. They were more focused on my own future.

However, Ned and Joan clearly had their own concerns held most dearly to their hearts. I was appalled to see how they ignored me and set about preparing to leave, just to save their own skins! Joan grabbed a number of essentials: a loaf, some ham, a knife, a cloak, and wrapped them in a blanket, while Ned grabbed a small barrel of, I assume, ale, before the two took their leave of me and bolted. I shouted after them, but they paid no attention to me, instead haring away at the best speed they could muster.

I could scarcely believe my eyes. Here was I, bruised, battered, utterly defenceless, and yet they were prepared to leave me to my fate without a backward glance. It was shameful to think that people could desert a man in need, as I was. Had our roles been reversed, I would have felt terrible guilt to have left a fellow waiting for the blow of justice to strike him. Not that it would have stopped me, of course, but I would have felt it nonetheless.

Although I knew it was pointless, I bellowed to them till I was hoarse, demanded that they should come back, begged them to come and help me, pleading for them to aid me, and all the while I tried to rise, looking desperately for a stick or staff I could use as a crutch, but I could see nothing, bar a besom in the corner. I rose to my foot and, using the table as a prop, hopped slowly to the broom.

It was a typical peasant's tool: the shaft an inch thick, twigs bound tightly to it by two cords, ideal for sweeping dust and rubbish out of the house. I pulled at the twine to try to remove the twigs, but it was strong, and my fingers could make no impression. I had no knife, for Clem had disarmed me when they bound my hands, but there must surely be something with a sharp edge here in the house.

If there were, it was well enough concealed from my eyes. After some minutes of searching, I found nothing. In the end, I decided to alter my attack and began snapping the twigs. In only a short time, I had managed to pull away six sticks from the first bindings, but then the second thong defeated me. Perhaps I could snap away the twigs where they protruded from one binding, then roll that binding away, over the remaining stumps, which would leave the one cord left, I wondered.

I set to my task with enthusiasm.

The stems of the twigs were so closely packed that it was difficult to separate them in order to pull them apart. It was hard work, but desperation made me persevere. I *must* fashion a crutch before Clem or Mal returned. They would both be happy to have me at their mercy, and I had no wish to be. No, if I could only fashion a support from this besom, I would be able to make my way . . . and then I paused.

Yes, I could escape from this house, but what benefit would that give me? My leg was too badly injured for me to escape on foot, and with the best will in the world, I could not mount my horse, even if I was able to reach the stable of the tavern with this leg. If I did get there, Clem would laugh at me before knocking me down and enjoying himself at my expense, with a stave or by simply punching or kicking me, and I could not hope to defend myself.

I stared at the mangled remains of the besom in my hands and then tossed it aside and returned to my stool. I didn't have long to wait.

It was less a knock at the door, more a steady pounding, as if the assailant was hoping to shatter every inch of timber. It sounded as though the door must shiver to splinters under that barrage, and I coughed as a fine dust fell from the rafters overhead.

That was when I heard the voices outside.

They were unenthusiastic, from the sound of them.

'You don't have to batter it like that, do you? Don't alarm her!'

'She won't do anything.'

'How do you know she won't? She's looked at me odd before.'

'Are you a man or a lump of foolishness? Just go and fetch him.'

That voice, cold and callous as a snake's hiss, was familiar, and I felt a shiver run down my spine at the sound of it: it was Agnes.

'Her and Ned – I mean, upset them, and you can't tell what will happen. They're family to Roger Rowle, and I don't want to upset him any more'n I want to upset David. They—'

'You *fool*!' she snapped, and I could have sworn I heard her stamp her foot. 'You think Ned or Joan would care about a traveller passing by?'

'She stopped us taking him to the gaol.'

'So what? She won't want to be associated with another felon, will she? That could bring danger to her tribe. Knock on the door again!'

'I don't like to.'

'*Oh!*'

I could picture the scene clearly. Agnes with her hands on her hips, glaring at her swain, while he stood shuffling his feet in the dirt. It was a more appealing vision than the one I had uppermost in my mind when I thought of him: the scene where he launched himself at me with his knife in hand, holding me against the wall in his noisome little saddler's chamber.

It wasn't him who beat at the door's timbers this time. No, it was her. Not that I could have told from the ferocity of her assault – it sounded like a man's thundering.

'Mistress Joan, we know you're there. Open this door!' she shouted.

Clem's voice was peevish and fretful. 'There's no need to shout at her, is there? Is she deaf, that she needs you to be so loud? Does she not usually answer well enough? Eh?'

I was a little surprised, even through my fog of fear. The lad was deferring to her. I had thought, after the way he leapt at me in his hostler's chamber, that he would be a more overbearing man, but he was definitely not the most authoritarian of the two.

'Hold your tongue, Clem!'

'Yes, well, I'm only saying you should knock *politely*, that's all, and ask if we may enter.'

'What are you scared of? She is not going to attack us, is she? She's an elderly woman.'

'I'm not scared, but there's no point upsetting people for no reason,' the lad said with evident sense, as far as I was concerned.

I heard a sigh, and then there was a quiet tap. 'Mistress, may I come in?'

'Certainly. For all I care, you are welcome,' I said without enthusiasm.

The door opened and Clem stood in the doorway, peering into the chamber with the anxiety of a schoolboy discovered stealing cakes. Behind him, gazing over his shoulder, I saw Agnes. When her eyes lit upon me, I saw her glower turn into something deeply unpleasant – a sort of malevolent leer, such as you would see on the face of a felon on coming across an unlocked safe. I did not like her look.

'Where're Joan and Ned?' Clem asked shortly.

'How should I know? I'm stuck here.'

'Not now, you aren't,' Agnes said. 'Get up. You're coming with us.'

'Why? Where do you mean to take me?'

'You're coming to the town's gaol. And you'll wait there until the Justices arrive to try you.'

'Why? What do you want with me? All I have done is be
attacked, and you want to see me hanged? You know I didn't
hurt anyone,' I said. I might have sounded as if I was pleading,
but really I was only attempting persuasion.

'You should never have come here. You shouldn't have taken
Daniell's money, and you shouldn't have puked all over me,'
Agnes said. There was some – I don't know – some vitriol in
her tone of voice that sent a fresh shiver down my spine.

'That was an accident. I wouldn't have done it a'purpose,
would I? A man cannot help it when he needs to throw up. I
just went to the window and didn't see you.'

Clem had investigated the room, and now he was convinced
we were alone, he seemed to grow in courage. He pulled out
his knife. 'You thought it funny, though. And you came to me
and said we were having an affair, didn't you? You even told
the Coroner and Mal this day that I was sticking the cuckold's
horns on old Mal.'

'Well, you were!'

'So? What's that to you?'

'Nothing,' I squeaked, for the knife was now very close to
my neck.

'But you betrayed our little secret,' he snarled.

'What, that you knocked me down?' I said.

He stopped for a moment. 'What?'

'On the night I was struck, someone knocked me down. It
was one of you two, I think. Someone was in your harness
room, but someone else knocked me down. Who would be in
the stables, but you? And if you had a lover, perhaps she was
given to visiting you in your chamber when she had a spare
moment? And that night, she saw a man win a large sum, and
she had been going to tell you of the man, and of the great,
swollen purse he carried, so that you could take it and share
it with her. Perhaps run away? And you heard all this and went
into the yard to see me while I pissed, and when I went into
the stable to look at my new pony, you struck me down, while
your lover was still in the chamber. I saw her shadow in there.'

'Very clever,' she noted, with a gleam, perhaps, of
appreciation. 'And then what?'

'You took my purse and made away with it somehow. You

stored it so that when you saw an opportunity, you could retrieve it and make free with my money. But, of course, the plan would only work as long as you both remained in there, safe. And your plans were all set to naught by the sudden death of Daniell, weren't they? If you were to run, suspicion would fall on you two, and you would be sure to be discovered if the posse sought you. There would be nowhere to run from the posse. So you chose instead to stay, and see whether you could cast more doubt on to a poor innocent traveller, whose only guilt was to have been caught up in the machinations of miners, felons and landowners. All I have done is be set upon, robbed, assaulted, captured, threatened with death, and now injured yet again.'

'He's not as stupid as he looks,' Clem said, and sniggered.

I suppose it was the most intelligent thing he had ever said. But, of course, that was soon to be forgotten. Because as he spoke, the door crashed wide, and there, standing and breathing stertorously, like a bull seeing a man crossing *his* field, stood Mal.

He had acquired a new cudgel, I noted. And it was now beating against his palm in a rhythmical manner that spoke of his inner turmoil.

'Agnes,' he said, and there was a sort of tortured tone to his voice, like a man who was struggling mightily to control his emotions after his favourite hound had bitten him.

'Mal, I—'

'I heard it all. You think me a fool?'

I didn't feel it was incumbent on me to comment at this point. Agnes was doing a splendid job of distraction, by the way. Her breasts were heaving in a manner that I found both convincing and captivating. I could not help but allow a smile to cross my face, and as I watched her give her husband a mooning look, as though she was delighted to see him at last, for she needed to be rescued from the ravisher, Clem, I was forced to drag my eyes away and see if Clem had realized she was about to desert him to save herself from the inevitable punishment she was most certainly due.

'Mal,' she said, 'I know it sounds terrible, but I thought the money would help us. You and me. I agreed to help get the purse, but that was all, and then Clem put his hand into my skirts, and . . .'

It was a picture. Clem had been all snarling fury before the door slammed wide, sneering at me in that particularly unpleasant manner of his. The instant the door opened, he had been enjoying the sight of my terror, and now he realized that something was going wrong. He had thought that Mal would be an ally against me, but now condign retribution was at hand for his injudicious and impertinent affair with his master's wife, and she was saying something that suddenly sounded less than helpful. I could see that my terror had transferred to him, and I rather enjoyed the sight.

Of course, Clem was a bully. I have often witnessed bullies who suddenly receive justice, and it is always a joy to watch. He was all too keen to threaten and terrorize me, but when a larger character like Mal hove into view, he showed his true colours. While I stiffened my back, as a true yeoman from London should, full of pride for my position and contempt for his, he slunk back like a cur ready to be kicked or whipped. The world had returned to her usual balance.

'Stay there, you bull's pizzle! You son of a goat! You would swive my wife, would you? You'd try to take her from me, would you? She's told me all, you prickle!'

'She . . . she what?' Clem said. His attention was fixed on the two of them, his head moving from one to the other like a man watching a game of tennis. 'What do you mean?'

'You raped my wife, you bitchson! You took her when I didn't have time to protect her, and you fondled her, and you wanted her to run away with you!'

'I . . . but . . .'

I could sympathize with the fool. After all, I have occasionally found myself in tricky situations, and similar conversations have been difficult to negotiate. I well recall that morning when I woke in my lover's bed to the enraged roar of her father, demanding to know my name, and the vicious trull waking and staring at me, accusing me of raping her, as if she had not herself invited me to her chamber. Not that her father would have believed anything I said, of course.

As for Clem, suddenly his attention was fixed on Agnes, and

with a kind of pathetic hurt, as he realized she had betrayed him. She gave a slight shrug, as though a form of apology, before turning her magnificent eyes on her husband again. 'I'm so glad I could tell you before he . . . before he took me.'

The lying bitch, I thought, but it didn't seem the right moment to raise any doubts in Mal's mind. With a sudden roar, he pelted across the room, his cudgel swinging, and it was all Clem could do to slip sideways and avoid it, holding his knife before him like a priest with a crucifix. He would never have survived in a London brawl; I could see that much. The return swing of the cudgel came close to my face, and there was a light tinkle as it caught the knife and sent it whirling away. Clem gave a little whimper, which made me smile, and then there was a crackling sound, something like the noise of an eggshell being crushed, with overtones of a cabbage being kicked, and I saw Clem's eyes widen, his mouth protrude into an 'O' of surprise, and suddenly his eyes rolled up into his head. He collapsed, his knees simply folding and his body sliding down until his rump hit the floor, and then toppled backwards. His head hit the rough packed-earth floor with the sort of thud you imagine a turnip would make. Only a turnip would have cracked open. Clem's didn't exactly crack, so much as squelch.

'You've killed him!' I said.

Agnes snapped, 'Shut up!' at me, and took hold of Mal's arm. 'Leave them, Mal. Come on, let's go back to the tavern. You need something to calm your spirits.'

'You killed him,' I said again. I was, I confess, shocked.

I mean to say, I have seen men stabbed to death, seen them eviscerated by cannon shot, hanged by the dozen, and everything in between that could cause a man to die. But although I have seen many clobbered over the pate, I've not seen someone struck down and destroyed so swiftly with one blow. And there was no doubt in my mind that Clem was dead.

'He shouldn't have tried to take my Agnes from me,' Mal said.

'Mal, come on. Let's go to the tavern,' she said again.

She had a determined, steely tone in her voice, and I suddenly realized her intention.

'Oh, no!' I said.

She looked at me, and there was real hatred in her eyes. And I felt a dreadful sinking feeling.

'Leave your club here,' she said, and, as if in a trance, Mal dropped it at Clem's feet. He submitted to her gentle persuasion, looking at her like a love-struck swain under the influence of a strong tonic, as she drew him gradually away from me and Clem's body, out to the door and through it.

As soon as the door closed quietly behind them, I tried to rise to my feet, but it was not possible. My ankle would not support me, and the knee was agony. I struggled to hobble to the table, but it was almost beyond me. Reaching it, I sobbed with the pain as my hands clutched the boards. It was a feat of endurance that I reached so far. I could not go farther. Instead, I stared at the cudgel at Clem's feet. It was beyond my reach, and as I stared at it, I was suddenly struck with the feeling that I did not want to pick it up. The handle was fine, but the head of the club had hairs, which looked matted and damp, and when I looked at Clem's head, I could see why. About his head there was a slowly growing pool of liquid, and I didn't need to be a physician to tell that it was his blood.

Yes, I knew what Agnes's plan was now. She would denounce me to the people of the town. I had already shown my hatred of Clem by accusing him of crimes, and now he was dead, at my feet, with the murder weapon almost in my hands. Clem had captured me and seen me dragged to Lydford, but that was no reason for me to murder him, she would say. And Mal would agree with her, of course. Because he saw me as evil. He was as bovine as . . . a bullock in his thinking. And I was here, stuck in this cottage with my injured leg, incapable of rising and escaping.

There was a sudden noise and I glanced at the door. Ned stood in the doorway, staring down at Clem like a man with a toothache. 'What now? Why him?'

'Agnes. She was having a game of hide the sausage with the stable boy, but when her husband found out, she told him Clem had raped her, I think, and she managed to have Mal kill Clem. Mal preferred to think Clem assaulted her than that she might have sought to run away with the boy.' I stared down at

Clem. Disgust fought with anger: after all, if it was Clem, as I suspected, who had knocked me down and robbed me, I might never now learn where my purse had been concealed.

'Where did she go?'

'She took him back to the tavern, I suppose. That's what she said, to give him a drink.'

'And you let her?' he snarled. There was a corresponding cry from outside, and once again I saw that damned raven at the window. If I had a sling, I would have taken a slug to the creature.

'What would you expect me to do?' I demanded, indicating my leg. 'I could hardly fight them, could I? I can't even stand, let alone run after them! And what does it matter? He may get completely blotto, but even if he's swine-drunk with bouzing, it'll make it easier to catch him, won't it? They will want to punish him, won't they?'

'For punishing the man who stuck cuckold's horns on him? Some may. But a man who's popular, who runs the best tavern in the town – what do you think? They'd prefer to accuse you of another murder and leave him in his place. After all, what better solution could there be? You, a stranger, no loss to any man here, or him, the owner of a well-run tavern where all the farmers and miners will visit occasionally. Some more than others. There's plenty of fuddling drink in his house, after all.'

'Then we should go to the tavern and speak with her,' I said.

'What about?' Ned asked, his face registering bafflement.

I didn't want to say, *My purse*, so I shook my head as if in disbelief. 'Her man has killed here, look. And a man who has killed once may have killed a second time, and go on to kill others. We should go and speak with him and, if we can, bind him so that he waits for the Coroner.'

He looked at me then. 'What of you?'

'Clem beat me that night, and I was robbed by him, before I returned to the tavern. Obviously, it wasn't me who killed Daniell. It was Clem! He's proof of my innocence.'

I stated it loudly enough for the Lord Chancellor in London to hear my declaration, but if I was expecting to see reciprocal understanding on Ned's face, I was to be disappointed.

'Mayhap the Coroner will believe you,' he said after a moment's pause. 'Come, I'll help you.'

I put my arm about his shoulders, and he gripped my waist and helped me hobble from the cottage. The raven, still at the window, watched us and muttered *caw* under his breath, or so I thought.

Of course, the scheme seemed, while I was sitting in that cottage with Clem's body at my side, only sensible. To return to the tavern, question the vicious wench as to where my purse was, and see to it that her husband was arrested for Clem's murder, there was but one flaw in my reasoning, which I dare say you have already considered.

It was this: while it all seemed natural and convincing to me, and while the Coroner had been content to believe in my innocence, before Clem captured me and bore me off to the miners' camp, after that he appeared to take Clem's and Mal's words against mine. Well, now Clem had been shown to be untrustworthy, and Mal would surely back me up on that, knowing that the man had tried to molest his wife (although personally, having seen her hips swaying so alluringly that day at the stable, I doubted that he had needed to try very hard, if you catch my drift). If his word could not be trusted, then perhaps people would be able to take mine instead. Of course, there was a risk that they wouldn't, but would that really affect me so badly? After all, I could not run or ride my horse away. I was stuck here in this brigand-ridden backwater whether I liked the fact or not, and there was little I could do about it. It would be better for me to speak up and convince people that I was innocent, even if it might be an uphill battle.

And find out where the foxy wench had hidden my money, of course. To think that she had it all along!

It took us a long time to cover the distance to the tavern. A very long time. We set off in daylight, with the damned bird flying from branch to branch before us, watching as if in disbelief that two humans could take such an age to cover so short a distance. If I could have bent down, I would have picked up a stone and hurled it at the bird.

'Why does that thing follow you around?' I said as we crossed a clapper bridge halfway to the town.

'What, him?'

'The raven.'

'He's not following us, he's leading the way,' Ned said.

I gritted my teeth and set my jaw. As if the bird knew where to go! I could tell when a man was making a pleasantry at my expense, and I saw no reason to give him the satisfaction of responding.

The end of this road brought us close to the middle of the town, such as it was, and as we came to the outskirts and turned right towards the tavern, I became aware of a sound in the distance. The raven's head rose, and it stared off to the south, towards the moors.

Ned lifted his head and stared.

'Bugger,' he said.

They came in an unending stream of battered and bloody bodies, limping, struggling, coughing, holding red-stained bandages to their heads, some using staffs to help them, while the Coroner rode at their head with an expression of stern resolution on his face.

He, of course, looked uninjured. That was no surprise. The knights of this world do not throw themselves into a fight with reckless abandon. They sit on their mounts, watching the peasants about them go in and get the first blows and injuries, before trotting off to the safest part of the battle, safe inside their armour, dealing a few slashes and cuts, before retreating to a safe distance and making sure that the battle is going as they planned. This battle, from the look of the poor devils in his cavalcade, had not gone to plan.

'So you are not yet in your gaol?' the Coroner said as they approached. His companions were clearly not of a mood to take interest in me or my position. He stared about him, and I could see that his attention was not fully on me.

'I fell and injured my leg,' I said.

Ned kept his head down, staring at the ground at our feet. The Coroner barely appeared to notice him, but merely nodded. All the while, the men filed past, one or two whimpering, others stoically gazing into the middle distance while trying to hold hands clapped over injuries.

'What happened?' I said.

The Coroner glanced down as if noticing me for the first time. 'We had a hard fight,' he said. 'The miners and Gubbingses attacked us together. I had thought that the miners would join us against the outlaws, but instead they joined forces. We were pushed back and back, all the way to the top of this path. Several men were killed up there, and the townspeople turned and ran. I could do nothing to hold them; they just bolted.'

His face showed a kind of wonder at the disaster that had just befallen him. I imagine he had thought himself leading a powerful force to an easy victory. After all, he was a trained knight, and the men in the mining camp and the Gubbingses were a mere rabble. They should be nothing against a man like him.

Alas, I have seen all too many men who thought themselves secure in their skills and intelligence, only to be beaten in an instant by others who should have been easily vanquished, but who had not seen the play. They didn't realize that they were intended to be the victims, and so threw themselves into the fray with happy abandon. The simple fact is, those who go into battle with a sense of complete superiority rarely plan for what might go wrong, whereas a disorganized rabble will very often demonstrate a cunning and speed of reorganizing that defeats those like the Coroner who have only education. But this was a rare occasion for him – a moment when he was brought face to face with failure.

'You mean you didn't defeat the miners?' I said, more to remind him of his embarrassment than to seek information.

'They will be here soon. They intend to catch you and string you up,' he said.

This was in an entirely calm, conversational tone, as though it was of little interest or importance to anyone. Indeed, it was said so matter-of-factly that at first I was struck with an urge to chuckle, as though he was offering some mild pleasantry, but a quick look at his face was enough to drive away any sense of amusement.

'What do you mean, they intend to string me up? You mean

they'll come here to hang me? They want to murder me? Well,
you must protect me, Coroner! You have a duty to the law, man;
you have to defend me!'

'With what?' he said, waving a hand at the townspeople
about him. 'These? They wouldn't be able to defend you
against a harvest mouse. Look at them! They have no courage
left.'

'You have a duty to protect me!' I repeated. After all, there
appeared little else for me to do. I couldn't force the man,
or the town, to defend me against the marauding hordes of
miners. If they were set against it, I would die. 'Will you do
nothing?'

'No. I will go to the tavern and consider the quality of Mal's
ale and wine,' the Coroner said.

I watched him as he spurred his mount into a walk, riding
off slowly, hunched like an old man. Which was something I
would never be, clearly, if I had to depend upon him.

'Sir Geoffrey is upset,' Ned said.

'Do I care about him?' I snapped. My thoughts were much
more focused on my own position, naturally. 'Where can I go?'

'All you need do is wait a little,' Ned said. 'I've sent Joan
for help. She shouldn't take long to come back.'

'Help? From where?'

'Our boy. He should be willing to help,' he said grimly.

We made our way to the tavern, hoping to arrive not long
after the Coroner and those with him, and when we arrived, we
found the place in a turmoil. Men were sitting at tables and
demanding drink, while the Coroner was looking morose as he
stared into a pewter mug of ale. Mal was walking like a pale
ghost among all the men, dispensing ale or cider from a pair of
massive blackjacks, barely responding when men spoke to him.

At least those in the tavern were the men with the fewest
injuries. There must have been forty or so, and the way they
were attacking their drink showed that their experiences up on
the moors must have been enough to appal them. I accepted
Ned's assistance to a bench, and sat with my back to the wall,
gazing about me and hoping to see any sign of support or
friendship. There was none. The men there must have known

my predicament, for none would meet my eyes, save only Ned.
And one or two others who appeared to find my situation
hilarious.

'What can I do?' I asked Ned, and repeated myself enough
to persuade him to glower at me.

'Be still! We'll soon have help, but until then you'll have to
be patient.'

'Patient? The miners could appear at any time, and as soon
as they do, I'll be murdered!'

I heard a faint *caw* from outside. It sounded like avian
amusement. If I could have bolted outside and lobbed a stone
at it, I would. But my leg prevented any such exercise.

Mal appeared with two more jugs. When Ned beckoned, he
shuffled over to us, but he avoided looking at me. I was beginning to feel like a ghost in that room, the way no one wanted
to acknowledge me. It was as if, were they to notice me, they
might themselves then be forced to try to defend me against
the miners. And no one was keen to do that.

Pouring ales for us both, Mal said nothing until Ned asked
where his wife was. Then his face became suffused with blood,
and we were both glad when he turned on his heel. He looked
like a man who had been dropped into Satan's pit for a while
by his best friend.

'Has she run away?' I wondered aloud. It would serve the
tavern-keeper well enough if she had done so. Personally, I
would be glad to see her gone. She gave me a feeling of anxiety
every time I saw her. Whereas at first I had thought she was a
potential willing playmate for a little mattress wrestling, since
seeing her in Joan's cottage, and her obvious attempt to leave
me with the body of her lover in a compromising position, I
found her less appealing.

'Best not to wonder while Mal's in hearing.'

'Aye, true,' I said. 'Come, bring my ale for me.'

I rose and made my way to the Coroner's table. He looked
up at me with a scowl, drinking deeply.

'How soon will they be here?'

'Too soon,' he said. He lifted his pot once more. 'I had
thought this would remove them from our side once and for
all. If the townspeople had been just a little more courageous,

we could have had them running. Now we'll be lucky if they don't divert the rivers from town, just from spite.'

'What does it matter?' I said. My own problems were still uppermost in my mind just then.

'They are a plague on all us landowners about the moors. They take our waters, threaten our best pastures, beat up our servants when they remonstrate . . . they are thieves and scoundrels. Rascals who threaten and rob at will, all because they claim the Queen's protection. Hah! And now I suppose they will petition her and demand compensation.'

'What of me?'

'If I were you, I should take my horse and ride far and fast.'

'I can't ride,' I pointed out sharply. 'My leg is ruined!'

'Then I suppose you are stuck here, just as I am,' the Coroner said. He upended his pot again. 'Hoi! Tavern-keeper, bring more of that piss you call ale!'

I saw Mal's face. He was still in Satan's pit from the look of him, but he obediently wandered out to the barrels. 'Have you seen him?' I said. 'He killed the stable boy in a cottage near the castle.'

'Why would he do that?'

'I told you: the boy, Clem, was enjoying the affections of Mal's wife. She persuaded Mal that the boy raped her, that it wasn't her agreeing to his advances, but that she was forced to succumb. Mal believed her, I suppose. I saw him kill the boy.'

'If she was committing adultery with the boy, I don't blame Mal.'

'Where is she, though?' I said.

'I don't care,' the Coroner said without looking at me. 'What of her? If she was adulterous, as you say, she deserves to be punished.'

For an officer of the law, Sir Geoffrey de Courtenay appeared more than a little careless of his duty to protect others. Of course, since the wench had been unfaithful, it was scarcely surprising if Mal had taken his belt to her. That was a man's right, after all. But I had more sympathy for her just now, since my own demise was imminent if this man and the townspeople didn't rouse themselves to my aid.

'This town is scarcely to be believed,' I said. 'You, the officer of the law here, will do nothing to protect me or her, but instead sit here in the alehouse and drink yourself to oblivion!'

'You should try it. Meanwhile, keep your mouth shut. Your constant whining grates like chalk on a tablet,' he snapped. 'If you want to run, *go*. If not, drink! And leave the rest of us to our own thoughts.'

I gazed at Ned, who appeared entirely comfortable with the way matters were progressing. As far as he was concerned, I felt, Agnes and I could stop by until the miners arrived, and be slaughtered by them. He did not seem to take any responsibility for our safety. It was atrocious and utterly reprehensible.

'Come, Ned,' I said.

It will scarce be a surprise to anyone to hear that I was not feeling any great urge to remain in the tavern, but when served this crushing disaster, my first instinct was, to be frank, to seek out the strongest ale or brandy I could find, and make myself as drunk as possible in short order. That is why I rose to my feet to go out to the back of the tavern and seek out the barrels. Rather than wait for Mal to come and serve me however he may, I considered it faster and easier to find them myself.

Ned shook his head and indicated he would remain in the chamber with the others, and I gave him a sneer of disgust. Surely even this wizened old fool could see that I needed protection? But no. No one in this God-forsaken town had any notion of civic pride or responsibility. They were all set on drinking themselves to foolishness without any thought for others, like me, who might be in sore distress.

The door at the rear of the tavern gave out to a short passageway. There were some doorways here. On the left was one which, when I opened it, presented me with a good-sized kitchen. At its side was another, which I guess led to the beer cellar. This was not below the tavern, but was just a room between kitchen and bar.

I opened the door, leaning against the wall, balancing precariously on my good leg, gripping my staff tightly. The door opened into a dark room with a solitary small window high in the wall. It reeked of ale that had been spilled over many years. On the left, I could make out some rubbish stored against the wall, and there was a pile of old blankets and trash on the floor. But above all the reek, there was also the smell of fresh alcohol, and I could just make out the shapes of barrels against the far wall. I entered carefully, and immediately fell down a slight step that was hidden in the dark. Swearing and muttering to myself about the ludicrous way that houses and inns were built in this foul little backwater, I made my way to the barrels, once I had clambered to my foot once more.

Gradually, as my eyes acclimatized to the darkness, I could make out a trio of barrels more distinctly at the wall, and smaller barrels which I sincerely hoped might hold brandy or sack. One of them, I judged, from the odour, to hold brandy. It was enough to bring a smile to my face, and I held it up, turned the tap and savoured the taste of good, strong brandy. I needed this.

But I was not comfortable standing balanced on one leg. My attention was taken by the blankets and things on the floor. They were appealing, in my present state. I hopped to them, the staff in my left hand, the barrel on my right shoulder, until I had reached the pile of material. Then I allowed myself to sink down and on to them.

And gave a short scream of horror.

I suppose you had already surmised, but I assure you that it had not passed my mind to think I was in the same room as a corpse. As my buttocks hit the blankets, I realized that this was no haphazard pile of old rags ready to be thrown out, but was a body concealed under some old clothes and blankets.

Springing, as best I could, from the body, I dropped my brandy barrel, which thudded to the ground and began to spray brandy from the tap, which I assume had broken on hitting the floor, and gave another scream when my injured knee hit the hard-packed flooring. I turned to sit on my backside, and scampered away from the body, going back to the door. I had dropped my staff at the same time as the barrel, and now I saw it was resting across the throat of the body. It was Agnes.

The silly wench had believed herself safe from her husband, I suppose. She had thought he trusted her, that he was entirely in her power. When I told him about Clem, I suppose that led to a bit of a doubt springing into his mind. When she told him later that it was a lie, and that Clem had tried to seduce her, or had raped her, even Mal's slow-moving mind must have started to work at a canter, and if he had heard any of Agnes and Clem's conversation while we were inside Joan's cottage, it must have ignited Mal's suspicions and fanned them into certainties. So he killed Clem and then came back here to his tavern and murdered his wife. She had committed petty treason and now had reaped the rewards.

But even while all this was hurrying through my mind, I was aware of a sound. It was the sound of the latch on the door to the bar area. And then I heard steps. All at once I was desperate to grasp my staff once more. I stretched forward: it was out of reach. I tried to rise to my foot, but couldn't with no support. In the end, I decided that I must crawl to it, but as I did so, the darkness grew thicker, as a massive figure appeared in the doorway.

I whimpered.

'Who's there?' Mal demanded, but I was relieved to hear not anger, but only fear. He didn't want people coming in here and finding his wife, I supposed. 'Where are you?'

Have you ever had one of those nightmares in which you spend the whole time fleeing from a terrifying enemy, and it doesn't matter how fast you run, he keeps on gaining on you? You can hide in a room, but then he's behind you; or you climb into a hole, and he grabs your ankles; you . . . well, this was rather like that, but instead of constantly being chased by Mal, I just had the feeling that wherever I might go, he was always going to be just behind me. When I was minding my own business in front of the fire with Frantz, Mal came in, if you recall, and it was only Frantz's quick work with his sword that saw Mal leave me in peace; then, on the moor, it was Mal who appeared, and who brought me back to town with Clem; now it was me in here with his murdered wife, and Mal was here again. He was determined to be my nemesis. And just now, with his massive form filling the doorway, I had every reason to believe he was going to be successful.

So you can picture the scene: he was there in the doorway, head down as he peered into the darkness; I was a matter of three yards or so from him, and a scant yard away from me was the huddled body with my staff lying across it. That staff was the only weapon within reach – but it wasn't, if you catch my meaning. It was about an arm and a half out of my grasp. Meanwhile, Mal was built heavily enough, after lugging barrels of ale about the tavern, to snap my neck like a twig. If he were to catch hold of me, he would be able to destroy me in moments. And I could do nothing to prevent him. My leg prevented anything in the way of self-defence.

From outside there came a sudden commotion. I heard a sudden clattering and the roaring of a lot of angry-sounding men. Mal clearly heard it all, too. I heard him sigh, and then he clearly reckoned that there was nothing to worry about in his cellar. It must have been a rat or something, he thought to himself, or so I fondly imagined, and turned to walk away.

You may think that I was instantly keen to shuffle across the room to fetch my staff, or perhaps I would rise to my feet and make my hopping way from that noisome chamber, but no. I have, over many years of danger and threat, learned that it is better, when caught, to sit quietly until danger has passed, and only then, when certain of safety, to rise and make my way to somewhere else.

So I sat where I was and waited. I heard the great door to the tavern open, heard the sudden extra noise of all those inside roaring and shouting, and then the door closed.

Now, obviously, I made the sensible conclusion: the door opened to permit Mal to pass through it, and then closed again when he was safely on the other side of it. It was, after all, the logical explanation of the door opening and then closing, was it not? What I did not appreciate was that Mal had gone to fetch a horn lantern, and once he had opened the door and entered the bar, it had been only to reach for the lantern. He had already lit it, and I assume he merely forgot to bring it with him when he entered his cellar. But now he had it, and just as I was attempting to rise and retrieve my staff, a sudden flash of light came and caught me full in the face.

I dare say it was an interesting sight, had anybody else been in the area. There was Mal, holding his lantern aloft to shine it into the chamber; in front of him, half-crouched, was the uncomfortable figure of the gentleman of quality from London, and huddled on the floor before me was the body of Mal's wife. I need hardly mention that on Mal's face was a ferocious expression of malignant pleasure, while on mine was a fixed resolution and determination. A fellow from London, after all, would not show himself fearful or alarmed at the sight of a mere peasant tavern-keeper from this land of mud and bogs.

'Hah!' he said after what seemed like an hour or two.

'Mal,' I said with as much hauteur as was possible, while still bent over, trying to straighten my good leg. The staff was still a good distance away. I noticed that my voice sounded a little unnaturally high and tried to imbue it with the confidence it deserved. 'It would appear that the miners have come to drink their fill. You will be kept busy.'

'You found her, then,' he said. He clearly had a mind that was difficult to move to a fresh course when it was sailing with the wind behind it.

'Who?' I tried, innocently.

'Agnes. You were right. You told me she was swiving the hostler, and I didn't believe you, not till I heard her talking to him today in Joan's cottage. That showed me the truth of your words.'

He took a step in, and I could see him reach around the doorway. There was a sudden gleam, and I could see that he had taken up a hammer of some sort. I couldn't help but emit a short bleat at the sight. I glanced down at the staff, but in the time it took me to look, he took two quick steps forward. I fell back, giving an anxious moan as I did so, convinced that at any moment I would feel that hammer on my pate, and that would be an end to me. To my astonishment, his forward motion took him past me and over to the barrels. He set the lantern on one barrel, picked up a fresh tap and hammered it into the nearer barrel. Then he put the hammer down, picked up his lantern and turned back to me.

That was when I allowed myself the release I needed. I shouted for help.

'Help! Murder! Help!'

And Mal stepped towards me.

*　　*　　*

I shuffled backwards urgently.

'You don't have to,' he said. 'I'll confess everything.'

He offered me his hand, and I stared at it. For one thing, it was Mal, and that hand could easily crush mine. For a second, if he picked me up, he could punch me in the belly with his other hand. To counter that, he could just as easily kick me in the belly – or the head – where I was now. Perhaps standing was the lesser of the two evils. I gingerly took his hand, looking up into his face. He didn't seem so fearsome now. In his face, when I looked at him, all I could see was a really rather terrible emptiness and loneliness.

'I loved her,' he said quietly as he lifted me. He left me standing at the door, fetching me my staff, and by the time I had it in my hand, the Coroner and several men from the tavern had joined us. My shout had roused the drunken sots from their shouting and drinking.

'Well? What is happening?' Sir Geoffrey demanded, looking from me to Mal and back.

'Mal has something he wants to say to you,' I said.

I looked at Mal and was assailed by doubt. He was staring at me, then down at the body of his wife, and for an instant I thought he would accuse me of killing her, but then he gave a great sigh, and all the energy seemed to leave him.

'I loved her. She was my little robin, always bright and happy, a darling to all the men who came in here, but always my woman. Always. Until the hostler came and took her. She said he tried to rape her, but I heard her talking to him, and she didn't sound like a woman who'd been forced against her will. She was talking as if she appreciated him. As if she wanted him. That was when I knew this' – he jerked a thumb at me as though I merited little more – 'man was telling the truth, even if he is from up-country. He said he'd seen her and Clem together, that they were affectionate. They were closer than they should be. So I killed Clem in Joan's house, and came here and asked her, and when she didn't speak the truth, I put my hands about her neck to stop her lies, and I couldn't help it, I kept on squeezing and squeezing, trying to stop her deceit and make her tell me the truth, and then, when I let her go, she just . . . and there she is. I didn't mean to kill her, I swear, but she had committed treason, and I couldn't bear to look at her after that.'

The Coroner looked from him to me. 'We shall need to have an inquest. You say you left the other body at Joan's cottage?'

'Aye,' Mal said. His shoulders sagged as he looked at the woman's figure. I suppose I have seen some dozens of bodies, and several murderers, but this was the first time I was so aware of the grief of loss. This poor dolt had adored Agnes, and although she would come and sit on a man's cods in the hope of winning some of his money, he had never doubted her love for him – not until I had made him aware of her infidelity. Now, with the knowledge of her betrayal, and the fact that he had snuffed the flame of her life, he was left in distress. He had no idea how to atone, how to . . . well, I suppose, how to live. It looked as if his life was ended with the death of Agnes.

I could sort of understand because, after all, she was a delightful little handful, but if the poor lurdan thought he was ever anything more than a passing fancy, he was obviously seriously mistaken. She looked on him as a useful protector, but nothing more than that, I'd guess. And the hostler was a more solid bet. Which was, I have to admit, a surprise. If she stayed with Mal, she would have a safe enough life in the tavern. It was hardly a dangerous place, as long as she avoided the Gubbingses and the miners, and as wife of the tavern's host she could expect a good life with plenty of wine and potentially a range of acceptable travelling fellows like me.

Like me. Yes, that gave me pause for thought, as we all traipsed back to the main tavern and the Coroner bellowed at people to fetch his clerk from the inn, while the majority of the men stood about glaring at the most recent arrivals, a contingent of miners who stood sneering at the townsfolk. That silly baggage could have spent more time with me, had she wanted to. I was a visitor with money. She could have entertained me, and if she had been successful, she could have joined me on my departure. I would have been a contented companion with her to warm my blanket on my way to the coast, and I was surely a better certainty than an impecunious hostler. Except, of course, she didn't really know me well enough

before my purse was stolen. For all she knew, I had no other
money in the world.

And another thought struck me now, a sharp thought that
hurt like a ballock knife in the chest: someone had taken all
that money, and while I knew that Clem had been out there,
someone else had struck me on the head. It was inescapable,
so I thought, that Clem was still in his little room in the stables.
Agnes had not been noticed leaving the tavern, but she was
always in and out, hurrying to the cellar and beyond. She could
easily have slipped out through the back door and so gone to
the stable. She knew how much money I had won, so it would
have been easy for her to come and find me in the yard, pissing
against the tavern's wall. A maid in a tavern will build muscles
quickly, moving barrels, filling and carrying heavy blackjacks,
walking about and topping up pots and cups all day. She would
have had the strength to whack me over the pate with a club
or something, and then liberate my purse.

But that didn't explain who had attacked and killed Daniell.
Agnes and Clem wouldn't bother: they knew he had no money.
No, it was still the mysterious man who was to have met him
that evening in the town. He was the man I wanted to see.

As I reached this point in my thoughts, I saw Ned and Frantz
sitting together in the corner nearest the smoking fire. I walked
to them laboriously, although after my experiences of the last
days, I was growing more competent with a staff as a crutch.

'Well met, Frantz,' I said.

He looked at me with that little smile playing about his lips.
'I am glad to see you again. I had thought you would be detained
by your companions on the way back here.'

'They brought me back,' I agreed. I didn't want to spend
long thinking about that journey with Clem and Mal. The
memory of that bog, and then my leg twisting and the crackle
as I fell . . . no, it didn't bear thinking about. 'You survived,
then?'

'Me? Oh, yes. I was inclined to take the side of the miners,
for they had brought me here to help them. It would be . . .
perverse of me to fight against them, would it not?'

'Yes. Of course. And you weren't injured in the battle?'

He smiled more broadly. 'That little mêlée? No, I saw to it

that the miners had the advantage. I walked on ahead to tell them where the townsfolk were waiting and joined them in the rout.'

There was something about his smile that made me want to punch him; I would have done, had he not been quite obviously fit and lean. As it was, I wondered about his abilities again. 'You did say that you could find anything with your sticks, didn't you?'

He nodded. '*Ja*, natural. It is a skill some men have. I can find anything.'

'What about a purse? A blue one, with coins inside?'

'A purse? Why, here I would find it hard not to find a purse. Every man carries one.'

'Oh!' I said. I had not thought of that. 'But if mine was different to all those here, would you be able to find it then?'

With a shrug, he pulled a grimace. Some of the townspeople had gone to the cellar and fetched a fresh barrel of ale, which they set on chocks on the bar, and began filling blackjacks to serve the men waiting more or less patiently, while Mal sat on a stool in front of the Coroner, who eyed him with disfavour. A man lumbered into my leg, and I gave a sharp screech before I remembered my other leg was the bad one. I glared at the fool, and he glanced down at me with contempt, but then Frantz shifted so that his great sword was visible. The clumsy man blenched slightly and disappeared quickly. A blackjack suddenly appeared on the table before me, and a trio of cups, and we filled them and drank.

'If you can describe it to me in all details so that I can gain a picture of it in my mind, perhaps I can find it. I have to be able to see, yes? To sense it, to know it. Perhaps if you take me to see where you last had it?'

'I see.'

'When I hunt for silver or iron, I can imagine those things. I can imagine the metal, the taste of it, the sight of the ore, yes?'

I nodded and slowly began to describe my purse. It wasn't terribly difficult, after all. A simple leather purse, with a couple of brass clasps at the top to hold it closed, so that it made a semi-circular shape, with a small *JB* in a diamond in the centre.

A leather smith had stamped the pattern, and painted the letters in bright red on a yellow background. I had been enormously proud when I had that made, only a few weeks ago . . . so very recently. And someone had cut the laces to rob me.

'You are sure of this, yes?'

'Oh, yes.'

He looked a little doubtful, asked me about the weight of it, the actual size, the way that it hung from my belt, where I used to store it, and then he asked me for my belt. Taking it in his hands, he half closed his eyes and felt the leather where the purse had hung. He sniffed at it, ran the leather through his fingers and sat for a moment before passing it back to me.

'Perhaps,' he said.

It was then that David appeared in the doorway with Nye and two other henchmen. He stood there, eyeing the room like a youngster making his first visit to a brothel. Seeing the Coroner, he walked to the knight.

'Sir Geoffrey. I am glad to see you sustained no injuries today. I feared that some accident might have befallen you after those Gubbingses attacked us all.'

The Coroner shot him a look, but the miner's face was all affable innocence. 'I thank you. I am happy you were not hurt either.'

'Oh, no. There were many miners about me, and my fellows here saw to my protection. But since we are the law on the moors, of course, we know how to defend ourselves from incursions. Like those of the Gubbingses.'

By now, you can well believe that the room had grown quiet as the two men stood a scant three paces apart. Neither wanted to be nearer than that. The knight had his left hand on his scabbard, while the miner had both thumbs in his belt, close to his dagger. I had no desire to remain there and witness a brawl or more serious fight, but just now I also had no desire to draw attention to myself, so I sat back and tried to avoid meeting anyone's eyes – not that anyone was particularly keen on watching me. Everyone's attention was fixed on the two men at the bar near Mal. I was happy enough with that. I didn't want to be noticed.

'What of the murderer of my father?' David said.

I grabbed my cup of ale, swallowed a large gulp and instantly choked. Ale shot from my nostrils, and tears sprang into my eyes. It was like washing my sinuses with vinegar.

Fortunately, my little explosion went unnoticed by the miners.

'He's here,' Frantz called out. He sounded quite merry about it. The bastard.

David glanced around. 'Ah, Master London. Come and join us, won't you? Since you are supposed to be a prisoner of the gaol at Lydford, I think it is safe to say you are a fugitive from justice. And we have a rope here.'

'You cannot hang him here,' the Coroner spat. 'He's a prisoner of the town.'

'He was ours first!' David snapped, and stepped forward a pace. His henchmen joined him.

I wished I had taken a seat nearer the door, not that it would have helped me in my current predicament. My leg would not allow me to flee.

Seeing David's move, the knight immediately took a step forward too, although it was noticeable that those around him tended to stay where they were. Not that he allowed the fact to stop him. He was only the same height as David, but somehow he managed to appear a foot taller, and seemed to loom over the miner.

'You will not hang any man here without the permission of the Queen's Justices. This man is to be tried here in Okehampton for a crime committed in Okehampton. He did not kill your father on the moors, but down here in the town. You have no jurisdiction here, *miner*!'

That last word was spat out like poison. I instinctively shrivelled like a salted slug. If it were not for my leg, I would have sidled out through the door. Well, my leg, the miners between me and the way out, and all the townsfolk who were looking at me none too happily as well.

The two squared up like boxers preparing to do battle, but even as they did, I heard the braying, snorting laughter of the ridiculous little clerk who had arrived with the Coroner. 'Sir Geoffrey, my Lord, apologies for my tardy appearance. My word, but it is difficult to pass along the street with all these

some of her clothing and carefully covered her. Mal gave a kind of sniffling sob, which may sound odd, but it was the case that the fool was for the most part bawling silently. Why did the great lummox kill her if it was going to make him so sad?

Anyway, when David tried to step forward, Ned roughly pushed him back again, so that Ned was standing between the Coroner and the miners. As if to support him, the raven fluttered down from the rafter and settled on his shoulder. I felt that familiar shiver run down my back at the sight of the creature. It didn't seem natural, as it fixed its beady eye on me. It looked like polished coal, as if it was not made of flesh and blood and feathers at all.

'This man hasn't killed anyone,' Ned said. He let his eye range over the miners present. 'You kill him, and you'll be letting the real murderer get away. You want that?'

There was some inconsequential foot-shuffling at that, as though many there were perfectly happy to see me swing even if I had nothing to do with the murder. It was a sport for them, rather than a seeking of justice, apparently.

Fortunately, Ned had an answer for them. 'If you let this man hang, you will be guilty of murder yourselves. He is not guilty found in a court before the Justice. You can't hang him without a trial, else you will be hanged, all of you.'

'Not if we take him to Lydford,' someone shouted from the back. There was a clonking sound, and then a sort of soft sigh. I couldn't see what was happening with all the men in the way, but there was all at once a strange atmosphere, as though the tavern was suddenly very full.

'Oh, aye? You think you can whisk him away and hang him there? But the Justices will hear what you have done, Ham Blackaton, and they'll want their pound of flesh. And it won't be the likes of David here who'll be hanged, will it? It'll be those like you, Ham, who catch their wrath. They don't like people hanging folk without them getting their pay for signing the death warrants, so they'll pick on them as might have been involved. That means you. And you, Jed, and you Paul. You'll all hang if you try to take this swinking fool here to Lydford.'

'I say you have fine words, Ned Gubbings, but they don't measure,' David said. He looked about him. 'Bring him. We'll

take him to the moors now, if these fine fellows don't want his
corpse hanging here in the town.'

And that was when I realized why the room felt so full.
Roger Rowle and his mother stepped forward with fifteen
Gubbingses. When I looked towards the door, there were five
more, three with bows bent.

It took David a little while to realize that the dynamics in the
chamber had subtly altered. 'Come on, take him,' he snarled.

Roger tapped him gently on the shoulder. He wore a happy
smile. 'I don't want to see my friend taken from here,' he said.

'Who are . . . Rowle!' David said, and his hand whipped to
the knife at his belt.

Joan slapped his hand away just as Roger slipped to David's
side and held his knife to David's throat. Holding it there, he
glanced over at me, beaming a smile. 'Shall I?'

'No!' the Coroner snapped. 'There has been enough killing
today!'

Behind Roger, I could see more Gubbingses slipping in
through the open doorway. Miners stood grimly as the outlaws
flowed in like quicksilver. Roger looked over at Ned, and I saw
the old man open his mouth, but Joan pushed him away and
shook her head firmly, although with a degree of reluctance.
'We want to help them, Roger. You can't keep fighting the
miners and everyone else. David here will be better off trying
to find out who it was killed Daniell. That's all he wants. Help
him find the guilty man and put his neck in the noose.'

'How do you know it wasn't this gaudy traveller?' David
said. I have to admit, he put a lot of effort into his sneer. I think
he could tell that his plan to have me dragged all the way to
Lydford, there to be hanged, was falling apart in a rather sensa-
tional manner. It was reassuring to see. But 'gaudy'? That was
hardly a fair comment on my excellent attire, even if it had
suffered a little in the journey here.

'I don't,' Ned said. That rather set me aback. 'But why would
he? He was knocked down and robbed, but would he be able
to get up and kill your father, David? Your father was a strong,
hearty man, wasn't he? Do you think a pasty-faced whelp from
up-country like this could kill him in a fight? When he'd already

been knocked down and weakened? Look at him! He's barely strong enough to knock down a new-born foal, let alone a man like Daniell, and you say he did it while he was still fuddled by a blow to his head? Is it likely?'

His words had an impact, I saw. True enough, he was not entirely complimentary about me. I mean, I was more than capable of wielding a knife, although not lifting a man's arm and stabbing him in the heart. That was a particularly cold-blooded way to murder. And a man the size and strength of Daniell would probably have enthusiastically deprecated a man like me lifting his arm to stab him. He would have more than likely taken a very dim view, and I could all too easily imagine that if he were to take offence at such behaviour, he would be very likely to resist in a highly effective manner. I was quite sure that if I had been the man who had attempted such an action, he would easily have overcome me and caused me to regret my presumption.

What was offensive was the way that all the miners and townspeople began nodding, albeit reluctantly, as if I was a mere weakling. It hurt my pride.

'So who could have attacked him?' the Coroner said after a moment's reflection.

Ned looked around him at the townspeople. 'You all know me. You know where I come from. You know I hold to my oath. I swear this on the gospels: I was here at the tavern that evening. I was outside, not in, drinking ale with Joan. And while I was here, I saw a man out there in the yard. He walked up from the town to the stables, and waited, hidden under the eaves where the thatch comes over the log pile. I saw this fellow roll out' – jerking a thumb at me – 'and he went to the wall to piss, before he wandered into the stable. And then I saw Mal's wife Agnes enter. A little later she came out with Clem. Clem walked off behind the stables and Agnes went back inside by the kitchen door. Then Daniell came out and went to talk to the other man. They walked round the yard out to the road to the castle.'

'What is all this? You never mentioned it at the inquest!' the Coroner said, and his anger was not feigned, I was sure. 'Why did you withhold your evidence that day? Eh?'

'You know full well, Coroner. Because it was *you* under the eaves; *you* who stood and waited; *you* who walked off with the miner; *you* who came back a little later and rode away. And you knew that this fellow had nothing to do with Daniell's death, since you saw him enter the stable, just as I did.'

'This is all nonsense!'

'I have made my oath. Will you do the same?'

The Coroner havered at that, and his face took on what was, to me, a rather delightful puce colour. Have you ever studied a ripe plum? At one side it may be a sort of greenish hue, while on the other it can be a deep purple. His face was more of the darker shade. I have been told that when a man blushes that way, it's best to call either for the physician or the undertaker – although, in my experience, a man is usually best served to call the latter rather than the former, thus saving considerable expense without altering the outcome.

Be that as it may, his clerk appeared to find the whole matter enormously amusing. He almost fell from his stool, he was chortling so strongly, and no matter how many people threw him looks of disgust, he only seemed to be sent into further paroxysms of delight. In the end, one of Roger's men wandered to him and tapped him on the pate with his sword's pommel. The clerk fell most delightfully silent and slowly slid from his seat, by degrees joining Clem beneath the table.

'Well, Sir Geoffrey?' Ned asked. His raven gave a loud *caw* as if in support.

'I had nothing to do with his death.'

'Why were you there?'

'We had arranged to meet,' the Coroner said, and I have to say, it was impressive that he could speak clearly with his teeth clenched so tightly together. He looked like a man with lockjaw.

'Why was that?' David pressed him.

'What business is it of yours?'

Sir Geoffrey seemed to be regaining a little of his composure, but on hearing his words, there were some angry rumblings from the miners in particular. A residual affection for their master, I suppose, although how any man could have any such feelings for the fellow, I do not know.

'It's the business of us all. Someone murdered my father and was happy to see this apparently innocent traveller take the blame. Worse, he tried to have me participate in seeing Master Passer unfairly accused and hanged. I would like to know that it was not you.'

Roger, still holding his knife to David's neck, nodded in approval and turned his smiling face to the Coroner. 'Well?'

'He wanted to talk to me about the pasture at the top of my lands. He had threatened to take them all and allege that there was tin there, gain a Queen's warrant to dig them up. We had been arguing about them for ages, him demanding money to leave my lands, me refusing to pay him, and we met here that evening. But there was nothing more to it than that. We met, we spoke and we parted.'

'Did you come to blows?' This was from David again. His voice was strained, as though his throat was constricted.

'No! We . . . I admit, I agreed to pay him to keep from my lands.'

'Did you pay him that evening?' Ned asked. He might have been a lawyer, the way he kept asking questions.

'No. I agreed to pay him later.'

I looked at him, and I was sure that there was a little glint in his eye as he said this. He did not look particularly sorrowful – then again, why should he? He was the victim of a blackmailer, and it would surely have been hypocritical of him to try to display some form of sadness. I wouldn't have.

And that was when the obvious struck me!

Daniell had been murdered by a man who stabbed twice: once in his breast, once under the arm. Two blows best suited to stopping a man's heart. But it was the one under the arm that snagged at my attention. It was such an obvious clue. The man who struck there was clearly a man who knew his way about a man's body, a man who had fought, a man who had served killing blows before. In short, it was almost certainly a knight.

I felt my mouth sag and fall open as I stared at him. And he turned and caught my expression. I have never seen a face turn so fierce so quickly in all my life.

*   *   *

I lurched back, away from him. His fist whipped out and grabbed my jerkin, pulling me towards him. I lurched forward, eyes wide in alarm as my nose almost crashed into his. My staff fell from my terrified hands, and I wobbled badly, eyes widened in horror.

'Um . . .' I said.

'You obnoxious little piss-bibber! What are you—'

'It was him, David! Don't you see? The Coroner! Who else would stab a man under the armpit? Who would know to look there? Eh? Only a man-at-arms, a knight or some mercenary would know to look there on the corpse, wouldn't he? That's why the Coroner was so keen to see me arrested and held, because it took all attention away from *him*! *This* is the man who killed your father!'

The Coroner shoved me away, and I tumbled back into the bar, bounced from it and fell to the ground again. My staff was just out of reach again. Looking at it, I was taken with the sight of Clem's body, just the other side of the table. He appeared to be staring at me with amused contempt. At least he wasn't making as much noise as the clerk, who was snoring fit to waken Clem and Agnes. When I looked up again, the Coroner was reaching for me, no doubt to repeat his successful 'Pull him, push him' exercise.

'You miserable, dishonourable—' he shouted, but then two men grabbed his arms and held him. They were miners, and the pair of them had arms like oxens' hams. It was a relief to see that the Coroner would be unlikely to be able to free himself and come and attack me again.

I had two men at my side, and they soon hoisted me to my feet again, one helpful fellow passing me my staff. Although I should have been grateful, I was aware that both wore broad grins, and one kept chuckling to himself, muttering something about 'the way he whimpered' or some such. They must have mistaken something I said. They were only foolish churls, after all.

David was before me again. Roger had put away his knife, and a sudden outbreak of peace seemed to have enveloped the tavern. David himself wore a childlike demeanour, just as on that first day I had met him. His round face radiated innocence, the gate to the field and had cut a length with a fork in it, although he had bloodied hands afterwards. I could have warned him that blackthorns are not the most amiable of bushes, but he seemed keen enough to learn for himself. Some of his language was impressive, although I have no idea what 'uneheliche' or 'kranken huere' might mean. It sounded like an interesting curse, was what I thought.

While he worked, I felt, rather than heard, a sound above me. When I looked, there was the raven once more. He cocked his head at me, and I got the impression the damn thing was sniggering. Why, I could only guess.

In any case, Frantz took the forked branch in his hands, palms up, the branches passing under his thumbs, and stood at the spot where I told him I had fallen. He looked about him, as though mildly interested in the surroundings, while muttering something under his breath, and suddenly the branch shot down to point at the ground. He stepped back, speaking again in some foreign tongue, and moved over the spot, and the branch repeated its downwards leap.

'*Ja*,' he said. 'It was here.'

'Are you muttering a spell?' Ned demanded with an edge. He had appeared from around the building, and I glanced up at the raven accusingly. I could have gambled half my lost purse that the damn creature was there to spy on us. He saw my glare, and I would swear the creature shrugged dismissively at me.

'No!' Frantz chuckled. 'I am asking, "Is this the place?" to learn where the man knocked our friend on the head. Now I ask, "Is the purse in the stable?" and it moves not, so no, it is not. Now, I ask, "Is the purse in the yard?" and see, the branch is still. I ask, "Is the purse nearby?"'

As he spoke, the stick shot down again, and Ned and I both jumped slightly. It was so unexpected.

'Is the purse in the yard?' he asked again, and the stick stayed still. He frowned a little, then began to ask, *Was it in the tavern? Was it within twenty paces? Was it within thirty paces? Was it within forty* – and the stick leapt once more.

'It is close,' he said. 'Is it concealed?'

A leap.

'Is it in the ground?'

Nothing.

'Is it in a hedge?'

Nothing.

He had wandered outside now and was peering about him. 'Is it in the wall?'

Nothing.

We walked about the yard, eventually moving down towards the gate to the field, and stood staring out past the buildings. There was the dungheap, then broken carts and a wagon, with tree-covered hills beyond. The stick seemed to be telling Frantz that the purse was near, and he paced back and forth, before finally closing his eyes and thinking. Ned and I stood, me wobbling rather with my bad leg, and Ned wobbling rather with the scrumpy, until Frantz suddenly snapped upright and stared ahead. He took two paces towards the dungheap, and then bent his head, muttering again. The stick jerked, and he began to laugh loudly. 'I know where it is!' he said.

We tried to hurry to him, but with the muddy path it was not easy. 'Where?' I called.

'Here, my friend. Here. You might regret your hurry!'

He was pointing at the dungheap. I stared. 'No, surely he wouldn't have put it there,' I said. It might have been almost a sob.

The dungheap was massive. It had the ordure from several years in its warm embrace, and just now there was steam rising from it in a thin cloud. I pulled a face to see it. 'Are you sure?'

In answer, he asked his stick again. The sudden flick down was entirely convincing.

'Ja! Yes, it is here. I would dig there,' he said, pointing at a particularly noisome area.

He began walking towards the heap, while I watched with my lip curled. To think that my lovely leather purse, with the careful stitching and colours, had been thrust into the horse shit and straw of the dungheap was distressing.

'Here!' he called.

We hobbled to him, and when we reached his side, I could see that the dung had, indeed, been disturbed here. All about this part, the dung had little green shoots and tiny leaves that were just visible in the gathering darkness. But in one spot, stabbed, he was so surprised he didn't even cry out. And then the fellow stabbed him a second time, and he didn't shout or roar. It must have been a terrible surprise to him, for him to have been so quiet.'

'Or he just had no breath after the first blow,' I said.

'I've seen men die, and often they'll bellow when they realize they've been stabbed,' Ned said contemplatively.

I looked at him. There was a degree of confidence in his tone, rather like other murderers I have known.

Nye looked to be almost in tears. 'But who would have done this, then? It could have been anyone in the town!'

'No,' Ned said. 'If it was someone Daniell trusted that much, it was someone he knew very well.'

Nye looked at him and nodded, and then his eyes widened and he stared at me and Frantz. 'Me? No! He wouldn't trust me to get that close if he was on his own. He was always cautious, was Daniell. He knew he had enemies, and he was careful.'

Ned nodded slowly, and I stared at him. If the fool wasn't careful, Nye might pull his head off for him! If he came to conclude that Ned was accusing him of murder, he might take real offence. I know the great lurdan had only a slow-moving brain, but once he had concentrated all his brainpower on one thought, sometimes he could react with surprising speed. And just now he was frowning at Ned with the concentration of a cat watching a sparrow.

'He doesn't mean you, Nye!' I said quickly.

'He knows that,' Ned said quietly.

'Eh?' I said.

'Like he said, even Nye wouldn't have got close enough to hurt Daniell. It was someone else. Someone Daniell would trust. There weren't many of them.'

'No,' Nye said.

And I rolled my eyes. These two were talking in riddles as far as I was concerned. 'Fine. Good,' I said, and poured more beer into my pot. It was a good brew, this. It didn't taste of acid and piss like the cider, anyway. 'So it was only someone whom Daniell really knew and trusted entirely. There can only be a few people like that.'

And then I stopped, because I realized what they were getting at.

Nye took his hand from my shoulder, which was a relief, because it had felt as though it was going to crush my bones like a rock rolling over a snail. He stood for a moment as if collecting his thoughts. It was a passable imitation, at least.

'Well?'

David Vowell had walked in behind Nye, and I think he had heard our conversation.

It made my back crawl.

'So, my friends, you have been busy exercising your grey matter, haven't you?' he said easily, slipping to rest on the bench opposite me, beside Ned.

I gulped. There was a sort of gleam in his eye, if you know what I mean – like the look on a bear's face just before he punches a mastiff and sends it flying. A sort of lethal, debonair expression, as though he knew full well there was nothing we could do. He was all-powerful here. It was his town now, since Sir Geoffrey was held in the gaol. Who else could stand against the head of the miners? There was no one who would dare to accuse him, and with the Coroner out of the way, only a fool would try it.

'No comments? I'm surprised. I thought you would want to ask me.'

'No,' I said, and could not help but babble slightly. 'We were outside looking for my purse, and found it. Do you know where that massive tarse Clem had hidden it? In the middle of the dungheap, the lunatic! Why shove it there? I suppose no one would look there, but—'

'What made you look there?' David asked, not unreasonably.

'It was Frantz here. The man you brought to look for tin,' I said. And then I thought: Frantz, who was told to wait in Exeter until just after Daniell had died. And then he was called to help search for tin on the moors. 'You asked him to come, didn't you?'

'Father always had a ridiculous superstition about diviners. He didn't use them to find water, but that was little problem on the moors,' David said dismissively. 'Who cares about finding

him to expect you as soon as we heard they were taking you
to the gaol.'

'How?'

'Our son keeps in touch with us. We have our ways.'

I supposed he did. A man who had once led a band of outlaws,
and who now lived in a castle, was surely capable of pretty
much anything he wanted.

'So you found Mal,' he said after a moment.

'Yes.'

'Poor man. Someone will have to persuade the coroner to
hold Mal's inquest.'

'Yes.'

'I feel sorry for Mal. He just couldn't live without Agnes.
Even though he knew she was unfaithful to him, he couldn't
face life without her, I suppose.'

Personally, I would have felt happier if the fool hadn't hanged
himself in a place where he could drip on me, but I didn't think
it a necessary comment just now. His body had been cut down
by two miners who appeared perfectly accustomed to their job.
It did at least explain the ladder lying on the ground. The poor
fellow must have kicked it aside when he leapt from it. A most
effective method of guaranteeing his demise, I supposed. It was
a horrible discovery for me, though. Usually, a man walking
in a wood like that would be aware of a body spinning in the
wind, but with my staff and poorly leg, my methods of locomo-
tion tended to be more hunched over, so I spent my time with
my head bent, scanning the ground for roots and branches that
might trip me, rather than a dead tavern-keeper's boots
that could brain me.

But yes, I did feel sorry for him. To have bought Agnes and
then see that she was untrustworthy, to the extent that he had
lost his temper and killed her, that was very sad. Especially
since he couldn't live with that crime afterwards. It was surely
a proof of his love for her that he had committed self-murder
so soon after.

We were sitting and considering this in contemplative silence
when the new arrival came in. What with all the noise and
disturbance of my finding the body, and the necessary admin-
istrative functions that followed (it was fortunate that the

Coroner and his clerk were still there – the Coroner was grumpy, but he did at least agree to hold his inquest), I had not found an opportunity to speak with the stranger.

He was a youngish fellow of some thirty summers, with a sun-burned face and bright blue eyes. From his build, it appeared he had spent much of his life in the saddle. His legs were bowed like a seaman's when he walked.

'Good day, Master. You will want a beer?' I asked when he appeared.

In short, he was very keen on the idea. Once he had been settled with a quart of strong beer, I began to question him about news.

'From London?' he said, and began to lecture me on the latest fashions, snippets of gossip about the Archbishop, and all other kinds of nonsense. If the fellow couldn't see I was already clad in the finest clothing London could offer, he was as unobservant as he was foolish. Not that my clothing was in the very best of condition, of course, after all the indignities it had been put through. Still, a man should have been able to observe the quality.

'What of the Queen?' I asked.

He shrugged. 'She isn't pregnant now,' he said with a little smile.

'And the Lady Elizabeth?'

'Oh, I believe she is well enough.'

I waited. 'Well enough' could mean that she was being held in less than salubrious circumstances in the Tower, or perhaps at Woodstock or some other place that was unappealing to a lady used to finery and comfort.

'She is at Hatfield, I believe,' the man said.

'And her household?'

'What of it?'

'Are they with her?'

He looked at me as though I was a fool. 'Where else would they be?'

'Oh, I don't know. I thought I had heard that there was a conspiracy. Some man in Suffolk said . . .'

'That fool? Oh, he's gone. It was obvious nonsense.'

I struggled to restrain myself. 'Nonsense?'

'Yes. There was nothing in it.'

I could have gaped. I could have reached to him and kissed him. I could have grasped my staff and beaten him to the floor. All these thoughts, and more, passed through my head as I stared at him, trying to maintain a calm, stoic exterior.

In the last week, I had endured hardships such as I had never before experienced. Even now I was battered and bruised, my leg all but useless; I had been threatened with hanging, I had been held in a gaol, I had been thrust into a war between three battling rivals, and could have died any number of times – and all because I had heard that my Lady Elizabeth was implicated in a conspiracy to topple Mary from her throne. And now, *now*, to hear that it was all entirely unnecessary left me bereft of speech. It was almost impossible to contain the emotions that cried out for release.

'Are you all right?' he said.

'I am fine,' I said.

There was no need to journey to the coast. I did not need to take a ship for some foreign land where they would not know how to speak English and probably had no use for a bath. I could stay here, in England, in civilization.

I looked about me. Well, once I returned to London, I could enjoy civilization again, anyway.

That was when this traveller looked over at my purse and smiled. 'Do you like to play dice?' he asked.

AUTHOR'S NOTE

Some aspects of this story may well cause the reader to consider that the author might have overstepped the mark. After all, the idea of Lydford Law, the Gubbingses, and the miners' use of extortion sound rather far-fetched.

Unfortunately, they were all much as depicted here in the novel.

William Crossing, a keen collector of folk tales and the history of Devon, gives the earliest mention of Lydford Law as:

> First hang and draw,
> Then hear the cause, is Lydford Law.

After the Norman invasion, Lydford became the seat of justice for Dartmoor. The Forest Laws, brutal and extreme rules to protect the King's rights over his 'forests', or hunting grounds, originally encompassed the whole of Devon. By Jack's day, the territory had reduced to only Dartmoor, but the laws were still severe and were used to protect and support the miners.

Annually, the miners brought in vast amounts to the royal Exchequer, and each ruler was keen to see the miners thrive. In the Middle Ages, any serf who escaped his lord's demesne could gain his freedom if he survived for a year and a day; however, a serf who ran to the moors could call himself a miner, and a miner was a servant to the King. The miner was, to all extents, free.

And miners made full use of the power that their position relative to the King conferred on them. Yes, they did threaten to dig up valuable land; they did threaten to divert essential water courses; they did demand money to go and trouble other landowners. Fights were common on the borders of the moors.

Richard Strode was instrumental in restricting some of their powers. He was a Member of Parliament, and the miners disapproved of his interference in their affairs. Captured while passing the moors, he was thrown into Lydford gaol and had to have a writ passed in government before he could gain his release.

By 1701, in Prince's *Worthies of Devon*, Lydford Law had become a proverb:

> I oft have heard of Lydford Law,
> How in the morn they hang and draw,
> And sit in judgement after:
> At first I wondered at it much;
> But soon I found the matter such
> As it deserves no laughter.

The Gubbingses, too, are not a flight of fancy, but were a noted tribe of outlaws who infested the gorge below Lydford, preying on local farms and incautious passers-by. They have been immortalized in many works of fiction – and I think I do them a service by bringing them and their exploits back to life in this book. In the past, writers have not been terribly kind to them.

In *John Herring* (1883), Sabine Baring-Gould describes a similar tribe, saying, 'The Cobbledicks had not arrived at that stage of civilization in which property becomes personal . . . They had never been civilized.' Charles Kingsley in *Westward Ho!* (1855) was equally unimpressed with them. But for my part, I have a sneaking fondness for them. It has often been implied that Devon folk are peasants with little to be said for them other than they make good farmers, that they are docile and gentle. That view is rather tested by the fact that Devon has for centuries filled the ships of the navy with piratical sailors and murderous soldiers.

More than a few young soldiers at Okehampton Camp soon learned that. Recruits fresh from unarmed combat training often came to regret taking a fancy to a pretty Devon maid and picking a fight with her boyfriend – a man who had been raised 'wrastling' steers from an early age.

If you would like to learn more about the Gubbingses, a good starting point is here: www.legendarydartmoor.co.uk/gubbins_lydford.htm.

Finally, I must mention one last detail. It is Frantz Lippert, the diviner from Nuremberg. This character is invented, but his was a common function, especially during Elizabeth's reign.

Dowsing has a very ancient history. In the fifth century BC, Herodotus described how the Scythians dowsed, but the Catholic Church disapproved of such practices. Even so, by the 1500s it was a procedure regularly used in German mining. A woodcut from *Cosmographia Universalis* by Sebastian Münster in 1544 shows clearly the diviner above ground searching for ores while miners toiled below.

It is a curious pastime, and as a man interested in science, I find it fascinating – especially since I have tried it, and have done so successfully. I know many people who have – most of them, like me, deeply troubled that such an activity can work. It shouldn't.

I have no idea how it can work. Yet it does. And it was a known skill that has been used for centuries.

Michael Jecks
North Dartmoor